Yuri Trifonov was born in 1925 into the privileged world of high-ranking Soviet society. His father, however, one of the Old Bolsheviks who had joined the Party before the Revolution, disappeared in the Stalinist purges, and his name was expunged from Party history. Trifonov, after having won a Stalin prize for an early novel, devoted ten years of his life to rehabilitating his father's name. It was not until he was forty-four that he found his true voice as a writer. There followed throughout the 1970s his series of short novels, culminating with *Another Life* and *The House on the Embankment*, that established him as one of the foremost novelists of his generation. He died suddenly on March 28, 1981.

Also by Yuri Trifonov in Abacus:

THE HOUSE ON THE EMBANKMENT

Yuri Trifonov

ANOTHER LIFE

Translated from the Russian by Michael Glenny

First published in Great Britain in Abacus by
Sphere Books Ltd 1985
30-32 Gray's Inn Road, London WC1X 8JL
Copyright © Novy Mir Magazine 1975
English language translation Copyright © 1983 by Michael Glenny

Set in Times

Printed and bound in Great Britain by
Cox & Wyman Ltd, Reading

'I dedicate this to my wife, Alla' – Y.T.

Again she woke up in the middle of the night, just as she had lately been waking up every night, as though someone had roused her with a familiar, malicious nudge: 'Think, think, try and understand!' She could not. Her mind was capable of nothing but self-torture. Yet whatever it was that woke her demanded obstinately that she try to make sense of everything: there must be a meaning; somebody must be guilty, it's always the family who are guilty; she shouldn't go on living, she ought to die herself. If only she could discover how she was guilty. And there was another thought, secret and shameful: 'Was death really the end of everything?' And then she would reprimand herself: 'What a fool I am. How can I think about death when I have a daughter?'

Yet she found it easy enough to think about death; it was something unpleasant but inevitable that had to be gone through – like, for instance, having to go to hospital for an operation. Thoughts about death were much easier to bear than memories; they caused pain, while thoughts of death caused nothing but a passing mood of reflection.

Now it was starting again. Long ago he used to come home from the museum on payday slightly drunk, usually from the Sevan, a bar next door to the museum, or else Fyodorov would take him back to his place, where they would stay up drinking much too late. Then when he came home he would go straight to bed and immediately fall asleep. He invariably woke up in the middle of the night, however, at three or four o'clock, just as she was doing now. He would keep her from sleep by shuffling into the kitchen for a glass of water or some food out of the refrigerator, while she would curse him angrily, half asleep. When he woke her up at those times she hated him: 'What a selfish child you are!'

At other times, behaving with great resourcefulness and cunning, he would hide the fact that he had been drinking; he was a very clever actor. She noticed neither the smell nor his reddened eyes, believed him when he said, 'I'm dog-tired,' pitied him, and quickly turned down the bedclothes. He would collapse into bed and start to snore, but later that night he would always give himself away by waking up long before morning. Now the same thing was happening with her. For her the equivalents of alcohol were memory and pain. By day she concealed them. No one must notice: at work, at home, her daughter Irinka, her mother-in-law – most of all her mother-in-law, because if she were to notice, the pain would be worse. So in the daytime she kept up the camouflage by exerting all her strength, but at night she had none left.

Sometimes he would wake up at night when he hadn't been drinking at all – just like that, for no apparent reason other than mere whim. It wasn't as if he were old; insomnia is something old men suffer from. It irritated her, because she was a light sleeper and would wake up as soon as he started sighing or tossing about, and particularly when he looked at his watch. He had a habit of picking up his watch from the lid of the blanket chest to peer at it, and the metal watch-strap would always clink against the chest. There had been many rows about that clinking noise. She would get furious. It was so stupid. The wretched man tried hard to handle the watch without making a noise, but somehow it never worked: invariably something, usually the metal strap, would brush against the lid of the chest – and a metallic 'clink' would ring out, sharp and clear in the night-time silence, and she would wince, having already awakened and lying there tensely waiting for the noise.

Her mother-in-law had continued living with her in the apartment. Where else could she go?

This woman firmly believed that the death of her son, in November of the previous year from a heart attack at the age of forty-two, was the fault of his wife. Living with his mother was difficult; they would have liked to break up the arrangement and part forever but were constrained because the old woman was lonely and if she were to part from her granddaughter, sixteen-year-old Irinka, she would be condemned to ending her life among strangers (her sister and niece showed no great enthusiasm for inviting her to live with them, and in any case she, Alexandra Prokofievna, would never have accepted such an offer). Furthermore, Olga Vasilievna had to think of her daughter, who loved her grandmother and without whom she would have been deprived of care when her mother was at work. All this had tightened itself into such a stone-hard, indissoluble knot that there seemed to be no way to undo it.

So she was waking up in the middle of the night and racking her brains in despair while by day her only relief was in leaving the house, scuttling away, disappearing. Nowadays she seized the opportunity thankfully whenever her work took her away from Moscow. She realised that this was wrong, that it was weakness, that Irinka needed her now more than ever – and she needed Irinka. Away on her trips she missed her daughter painfully, always hastened to come back, spent at least five roubles every evening talking to her by telephone, and on returning would discover that her daughter, absorbed in her own little concerns, had managed perfectly well without her. Far from comforting Olga, this only increased the pain, so that she would once more feel the urge to get away again, to escape, knowing in advance that it wouldn't help. Oh, how she would have pitied, how she would have appreciated the old woman, if only she lived somewhere far away! But in these little rooms, in that tiny little hallway, the years they had all spent together stood crammed tightly one against another, blatant and unadorned, like the patched carpet slippers in the crude wooden box that Sergei had knocked together and that still stood under the coat rack. Here, in all this overcrowded muddle, there was no room for pity. Her mother-in-law might say, 'You used not to buy biscuits like these before. Where did you get them? In Kirovskaya Street?' That one sentence instantly destroyed all the sympathy for her mother-in-law which Olga had been scraping together crumb by crumb. It meant: You never treated *him* to biscuits; but now, for yourself, you've started buying them. Trivial things like this, so petty and stupid as to be ridiculous, wounded her like a blow from an iron bar – because they were deliberately spiteful and meant to hurt.

As painful as the biscuits had been the business of the television set. Long ago, while Sergei was still alive, they had wanted to buy a new, big one in place of their little old set with its antediluvian screen and had put aside the money. Yet Sergei's TV watching had often infuriated Olga – perhaps it was wrong of her to have been so annoyed, so unfairly and stupidly irritated (though to be frank, she had good reason for it), because of the way he used to sit for hours, oblivious to everything else, watching endless sports programmes. He would collapse into the green armchair, legs crossed, cigarette between his teeth, the round ashtray with a little fish on it beside him on the floor – and then stay there as though glued to the TV, deaf to questioning or even shouting. But why *all* the programmes one after another? Surely they can't all be equally interesting? 'I'm relaxing! I have a right to rest and relaxation, haven't I?' His anger was slightly calculated, put on to make sure that everyone realised how incredibly tiring his work was.

In fact, he really did get tired at work, and he had troubles there too. But then so did everyone. He lacked the necessary coolness and stamina. What's more, he would often cover up and keep quiet about his problems, many of which she heard about only much later. When she had difficulties at work she always told him about them and it made her feel better, but he

3

concealed his, ashamed of his failures. And then, slouched in front of the television, he would complain, half genuinely and half acting the fool: 'Gentlemen, my nerve cells need rest. Dogs eat grass, intellectuals listen to music, and I watch sports – it's my therapy, my bromide, my holiday, damn your lack of perceptiveness, gentlemen . . .'

Just the usual buffoonery, but his mother, Alexandra Prokofievna, felt impelled to intervene in her son's defence. Sometimes, to support him, she would sit down beside him and watch ice hockey or volleyball – it didn't matter to her what it was – and exchange comments with him that made Olga almost burst out laughing. On occasion, subtly and covertly but always so that Olga realised it, he would make fun of Alexandra Prokofievna during these conversations in front of the television, but the old woman obstinately pretended that sport greatly interested her. Ah yes, thirty or forty years ago she had been a keen hiker. And not long since, she had donned an ancient pair of khaki-coloured trousers and an outlandish jacket dating from the days of 'war communism' in the early twenties, shrugged into an old knapsack that had once been used for collecting scrap metal, and set off quite alone by train out into the country. She had, it seems, been taking a trip to the places where long ago she had gone walking with her husband, Sergei's father, a mathematics professor who had been a passionate hiker, tourist, and photographer. (Sergei's father had joined the Volunteer Reserve in 1941 and had been killed that autumn in the defence of Moscow.) Alexandra's bizarre hiking gear dating from the twenties gave her a tragicomic look. Sergei took it all calmly – he allowed no one else to make fun of his mother, or even to smirk at her behind her back – but Olga found herself upset by the whole thing. If people were able to understand and forgive the old woman's pathetic eccentricities, why could they not understand her, Olga Vasilievna? Why couldn't they see her grief? There seemed to be absolutely no way of making her mother-in-law – a woman by no means stupid, with a law degree – acknowledge Olga Vasilievna's right to suffering.

'But of course buy a new TV, buy it, don't hesitate!' she said when Olga stupidly decided to ask her advice.

Irinka was desperate for a bigger television. Olga didn't care about it, but in a nearby shop, in the next-door building in fact, where Irinka was always popping in for this and that, they were selling a very good brand of TV set which was rarely available, and a decision had to be made.

'I tell you: buy it. Why deny yourself the pleasure?'

Olga said that she was not in a mood for pleasures.

'I understand, but on the other hand you're not planning to shut yourself up in a convent.'

'No, I don't want to go into a convent, that's true.'

Olga purposely gave the older woman a sour reply, in order to hurt her – after all, it was she who had meant to cause Olga pain with her remark about pleasure.

'So don't upset yourself, take out the money, Sergei put it aside for that purpose, it's what he would have wanted . . .' The kind smile froze on Alexandra Prokofievna's flat, high-cheekboned, Tartar-like face, and her eyes – narrow, bright-blue slits, Sergei's eyes – stared at her coldly and without pity.

Embittered by these malicious digs, Olga decided not to buy the television, just to spite the old woman. She shouted at Irinka, who burst into tears. But later, still more embittered, Olga changed her mind and bought it. For four months her mother-in-law never once watched television. She explained that she was sparing her eyes and was afraid of radiation, but it was also meant as a demonstration. One of Olga's friends tried to reassure her: You must find a *modus vivendi*, be tolerant; you both share the same grief and you both love the same little girl. Olga also thought that things would somehow settle themselves, but after a certain incident she realised that it was no good, it would never work out.

It happened less than two months after the TV incident, in January, when her anguish became intolerable. It was at such moments that she no longer wanted to go on living. One night, tortured by insomnia, Olga got up and went into the kitchen, where she burst into helpless tears. She took a sedative, then drank some cold tea from the teapot. Suddenly she heard Alexandra Prokofievna shuffling into the kitchen; she couldn't sleep either. That shuffling sound pierced Olga Vasilievna to the core because it was so familiar: Sergei had shuffled along exactly like that in those same backless slippers, which the old woman had for some reason taken to wearing around the house. And it seemed to Olga that it was Sergei walking in them. He used to come into the kitchen when all three of the others were sitting there, stand in the doorway wearing a hat made out of newspaper, raise his hand and say, 'I greet ye, my people!' Irinka, of course, would collapse with laughter. He was always trying to bring them all together, make them feel closer, united, even if only for a minute, even if only by jokes and clowning. And now, suddenly, the shuffling sound brought it all rushing back to her and she sobbed aloud, unable to control herself. It was terrible, unforgivable, because no one should ever see her tears.

Alexandra Prokofievna came in wearing a nightgown, her grey hair unkempt, her face yellow and disagreeable-looking. She glanced at Olga, walked over to the cabinet, took down a cup, and filled it with water. No, she was not going to give the water to Olga; she needed the water herself.

She acted as if she could neither see nor hear Olga Vasilievna sobbing, and merely asked in her usual querulous voice, 'Where do we keep the bicarbonate of soda?'

Without answering, Olga went out of the kitchen.

She could not forget the question about the bicarbonate, the unseeing eyes – because something that was kept concealed in daytime had suddenly come out into the open. The truth is laid bare at night. Olga was crying; yet the old woman had looked at her with hatred.

It had happened in the past that Olga and Sergei had some of their bitterest rows at night. He had said one night that if it weren't for Irinka he would leave Olga, and that seemed to her such a lethal truth that she had hardly been able to live through till dawn. Yet the next morning he was making jokes and talking nonsense, having remembered nothing, and their night-time argument evaporated without a trace, like a nightmare.

A few months later he suddenly announced that he intended to go away alone for a holiday at New Year. This frightened Olga. She refused to let him go by himself and demanded to be taken along. In those days it was easy enough to get ten days' unpaid leave, but there was a problem about leaving Irinka, because Sergei's mother was slightly unwell. It was nothing serious, and if Sergei had needed a holiday she would have let them go without hesitation. But on this occasion, realising she was doing it mostly for the benefit of her daughter-in-law, she flatly refused to be left alone with Irinka. As part of an outright conspiracy, Alexandra Prokofievna invited her sister Vera over, along with Vera's daughter, Sergei's cousin Tamara, who was a neurologist at an exclusive clinic.

Olga had never liked Tamara and did not believe a word of her long, pedantic explanation of Alexandra Prokofievna's illness at the dinner table; she was obviously exaggerating things in order to confuse everyone. Not wishing to start an unpleasant argument, Olga said nothing and took it all impassively, even though it was an obvious plot. But that night she could restrain herself no longer and woke Sergei with a question – only to experience that same nightmarish feeling that everything was collapsing, the ground sliding away under her feet.

'Come on, admit it – there's someone else you want to be with, just the two of you, isn't there?'

'Yes, there is, there is,' he said in a whisper, instantly awake. 'That someone is myself. I want to be alone with myself. I want a rest from you, from mother, from all of you, all of you.'

For a moment she believed it – she was used to trusting him – but then she had second thoughts: Did he really need to be alone? She could think of no reasons why he should want to go, all alone, hundreds of miles away from Moscow. So although she was usually inclined to take him at his word and was easily reassured, this time she did not altogether accept his reason. In her heart of hearts she was nagged by a doubt that provoked the sickening thought: 'He's got someone else!'

He liked small blonde women. She found this out one day quite by chance. He had a penchant for miniature women that he could cradle in his arms. One day he had said tenderly to Olga, 'What a pity you're so solidly built. I would like to be able to carry you in my arms.'

Yet all his women were on the large side. Pure coincidence; it just happened that way, he used to say. He had had five women, four before Olga; she was the fifth. Maybe there had been others as well – in fact almost definitely, it was indubitable – but she knew for certain about those four and could only guess and suspect there were others. About the four, though, she had gradually wormed all the details out of him and could name them all – Valka, Svetlana, and so on – and never missed an opportunity to say something cutting, to make some sarcastic gibe about them and about him simultaneously. She hated them, these she-devils, these sluts, two of whom had been older than he was and had taught him all kinds of disgusting things; one had been the same age as Sergei and had fancied herself as a high-minded intellectual, although in fact she was an oversexed bitch who had schemed by fair means or foul to make him marry her. He, thank God, had resisted her wiles and had treated her firmly although maybe not entirely decently, but she deserved it, the bitch. Then there had been a pudgy pink-and-white creature with whom he had worked in the museum, empty-headed and affected but very beautiful, who was always running away from him while he chased after her. One day he got fed up with this: she ran out of the house where they were meeting; this time he didn't chase her, and it all came to an end.

Despite her hysterical behaviour, this fourth woman was generously built and he called her Brünnhilde. He used to say

7

that her breasts were as heavy and round as soup plates. Olga felt a special hatred for her. She hated them all even now, all four, because Sergei still caused her pain and continued to do so. And so, she thought, he never did have any tiny little blondes, and that was perhaps why he had a longing for them. Once he went away on a twelve-day holiday without her, to a place called Peresvetovo, between Moscow and Gorky. She found this unforgiveable, not simply because she thought he was bound to be unfaithful to her in Peresvetovo but because he had gone in spite of her desperate plea. Yet three days later came a telegram: 'Lovely here. Bring Irinka.' She asked for a day off work, took the train with Irinka to Peresvetovo, and, of course, he was forgiven. They went sledging down the hills on a Finnish sledge, and next morning, seeing them off on the train, he mumbled, 'What a silly, silly woman you are!' – and kissed her, scratching her mouth with his unshaven face. And not long ago, when they were applying for a holiday at a spa, the doctor had pronounced Sergei 'Effectively healthy'. Everything had been fine – blood tests, heart, blood pressure. And then what had happened? No one could understand. And she could not understand how she was to live without him. Yet somehow she had managed it thus far – thus far for five months and twenty-five days! She could not conceive how she had done it: the time had just passed, senselessly, dragging; she had simply kept going . . .

The alarm clock would ring at seven. For another hour and a half she would lie sunk in oblivion, not the oblivion of sleep but the oblivion of a vanished life. Then slowly she would get up, put on her quilted nylon dressing-gown, Sergei's present to her on her last birthday; or sometimes without even her dressing gown, just in her nightdress, uncombed, because she no longer bothered about her appearance. She would wander into the kitchen, put on the kettle for tea, a saucepan of water for kasha and another for eggs, and take the cottage cheese and yogurt from the refrigerator, so what while she and Irinka were washing and getting dressed the cottage cheese and yogurt would warm up a little in the heat of the kitchen. She would switch on the radio, which stood on top of the cabinet. And all the time, no matter what she was doing or what she was thinking about, she could feel an emptiness and coldness behind her back.

There had been a boy called Vlad, good, kind, boring, hopeless, but intellectually gifted; he had a broad, pockmarked face and was slightly popeyed, which gave him a look of earnestness and devotion. He wore spectacles in a tortoiseshell frame. Whenever he laughed – which happened rarely and always unexpectedly – he would cover his mouth with his hand, because his upper lip had slightly more of a cleft in it than was normal. It was not a real harelip, rather a kind of a hint at a harelip. Vlad was a medical student, and even then people were predicting a great career for him in medicine. Olga Vasilievna's mother (for whom all *externals* – whether a person's looks, an overcoat, a bookshelf, curtains, even a bunch of flowers – were of absolutely no significance at all, and who was influenced only by a rather vague, debatable quality that she claimed to detect with her inner eye and which she called *essence*) very much wanted her daughter to marry Vlad. But Olga simply could not accept this idea, even though she was as aware of Vlad's qualities as her mother was. Just think – to have to spend the rest of your life looking at that vast, pockmarked face . . .

And so it dragged on, half feeble courtship, half childlike friendship, hopeless for Vlad, joyless for Olga, lasting two or three years (she was simultaneously being bored by the attentions of another young man, called Gendlin, an engineer and a total nonentity, even though her mother approved of him too), until the fateful moment of graduation, the start of real life, a job teaching in a school in Pulikha Street. She was twenty-four, with no line of retreat; all her girl friends, damn them, were already married. And suddenly Vlad appeared with another young man, named Sergei. They had met the previous winter at a student camp in Zvenigorod and had instantly become friends. Vlad was in general a lover of his fellow men: he developed great enthusiasms for people, although it must also be said that his judgment of them was often less than brilliant. He regarded Sergei's mother, for instance, as a paragon among women; he trembled before her, tried to ingratiate himself with her, and all because Alexandra Prokofievna had once been a typist in the Political Department of the Red Army during the civil war. But that, of course, came later; before Sergei, he had first befriended some pilot in the Air Force, then a wrestling champion who looked like an ape, then a secondhand bookseller who dealt in very old detective novels and who was a garrulous know-all and a morphine addict. Vlad's new friend Sergei was a historian who had recently graduated and now worked in some obscure institution in a job that was not in his field. In addition, as Vlad announced when he introduced him, Sergei was the undisputed champion of the Zvenigorod region at various word games, such as saying words backwards.

In fact, on that first evening he had amazed Olga with this bizarre skill. Vlad would shout excitedly, 'Dining room', and his friend would reply, 'Moorgninid'. 'Glance' cried Vlad, and immediately came the response: 'Ecnalg'. 'Briefcase', Vlad suggested slyly, secretly rejoicing at his friend's inevitably successful retort. And with only a moment's hesitation Sergei answered, 'Esac . . . feirb'. 'What was that?' cried Vlad. 'Say it again, please! We must check it.' They checked it, and it was faultless. It produced an enormous impression. Vlad added to the excitement by announcing, 'But he's a genius. A plain, ordinary genius.'

In those days Sergei was slim and well built, with a shock of thick hair and a spring in his walk; he had an odd but infectiously cheerful way of talking, and he was unlike anyone else Olga knew. She felt that something had happened. Suppressing her nervous excitement, she joined in the game and asked, 'Earthquake?' 'Ah!' cried Vlad. 'That's a very difficult one.' The new visitor looked at her for a second as though agreeing – yes, that's difficult – then said quietly but firmly, 'Ekauqhtrae'.

This mysterious word pierced her like a needle. It was, perhaps, the uttering of a password that heralded a complete change in her life. A crazy, unheard-of, unwritten word: 'Ekauqhtrae', but it was a mirror image of another, a real word, in which she had always believed – 'earthquake'. That game, that funny, absurd first meeting and the nonsense they talked as they drank vodka and ate sardines, stuck in her memory forever, because it had given her an inward shock and was the omen of a change in her destiny.

Added to this, it was at the beginning of spring, a vaguely unsettling time whose meaning had to be guessed, like the word 'ekauqhtrae', a time when all the people around her, holding their breath in expectation and conjecture, were constantly whispering and arguing about something. The new guest, however, displeased Olga's mother because on that first visit he rushed out of the house to buy a bottle of vodka. When she came to know him better, Olga guessed that it had not been fondness for alcohol but plain shyness and a particular, excessive nervousness that made him do the stupidest things. For years her mother could not forget Sergei's *faux pas*. 'And do you remember,' she would say whenever her son-in-law did something wrong, 'how he ran out for a bottle of vodka the very first evening he was here?' Her mother, who strove so hard to grasp the 'essence' of things, was incapable of perceiving that this silly behaviour did not represent the 'essence' of Sergei's character at all. She was firmly convinced that Vlad was the most suitable for her daughter: that, for her, was the essence of the situation. Poor mother – for all her love for her daughter, she could never rise above the naïve egotism that was so characteristic of her – naïve because it never entered her head to detect a trace of egotism in herself. Quite the reverse: she saw herself as enveloped in a positive cloud of altruism; in her own eyes she lived only for others. There was a certain truth in this, except that on closer examination it was plain that 'others' meant only one person – Georgii Maximovich. At any rate, she insisted that Vlad was the better one for Olga, imagining that she was concerned about her daughter, whereas in fact she was really concerned about herself; Vlad was more suitable from *her* point of view. She had also disliked the word games that first evening, and Sergei's story of how he and Vlad visited a mental hopsital. And Sergei was brilliant at telling stories. Georgii Maximovich, who came into the studio for a cup of tea while Sergei was telling that story, also looked at him disapprovingly.

There was a remarkable synchronism between Olga's mother and Georgii Maximovich. Whenever her mother pronounced some opinion, Georgii Maximovich would nod in confirmation, accompanying his nods with such phrases as 'That's so' or 'I'm afraid you're right.' Olga's real father had died long ago, when she was six. Her mother had met Georgii Maximovich during the wartime evacuation, when they were both working in the same factory, she in the planning department and Georgii Maximovich as decorator and painter in the workers' club. He was an artist who had studied before the revolution under some famous Greek, had travelled and taken part in exhibitions abroad. He was arrested and 're-educated', and after his release could not re-establish himself as an artist; gradually he lost heart altogether, so that by the time he was evacuated to a remote little town in the Urals he had degenerated into a mere starving sign-painter.

But when Georgii returned to Moscow with his new family, Olga and her mother, he was given a studio and a room in an artists' co-operative. He began to be recognised again; he was mentioned in the press and given commissions. He had not, it seemed, wasted his time during his wartime evacuation to the Urals but had worked like an ox – because art is made by oxen, according to Jules Renard, who was Georgii Maximovich's favourite author – and had drawn a whole gallery full of studies of industrial workers entitled 'Urals Steel'; these drawings were exhibited several times, were reproduced as prints and even made into postcards – and Georgii Maximovich underwent a kind of renaissance, a second youth, or as he put it, 'my rosy period'. All would have continued to go well had Georgii Maximovich not become ill just then, in the late forties. He had headaches, then something went wrong with his eyes. He was forbidden to work and went away to a sanatorium. After that he developed heart trouble, and shortly before Sergei appeared, Georgii Maximovich had a heart attack. How old was he then? Olga's mother was seventeen years younger than he; she was forty-three when Sergei came on the scene, so Georgii Maximovich was sixty.

He still walked with a straight back and his handshake was firm. When meeting someone for the first time, he had a habit of looking hard and intently into the person's face and unceremoniously staring them up and down. New acquaintances found this disconcerting. Sergei admitted later that he had been slightly taken aback by his first encounter with Georgii Maximovich? 'He looked at me as if I had stolen something.'

Georgii Maximovich, however, also had another habit: having thoroughly studied a new person he would announce that he had 'an interesting face' and that he would be 'very interesting to paint'. In the tone of these remarks there was undoubtedly something of the slightly patronising attitude of the artist standing above the rest of humanity, but they were at the same time an innocent flattery that everyone enjoyed hearing. Georgii Maximovich never made these comments to Sergei, however. He was on his guard from the first. Of course Georgii Maximovich's reactions on such occasions were not really his own: like a sensitive membrane, he simply picked up the vibrations given out by Olga's mother. She and he were, in fact, perfectly attuned to each other. And a very good thing too – 'Thank God for it', thought Olga.

She had never been jealous; she hardly remembered her father, and Georgii Maximovich treated her mother well. He obviously loved her, while she, poor woman, positively adored him, and over the years they had grown to have the same tastes, the same opinions about people, about art, books, money, everything. Her mother was constantly absorbed in his problems and his illnesses. She simply had no time for anyone else's life.

When Irinka was born, Olga's mother was at first torn between her granddaughter and her husband; she wanted to be useful, to be everywhere at once, but she lacked the strength for it and gave in, surrendering her role to the child's other grandmother. Olga forgave her. For some time they lived with neighbours in the flat next door to the studio in Sushchevskaya Street, where her mother and Georgii Maximovich lived; next they lived with her mother and Georgii; then Sergei's mother suffered a grievous blow – the death of Sergei's sister, her unmarried daughter, a sick, unhappy girl whom she greatly loved – and they decided to move in with her in her two-room flat in Shabolovka Street.

It was here that Sergei had spent his childhood. Everything in the place was familiar to him and much loved, and although Olga sensed at once that living with her mother-in-law was not going to be easy, Sergei very much wanted it and said they ought to meet the old woman halfway – although, incidentally, she was hardly an old woman but a noisy, bustling, middle-aged lady. They could at least give her a granddaughter. It was sad for Olga to leave her mother, but there was nothing to be done about it. All this had happened of its own momentum, beginning that evening when Sergei first arrived – tousle-headed, wearing his lumberjack shirt and a jacket with padded shoulders – and said words backwards.

After that first evening came spring, meetings in backyards, doorways, cafés, bars; then summer, Vlad still totally unaware of what was happening, scraping together the money for a trip south – heat, cool sea, liberation. Four of them went together: Olga and Rita, her friend of those days who later vanished without a trace, and Vlad and Sergei. Vlad had a friend – or rather, a friend of his father's – a general in the army medical corps, who owned a house at Gagra, on the eastern shore of the Black Sea. He had promised to rent them rooms. They needed two: one for Rita and Olga, one for Sergei and Vlad, but there turned out not to be room enough for them all in the house. The summer was burning hot and Gagra suffocatingly humid. In the end, Vlad's friend – whose name was apparently Porfiry Niko-laevich, or it might have been Parfenty Mikhailovich, a vague man who had once worked in some important institution in Moscow but was now living on a pension in his house in Gagra – could rent out only one small and rather unpleasant room; he also offered them a summerhouse in his garden. The boys were given the room and the girls took the summerhouse; right by the beach. It was a flimsy, shack-like structure that would nowadays be called a bungalow and has become the fashion all along the Black Sea coast. At first everything was fine, but then certain disadvantages came to light. The girls, for instance, had to go through the garden and into the house to go to the bathroom.

Apart from that, the other house guests, Porfiry Mikhailovich's relatives, friends, and acquaintances, who were many and of whom more were constantly arriving by car, led a noisy, hectic kind of life. They spent all day and every day drinking, fooling around, shouting songs, playing records loudly and dancing on the veranda, barbecuing kebabs in the garden; in the evening they would all flock down to the sea for a swim – down the garden path, through the gate in the fence and out onto the pebbly beach. The house stood just above the shoreline.

Parfenty Nikolaevich's rowdy guests would invite Vlad, Sergei, and the girls to join them. The boys never refused, since they had no money, Gagra was an expensive place, and the wine and Georgian brandy flowed freely. Rita, an unattractive, scheming girl, fed up with her lonely life in Moscow, also plunged into this whirlpool, which looked dangerous but tempting.

Olga, however, said firmly, 'No'. There were occasional louts among the people who wandered through the garden in the evening, and once someone tried to break into the shack at a late hour; the door shook, stupid Rita giggled, but Olga guessed that it wasn't Rita they wanted. 'Hey, Miss High-and-Mighty,' they shouted from outside. 'Come for a swim with us.' In a stern voice Olga threatened them with the police.

Next morning she complained to Vlad, who ran into the house to fetch Porfiry Parfentievich's wife, a graceful lady who always wore white; her black hair was streaked with grey, and she had gold on her fingers, gold in her ears, and when she opened her large purple lips she revealed a great deal of gold in her mouth as well: 'Please forgive my hooligans, girls. They are children of the South. The sun is in their blood. The sun makes people crazy.'

Sergei was brilliant at swimming and diving. He and Rita would swim far out beyond the line of buoys, while Olga and Vlad splashed about near the shore. For all his clumsiness or shyness in practical matters and in personal relations, Sergei was physically very brave. He could never bring himself to ask Porfiry how much rent they should pay for the shack, or to tell him about the bathroom, which the house guests often kept occupied in a long, continuous succession, thereby putting Rita and Olga in an embarrassing situation; afraid of causing offence, he would postpone any encounter with their host in a cowardly fashion, but at the same time he never turned down the offer of a drink, or an invitation to join the other guests on the veranda, and she detected with annoyance a vacillating and unmanly streak in his character. Yet he was always ready to get involved if there was a fight on the beach, and he thought nothing of diving into the water from a height of thirty-five feet. Each day she became more aware that she was hooked.

Never before had she fallen for anyone quite so hopelessly, or desperately. Nothing else existed any longer. All other thoughts vanished. Only a few days had passed – what could have changed in such a short time – yet everything around her seemed to have altered: the colour of the sky, the smell of the sea, the taste of kebab. It was as if a needle on some inward dial had moved forward: everything inside her was churning much more rapidly than before. She also felt something new and disturbing, as though some extra, superfluous source of gravitational pull was causing her torment and discomfort. She couldn't bear it, for instance, when he went into the house and stayed there for a long time. Of course it was nonsense to feel like that; yet she went through agonies: Why is he in there? Who is he with? Whose laughter is that coming from the veranda? Male laughter upset her as much as female. It meant that he was enjoying himself more in there than out here with her. These torments were strange, divorced from reason, born of pure instinct. After all, he wasn't her husband, they hadn't even made love yet; that idea, in fact, was only just beginning to take shape in her secret fantasies; yet from her feelings and the pain she experienced they might as well have been lovers.

One day she could stand it no longer and walked up to the veranda to call him. Vlad and Rita were getting ready to go to the beach, but Sergei had taken the chess set indoors with him. She had started learning to play chess, wanting to do everything that he did (one day, overcoming her fear, she had even dived off the ten-foot springboard), and as she opened the glass door she saw several people, men and women, sitting around a table drinking. They were all looking at Sergei, who was standing a little apart so that everyone could see him, and doing a piece of mimicry. He was an excellent mimic; two of his best acts were 'the old chemist' and 'the soccer fan'. He had, in fact, many talents – he could draw, he sang well, and he had taught himself to play the guitar.

At that moment on the veranda she suddenly felt a fierce wave of revulsion towards him, like an attack of nausea, and towards the people around the table staring at him with cheerful, boozy amiability. As they clapped, shouted 'Bravo!' and raised their glasses to toast him in Georgian – '*Allaverdi Sergo!*' – she completely lost her temper and said angrily, 'All right, now you can say a word backwards – "buffoon", for instance – and then say goodbye. They're waiting for us on the beach.'

He stared at her in amazement with his narrow blue eyes and actually opened his mouth to say something in protest, or maybe even to say 'buffoon' backwards, but she took him by the hand, he silently obeyed, and they went out.

On the way to the beach she gave him a lecture, deriving keen pleasure from the fact that he took it in silence while she scolded him with motherly severity: 'Don't you see how shameful, how disgusting it is to demean yourself in front of those drunken fools? You, an intellectual, clowning to amuse those rich, idle ne'er-do-wells.'

He defended himself good-naturedly. 'You're too much of an extremist. Take it from me as an historian – extremism never leads to good results.'

Yet he seemed to enjoy being held by the hand, to enjoy her indignation on his account. It was perhaps at that moment that her mind created the model which for years she was to keep before her as the ideal form of their relationship, towards which she would strive with her utmost strength, and to which he cunningly pretended to submit while remaining in fact remote and uninvolved: to lead him by the hand and teach him what was right, no matter what the cost in pain and heartache. On the beach, when Vlad heard her attacking him, he rushed to his friend's defence: 'You don't know the local customs. Here, if they offer you a drink or invite you to join a party, you can't refuse.'

Rita, who had long been nursing a grudge (even her little mind had finally grasped that neither Vlad nor Sergei was interested in her, and she was gradually starting to hate Olga), said that Olga was, as usual, making a mountain out of a molehill. As for Parfenty and his house guests, in Rita's opinion they were perfectly normal, decent people and Olga was wrong to despise them. 'There's no need to look down your nose at them' was her expression. But what did these people do for a living, for God's sake? Where did they get the money for such fabulous generosity? It's rude, it's bad form to ask questions about other people's money. They're obviously not crooks, because if they were they would be in prison. Thus ran the logic of this stupid creature, with whom Olga had inexplicably struck up a short-lived friendship. Rita was a thin girl with reddish-blonde hair, freckled white skin, blue eyes, and a sharp little nose. She had never lost the firm belief that she was beautiful, and the years passed for her in a state of unremitting perplexity: Why did no one else ever notice it?

Although they were an ill-assorted foursome, they went everywhere together: to the bazaar; to the cinema; to the little smoke-filled snack bar where Datiko, a fat man with a tiny head, served them wine and small, fat-soaked Georgian meat pies called *chebureki*; along the promenade; among the white-clad crowd sauntering up and down the main street; to the tennis courts to watch the good players, whom Sergei and Vlad watched with jealous fascination. Later in the day they too were allowed to leap around the court for a bit. Both of them were only just starting to learn, taking lessons from the professional, Otto Janovich. Vlad was useless at tennis, but Sergei showed promise, and every evening he got better at it; if he had wanted to, he could have become a real tennis player – with his natural talent he could have become a real anything: a real swimmer, musician, draughtsman, even a nuclear physicist. Otto Janovich said that his movement was 'excellent', but the boys couldn't afford rackets of their own and pay for lessons too, for they had to economise to pay the fare home.

Olga and Rita sat on long benches in the shade of a row of poplar trees and watched them play. The sight of Sergei in his white T-shirt and white peaked cap, his thin sunburned face, his powerful well-rounded legs in the short socks that he had brought from Moscow specially to wear with his gym-shoes (he had no idea he would be playing tennis but thought he would be playing volleyball, for which he was a fanatic), made her heart thump with happiness. It gave her a warmth to watch him when he couldn't see her, to see his enthusiasm, his exertion, his irritation, his delight – it was all laid bare for her. One day Otto Janovich, a gnome-like little man with a beard, surreptitiously passed her a note. Unfolding it carefully so that Rita wouldn't see, she read: 'Come tomorrow at nine o'clock in the morning. I will teach you free of charge and for as long as you like.' The little gnome charged a high rate for an hour's instruction, and he was said to be a rich man. She smiled at him and shook her head. Otto Janovich made a face expressing profound disappointment. And there were many others that summer who wanted to teach her free of charge and for as long as she liked!

No doubt about it, she was pretty then. She had not yet started to put on weight. Everything about her was in harmony, coordinated, her body smooth and firm, and although she couldn't swim, she ran fast, played volleyball, and could turn a perfect cartwheel. She couldn't possibly do it now, but in those days it was nothing for her to turn ten cartwheels in succession without a trace of strain. Men stared at her on the beach. At that

17

age she tanned very evenly and quickly, an ability that she later somehow lost. Foolishly, she would lie in the scorching sun for hours, regardless of the effect on her. She wore her hair shoulder length, in the way that was fashionable at the time, loose and unkempt. Sergei used to call it 'the head of the Medusa'. But it greatly suited her – that thick, luxuriant, dark-auburn mass of hair above her clear, rounded, pure forehead, as yet without a wrinkle. It was probably the best year of her life, the year of her prime. She realised this from the way men watched her; the Georgians would stare at her as she came out of the water, insolently clicking their tongues and smacking their lips. And of course they pestered her shamelessly, always trying to make friends, to strike up a conversation or share the book she was reading, and inviting her to play volleyball. Sergei and Vlad spent their time in constant expectation of a fight.

Her admirers included a bunch of men from Leningrad, a naval captain staying with Porfiry called Tsnakis, and some actors, tanned almost black, with one of whom Sergei had a scene in which he hit the actor with an inflatable rubber dolphin, inflicting a minor scratch that led to much fuss and shouting. The police appeared, and only Porfiry saved Sergei from getting into trouble. And then there was someone else who made a pass at Olga in the forest when they drove out on a trip to Lake Ritsa. There was also a funny little middle-aged creature with an olive complexion, one of Porfiry's house guests, who made a simultaneous play for both Rita and Olga. Thoughtful and obliging, he went every morning to the bazaar and bought them salad, buttermilk, and fruit. He treated Vlad and Sergei with paternal benevolence, apparently not regarding them as serious rivals. He would follow them down to the beach and exasperate them with his boring conversation, from which it was all the harder to escape because the little man himself had such good manners. One day, under an oath of secrecy, he showed Rita a medical certificate that stated that So-and-So, while possessing normal sexual potency, was incapable of procreation owing to inadequate fertility, confirmed and signed by Dr Such-and-Such, medical director of a polyclinic. Naturally Rita divulged this news to the others, which provoked much hilarity. The little olive-skinned man vanished soon afterwards and did not reappear.

Sergei taught Olga to swim. How they enjoyed those lessons! It would have been boring if she had been able to swim as well as he could. He held her with his arms, she floundered, clinging to his neck, laughed, sank, surfaced again blinded by spray, all the time feeling his hands, which in the water were very bold.

Vlad watched them, straining his eyes – he could not wear his spectacles in the water – trying to make out what was going on over there among all the laughter and the splashing, and sometimes he would offer, 'I could teach you too, if you like. If Sergei gets bored . . .'

Ever gallant, poor Vlad was not much better in the water than Olga was. He was misled by the brusque and apparently irritated way that Sergei shouted at her: 'Won't you ever understand, woman? Move your legs like a frog!' He loved calling her 'woman', as though they had spent a lifetime together. There were other terms of affection, such as 'elephant child' and 'elephant cow'. People who knew them found it odd that she put up with being called such unflattering names, but she liked it: she knew what was happening when he used them. Vlad would bob alongside, trying to teach her, and they couldn't help laughing because it all seemed so funny. Puffing out his cheeks in his conscientious efforts to help, Vlad never realised that he was an unwanted intruder. Rita, who understood this and the reason for it very well, grew quietly furious; she was under the impression that Sergei had been invited for her, so she interpreted these developments as treachery. Sergei and Olga regarded each other as a joyous fount of mutual pleasure and fun; every word, every childish joke, set off peals of laughter.

One night Rita started a quarrel by demanding to have the window shut. Olga protested; the shack was very stuffy.

'But I'm cold,' Rita asserted obstinately.

'It's stifling.'

'I don't intend to catch a chill just to please you.'

'We won't be able to sleep with the window shut.'

'You'll sleep perfectly well. I'm not worried about you.'

They bickered like this for a long time and Rita, of course, won: the window was shut. Olga felt self-assured and happy. Rita's animosity did not subside; she began accusing Olga of selfishness.

'What a fool I was to agree to come with you. All you ever think of is yourself. Living with you for even ten days is intolerable, you're such a complete egotist.'

Listening to this tirade, Olga felt no hostility and no urge to answer back: deep in her heart she actually pitied Rita. But how could she help her? It would be wonderful if only Vlad would show even a faint sexual interest in Rita, but Vlad persisted in treating her with nothing but comradely good nature, which was not at all what she needed.

'I don't know why I'm an egotist,' said Olga, yawning and smiling through her drowiness. 'Let's go to sleep, I'm tired.'

'Of course *you're* sleepy – you've been rushing around and shrieking your head off all day,' grumbled Rita. 'The reason why you're an egotist is because you think of yourself the whole time. You never give a thought for other people. I've never had a worse holiday in my life. It's been hell, like a nightmare.'

Then, to crown it all, Rita threw a fit. Olga ran indoors for Rita's pills and water and woke up the others. Lying there in the shack with a wet towel around her head, Rita cursed her fate in a pathetic voice and begged for a ticket back to Moscow. Olga murmured some nonsense to calm her down, but she was thinking: 'Tomorrow, in the sea . . .' No one else's tears or heartaches could dim her happiness.

Rita found a woman friend who was holidaying in nearby Akhali and moved out to join her. One day they saw her walking arm-in-arm with this friend, a middle-aged straw blonde, accompanied by two men in pyjamas – in those days it was the fashion in the South for men to stroll around town wearing striped pyjamas as if they were summer suits. All four were talking noisily. Rita glanced at Olga in passing and walked on with barely a nod.

At first, sleeping alone in the shack made Olga uneasy. She did not fall asleep until dawn, listening to the roar of the surf, suffering alternate agonies of elation and depression and of something else incomprehensible: the unknown. There were sounds of people walking through the garden; the rasp of cicadas; a car honking; someone driving out through the gates. Where, Olga wondered, could they be going at this hour of the night? To the bar for some wine, perhaps? In the morning she would complain to the boys that fear had kept her awake all night. She was not telling the truth: her restlessness had been caused by unbearable expectation, a welter of confused thoughts.

In fact, from her first night alone in the shack she was waiting for him to come. Then one morning the boys promised they would stand guard over her. And they would all go swimming that night.

The night was pitch black: nothing could be seen beyond two paces; a starless, southern night. The clouds hung low in the sky and breathing was difficult. On the beach were sounds of talk, of footsteps on the pebbles; many other people were sensible enough to swim at night. They conversed in undertones, some in whispers; the air was charged with a certain mystery, of which

Olga was thrillingly aware, although she thought it was her imagination and the mystery was within herself. Then she discovered that people really were whispering, that the mysteriousness was genuine and had nothing to do with her feelings. After a while her head began to reel and her legs felt weak from the sultry humidity, from the thick darkness and a premonition of mystery. The darkness was so thick that you could bathe naked. Olga walked towards the sea, unable to see the water. Never in her life, neither before nor after that night, had she bathed in such warm water; its temperatures must have been at least a hundred degrees. There were no waves, only a flat, quiet calm, as though this were not the sea but merely a mass of warm water as in a swimming pool, with only gentle splashing sounds and an indistinct murmur of voices to be heard amid the utter blackness.

She sensed there was something unusual about tonight. Vlad had disappeared. Though he might be nearby, he was silent, not giving away his whereabouts. She could not see Sergei when he took her by the hand and led her into the deeper water. They stopped when the water was up to her shoulders. He said it was like a sacred rite, like bathing in the holy waters of the Ganges or the Jordan, or in tropical rivers where the water was like steaming milk. Vladimir, grand duke of Russia, had been baptised in the Dnieper – although it must have been a great deal colder.

She laughed at him: 'Don't you know a lot!'

He asked, 'Would you like me to teach you to swim?'

She was surprised: he had been doing nothing else all day. She waded close to him and clasped him around the neck, and they stood and kissed for a long, long while. It was the first time, but it was as good as if they had kissed many times before; the only strange thing was that there were people all around but no one could see them. Vlad called out to them from far away. She felt embarrassed and started to pull away; they struggled, then ran out of the water and collapsed onto the rocks.

The rocks were warm: yet she soon felt cold and started to shiver.

'Hey, where the hell are you?' Vlad shouted.

Sergei closed her mouth with his hand. Unable to contain themselves, they both burst into giggles and rolled off the rocks on which they were sitting.

'Ah, there you are . . . hiding in the dark.' Vlad sat ponderously down beside them. 'Well, I've fixed up my ticket.'

Chilled to the bone, Olga was afraid to ask 'What ticket?' lest her voice betray how much she was shivering. It was ridiculous to be shivering on such a sultry night, but she didn't want Vlad to guess what was happening to her. He explained that he had made arrangements with one of the clinics of the First Moscow School of Medicine to work there during August. He was still a medical student then, in his fifth year, even though he was three years older than Olga and Sergei; he had started university later than they had.

She realised from his voice that he had guessed. She felt very sorry for him. Tongue-tied, he mumbled some nonsense – pathetic instructions about what they had to do before his departure. The conversation on the beach continued painfully until about two in the morning; then she announced that she wanted to go to bed. It was not that she really wanted to sleep – her brain was wide awake and racing – but something made her say it; it was simply impossible for the three of them to go on sitting there any longer.

Always the gentleman despite everything, Vlad asked whether she needed anyone to stand guard. What an excellent husband he would have made, if only . . . Olga's mother thought there was 'a little bit' of Pierre Bezuhov in Vlad. Since Pierre in *War and Peace* was her favourite hero, coming from her 'a little bit' meant a great deal. Georgii Maximovich used to say that Vlad had a face like the Mordovian god Keremet, that it would be interesting to paint him (he did paint him, in several long sittings that caused Vlad much discomfort) and that he very much wished everything would work out between Olga and Vlad: 'Don't play hard to get; you'll never find a better husband.' Now he's a professor, head of his department. He has three children and a wife – a kindhearted shapeless cow of a woman with a broad, fat bottom; she is a doctor too, a radiologist. But that night he was crushed, miserable, and could only ask in a defeated voice, 'Do you need anyone to stand guard?'

Both men went away, leaving her alone, her wet bathing suit spread out on the wooden sill to await the sun. She couldn't sleep, but not because she was afraid; that night there were no footsteps, no voices, nothing. She lay with open eyes, her heart thumping; she knew it would not stay dark much longer: he must come soon. After about twenty minutes he came. Again the thought of Vlad worried her: suppose he had noticed Sergei leaving their room and had guessed where he was going? She asked him why he hadn't waited until tomorrow, when Vlad would be gone.

In reply he asked, 'What's Vlad to you?'

In truth Vlad meant nothing to her.

'I couldn't wait till tomorrow.'

There was no talk – no promises, no vows; she simply entrusted herself to him forever.

Later there were many, countless other nights, in Moscow and in the country, in the summer, in wet weather, in the chill of the autumn when the heating was not yet on and the room was warmed by a portable electric heater; they made love almost every night. Theirs was a rare gift; her girl friends sometimes exchanged intimate details of their love life, but Olga never did. If she had told them about it, they wouldn't have believed her and would have thought Olga was telling the same sort of lies that they themselves invented, but the secret was very simple: what one of them lacked, the other possessed, and what they both possessed was merged jointly and fully into a wholeness – although of course this didn't happen all at once; it didn't happen on the first night, not even in their first year. Then she realised that with anyone else it could never be as it was with him. What was it like that night in the shack? A sultry, airless night, long forgotten . . .

The superfluous Vlad hung around their necks for one more day. In the water Sergei never once came near her. He spent all the time with Vlad, even seemed to be avoiding her. This alarmed her; then she calmed herself with the thought that he was cunningly acting this way on purpose; after all, he knew and she knew that he would come to her again that night. Then some man invited Vlad to go swimming; they swam away from the shore and the man gave Vlad some news. At that time all kinds of rumours and snatches of news were going around. She had forgotten what this particular piece of information was; she remembered only that Vlad and Sergei became unusually excited and were going to run to find Porfiry, but their host, the man said, had left for Moscow, that his wife was ill and couldn't see anyone, and that all the other guests had also left and gone home. Not a single car remained in the drive.

They went into town to wander around the bazaar and the little shops. Whenever Vlad moved away or turned aside from them, Sergei would take her hand and squeeze her fingers, contrive to touch her or press up against her. Vlad and Sergei argued a lot that day, talking very noisily, but she could think of nothing but what would happen that night. In the bazaar, they were selling the first grapes of the season. She realised, of course, that the news might be interesting, but she was obsessed

23

with another event and also slightly perplexed: On *this* day of all days, how could Sergei be so absorbed by something else, and how could he, for instance, even fail to hear her when she asked him a question?

The Greek maid, who had a pronounced moustache, was pottering around the garden with a rake, while Titan, the Alsatian, lay sprawled miserably on the porch, his head on his paws. The family and guests had all dispersed, vanished; even Porfiry's wife, the elegant lady with the blue lips, looking like a Gogolesque corpse, had disappeared somewhere.

How good they were, those few days when Olga and Sergei had the house virtually to themselves. The Greek maid was frightened of sleeping in the house alone and had invited them to share the second-floor veranda. They spent five days there. Everything in the house was built to gigantic proportions; the divan on the veranda was apparently designed to accommodate an orgy. The rooms, as yet unaired, were still full of the sour, stale fumes of wine mixed with a faint smell of dog, but out on the veranda the sea air blew, at once enervating and bracing. They talked steadily day and night, insatiably learning about each other. For them, everything was already settled. Yet in October, Vlad was amazed when he was invited to their wedding. It had, apparently, never occurred to him that things were going so far or so fast.

After all, they had only just met – and already they had lived through an idyll on a veranda over the sea, no secrets between them, closer to each other than they had ever been to anyone else. August brought difficult encounters with his mother, but it changed nothing. Perkhushkovo in the autumn, electric trains in the evening, meeting at suburban stations; it was then that Svetlana had shown up, a nightmare that for a long time would not go away and that almost suffocated her.

When did she first hear about Svetlana? Was it from his mother?

No, when his mother spoke the name, Olga had shuddered: it was already known to her, already embedded in her mind like a tiny splinter, inflaming the surrounding tissue, causing a slow, painful swelling. Sergei was open, thoughtless and indiscreet and blabbed a great deal about his past, so she had heard about the bespectacled Svetlana who would stop at nothing to hold on to him. At first Olga had not taken her too seriously, because everybody had a past, including herself: there had been Gendlin, for instance. He had been totally ousted from her life, buried several millennia ago, like Pharaoh Tutankhamen. They had met, she seemed to remember, at a recital at the Conservatory. He was an engineer or some other variety of technician, tall, with a rather odd walk that at every step made him seem about to sit down. Her mother's reproachful voice saying 'Gendlin called again' always made her feel guilty – not because of Gendlin but because of her mother. Getting rid of Gendlin had been no problem; he had quietly dropped away of his own accord like an autumn leaf falling off a branch, but she had nevertheless said to Sergei proudly and somewhat didactically, 'So I told him absolutely straight that he must stop ringing me up, because it was pointless. He understood, and that was that. You have to break it off with one good sharp tug, like pulling out an aching tooth.'

Sergei had agreed – yes, yes, of course. Like an aching tooth. Since she was still unacquainted with his capricious and unstable character, his submissive nods and his instant unforced agreement with whatever she said gave her a sense of ease and security. This did not, however, last very long; it lasted only until her first meeting with her future mother-in-law.

The room in that house in Shabolovka Street amazed her; hexagonal in shape, with an unusually high ceiling, it had been sliced out of what had once been a much larger room, leaving several plaster cupids ruthlessly cut in half through their rumps. One foot and a little wing adorned the cornice of the hexagonal room, while the other foot and a small hand, holding a bow, projected into the hall. None of the cupids had any heads; these were now on the other side of the partition that divided the flats. The walls, papered in dark cherry-red wallpaper, ornamented with a white basketwork pattern, were hung with innumerable photographs. Sergei at once drew her attention to one of them: a pyramid of bewhiskered men in military tunics, fur hats, and greatcoats, and, barely noticeable in one corner, a small figure in a white headscarf with indistinguishable features.

'That's my mother in the Red Army Political Department. In 1920.'

It was emphasised from the very beginning that his mother was not to be compared with other, ordinary mothers; she was not an ageing lady but someone who had Made History. Olga Vasilievna, however, had approached this woman – very wrinkled and thin-lipped, with narrow eyes and prominent cheekbones – with enormous sympathy and a sincere desire to love her, not because she had Made History (she was indifferent to all relics, ruins, and witnesses to the past) but because she was Sergei's mother. They drank tea out of small and very cheap cups that might almost have belonged to a child's tea set. His sister came, wrapped in an old-womanish shawl, a fat, ungainly girl, completely unlike Sergei, with a vaguely wistful, enigmatic smile. Whenever she talked, she would assume this lopsided smile and look away to one side. She was three years older than Sergei.

Everything in the house – the walls, the ceiling, the china, the furniture, and the people who lived in it – was distinguished by a peculiar kind of incoherence. Yet how she loved it all! He ran out to the shop for a bottle of Georgian red wine – they had developed a passion for red wine in Gagra. And then, when Sergei's sister went into the next room and Olga was left alone with her future mother-in-law, the old woman suddenly asked, 'Do you know anything about Svetlana?'

Olga admitted that she did know about her, but only vaguely.

'Well, I've news for you, and there's nothing vague about it.' Her eyes, narrow blue slits with steely pupils, bored into Olga's eyes. 'This Svetlana, whom I had never heard of until the day before yesterday, is expecting Sergei's child.'

This creature, it transpired, had come to the house and told them her story, with much hysterical embroidery (later it was proved to be a very ordinary attempt at blackmail; she was relying on their credulity), and now Olga was being put on trial to see how she reacted. The shabby little living room was suddenly transformed into the setting for a kangaroo court; the only things missing were the commissar's leather tunic with a Mauser in its wooden holster.

'Are you sure you can be happy at the cost of another person's unhappiness?'

Olga stammered, 'I don't know . . . Are you sure this is true?'

The woman with the steely eyes nodded coldly.

'But we love each other. They will have to give each other up . . .' In a miserable voice Olga tried to resist the onslaught.

'You're speaking of the way scoundrels behave. My son is not a scoundrel. He's simply irresponsible.'

Suddenly the sister reappeared, having heard everything. Twisting her mouth into a smile, she said tensely and forcefully, 'Don't pay any attention to her. As usual she is distorting and oversimplifying everything.' Turning to her mother, she angrily spat out, 'You're talking nonsense again. It makes me sick to listen to you.'

The old woman subsided. Sergei came running in with the wine, and Olga summoned up all her strength to stop herself from bursting into tears. Sergei understood completely and began to cross-question his mother. If it was impossible to discover what he and his mother and sister really thought about this snake, Svetlana, because she did not seem to exist: what mattered to them was a principle, over which all three quarrelled fiercely, each insisting that he or she was in the right.

Olga could make no sense of it all. One thing, however, she did understand, or so she thought: *They did not want her*. Inconsistency lay in the very nature of these people, and to draw any hasty conclusions from what they said or did was likely to be a mistake. Sergei said that Svetlana was lying. She believed him. Yet somehow he found it very difficult to break with Svetlana: she threatened suicide, he was tormented with guilt, visited her relatives, and had several meetings with Svetlana's brother, a boxer. He went to see doctors and she had pregnancy tests done at a laboratory, but they were negative. It was quite obvious from Svetlana's behaviour that she was pulling a con trick: unfortunately Sergei's mother was easily influenced by persistent liars, even though – so Olga guessed – the old lady wanted Svetlana even less than Olga as a daughter-in-law.

The whole nightmare lasted for three weeks of September, and at a certain moment it looked as if Svetlana had succeeded in her aim of pulling Sergei, if not over to her side, at least away from Olga. So lethal was the blow delivered by this scheming bitch that Olga actually decided to break it off with him. Something stayed her hand, however, and she held on.

A ring on the doorbell at midnight. There stood a drab-looking, dishevelled, bespectacled girl on little bandy legs. Are you Olga? Yes, I am. Olga at once realised who it was and felt the blood rush to her face. Her hatred for this female was terrifying: she wanted to pick her up, throw her downstairs and break every bone in her body. Instead, of course, she politely asked her to come in, and they talked in the hall. Svetlana tried to convince Olga that Sergei did not love her, could never love her. It was no use for Olga to try to deceive herself: he couldn't abide 'women like her'; it was just a temporary thing on his part, an aberration that would pass; they would be 'very unhappy', and more hysterical nonsense of the same sort. Olga felt as if something were squeezing her guts. Speechless, she stared at the thin, triangular little face with its sharp, trembling chin and huge eyes, the magnified pupils quivering behind thick lenses as though Svetlana were in pain. To prove she was telling the truth – this was her reason for coming – she announced that Sergei had recently spent two nights with her, in August – after he had come back from the South.

Olga responded firmly, 'You're lying!'

She did not believe it for a moment, even though Svetlana took great pleasure in mentioning a particular detail that she could not have known if she had been lying.

Olga still did not believe this naïve little fool. Next day, as she ran through the rain to the shop near the Hotel Metropole, where they had agreed to meet – her intention being to tell him, finally, to go to hell – in her heart she felt absurdly calm and secure. She secretly believed he would be indignant, would explain, try to vindicate himself, and dispel the horror of this sudden threat. Never in her life had she experienced anything like this. She had confided nothing to her mother or her stepfather; she was fighting this battle on her own. Now she had to reach a decision within a matter of seconds.

Sergei, his features darkening into a scowl – it was at this moment that she began to notice a strange side to his character – said, 'She's a little slut, but she's telling the truth. Except that I spent one night at her place, not two.'

My God, but why, why? Why did he do it? Why tell her about it even if it was the truth?

'I felt sorry for her. I knew I was going to leave her, and I pitied her.'

He took pity on *her*; yet he was quite ready to make a casual admission that caused extreme pain to the woman he loved. There, in the rain, outside the Metropole, they wandered up and down like lunatics, bumping into people – something large and impressive was under construction there, the building was covered in scaffolding, and now and again when it started to rain harder they would huddle under the projecting boards for shelter – and talking, talking, talking as they tried to work out how to go on living, whether they should stay together or part, perhaps forever. She wavered from one alternative to the other, but with every minute her resolution to leave him weakened. Suddenly it occurred to her that this had been sent by fate to test her and that if she could only fight back she would be happy. It ended with their going into the Metropole restaurant and eating a good lunch; he had received his pay from the museum that day, and they spent half of it on the meal.

The wedding took place a month later. It was the end of October, cold but sunny; they sealed the windows with newspaper to keep the guests from getting chilled and borrowed a record player and some records from their neighbours. It was not so much a wedding reception as an ordinary party, with vodka, snacks, and chicken Kiev brought in from a nearby restaurant. Sergei composed and typed out some hilarious invitation cards, along the lines of:

Dear Friend!
   If your soul longs for respite and you wish to forget for a while the cares of family/bachelor/factory/school (delete whichever is inapplicable) life, come to our domestic wedding and/or concert . . .

The programme of the 'concert' was a farrago of delightful nonsense (Sergei was brilliant at such things) made up of the bridegroom's party pieces – impressions, saying words backwards, songs, a lecture by Dr Polysaev on the benefits of starvation, and God knows what else, but it was all forgotten now, vanished – no, there was one thing:
   Gastronomic orgasms.
   By kind permission of the bride's mother, henceforth referred to as mother-in-law.

She remembered this because it had been the cause of a minor quarrel that broke out late that night when they were doing the washing up – Olga, her mother, and another woman who came in to help, with Georgii Maximovich doing the drying. Sergei, dead drunk, was snoring in another room.
   Georgii Maximovich announced that he was puzzled: What were gastronomic orgasms? If it was meant to be a joke, then it was in rather dubious taste. If it wasn't a joke, then what, he would like to know, was it supposed to mean? Did it refer to some sort of disease, or what? And why the reference to the 'mother-in-law'? All the jokes about mothers-in-law had been played out about the year 1900. Olga's mother smiled ironically and said that she wasn't in the least offended by that sort of humour, and as far as she was concerned they could go on making such jokes. Even if she had felt offended, she would never have admitted it. Later it emerged that Olga's mother detested the idea of playing the role of mother-in-law and she did not like the word; least of all did she make any claims to excellence in matters gastronomic.
   No marriage is simply a union of two individuals, as people think, but a merger or a collision between two clans, two worlds. Every marriage is bipolar: two systems collide in space and are fused into a dual entity forever. Who will dominate whom? Who wants what? How will they get it? His world, his relatives, arrived and opened their eyes in wild curiosity at the sight of her

relatives, her world; and although there was never again in the whole seventeen years of their married life such a full-scale meeting, such a frank, uninhibited encounter, the collision of the two worlds began then and persisted all those years, often unseen and unheeded by any of them. And now Sergei was dead – but the old war still went on.

There was not, of course, any actual warfare. Everything was settled calmly and peacefully, if one didn't count a few mild subterranean tremors. Nevertheless, Olga felt nervous: she sensed that her future mother-in-law could be awkward and prickly, and that Sergei's slightly eccentric sister was the sort of girl who might easily do something unpredictable. She was worried, too, about her mother's brother, Uncle Petya; he and his family were apt to be loud and tactless.

Before they sat down at the table, Georgii Maximovich invited all the guests to see his studio. To get there they had to go down a long corridor; along the right-hand side was a row of doors leading into other studios, while on the left were the communal bathroom, the communal kitchen, and the communal lavatory shared by all the inhabitants of the third floor. The house was a typically bad design of the 1920s. The guests proceeded, shuffling, along the corridor, while other, inquisitive tenants stood in the doorways of the communal kitchen and bathroom – the wives, mothers, and children of the artists who shared the house – and the artists themselves opened the doors of their studios and stared out at the crowd. The artists' wives and mothers were not exactly well disposed towards Olga and her mother, although the two women had been living in the house for eight years, a period in which it would have been perfectly possible to get used to them and accept them. But for some reason the artists' wives and mothers had fond memories of Georgii Maximovich's first wife and his son Slava, from both of whom Georgii Maximovich was separated several years before the war.

The procession of guests moved in total silence, and at first there were several rather embarrassing minutes – clouds of soapy steam billowed out of the bathroom, where someone was doing his or her laundry, the toilet in the communal lavatory gurgled incessantly – then suddenly Sergei squeezed Olga's fingers and started singing Mendelssohn's wedding march in a loud, raucous voice: 'Póm, pom, pa-pá-pa-pom, póm-pom . . .' Someone else joined in, people laughed, began talking, and the awkwardness vanished. At that moment the red-haired Zika, wife of an artist called Vasin, appeared with a bunch of roses.

Without a word she pushed the bouquet into Olga's hands and bent forward – she was tall and clumsy – to kiss Olga on the cheek. Olga hardly knew Zika, but later she came to know her well.

Georgii Maximovich's studio was unusually tidy, which no one, of course, noticed. Everybody crowded into the middle of the large room under a 200-watt lamp, where Georgii Maximovich displayed his paintings, one after another, on an armchair that served as a temporary easel. Olga had never liked these pictures very much, but no doubt the fault was in her own lack of understanding, because all the other artists in the house spoke of Georgii Maximovich with respect, showed him their efforts and asked his advice. Yet Olga felt that all these oil paintings of ponds, birch groves, streams, and ravines, all these old men, children, dogs, hands, and heads drawn in sanguine on large sheets of paper, were exactly like countless other paintings and drawings done long ago by other artists, and she could not see the point of repeating what already existed in the world.

Evidently, though, there was some point to it, because Georgii Maximovich's works were accepted by an art-purchasing commission, people bought them and Georgii Maximovich was no pauper. A kind, well-educated man, he had studied in Paris, had known Modigliani and Chagall, and he loved to pepper his conversation with French words, even though he read and spoke French very badly. At one time he had been called 'the Russian Van Gogh', but Olga couldn't help wondering how he managed to understand so much about other people's work while he had so little insight into his own. It was said that as a young man he had painted quite differently, but for some reason none of his works from that period had survived.

Georgii Maximovich loved to invite people into his studio and baffle them, overwhelm them with a display of his work. Clearly he was quite genuinely proud of all these ponds and birch groves, and it was forgivable in an old man who had never enjoyed a surfeit of either fame or prosperity, and in any case Olga's mother loved him so much – but to drag everybody into his studio on her wedding day was really going a bit too far, and Olga felt more than a little angry with her stepfather. He had no qualms, for instance, about showing them a series of drawings of a nude woman on a divan, a woman with broad hips, a pronounced waist, and dishevelled hair, although her face wasn't visible. No one knew that this was her mother; yet it made Olga feel uncomfortable, and she tried not to look at the

31

drawings. Everything would have been fine, the guests were nodding appreciatively and saying, 'Ah, yes . . .' as they sighed gently, when suddenly Sergei's mother asked a tactless question, unconnected with Georgii Maximovich's work.

'Er, please tell me,' she said, 'what is that picture?'

'That's the famous *Guernica*,' Georgii Maximovich replied hurriedly, not wishing the attention of the others to be distracted from his own works. 'It's a reproduction, not an original picture.'

'Why is it famous? This is the first I seem to have heard of it.'

Later that remark of Alexandra Prokofievna's – 'This is the first I seem to have heard of it' – became a sort of byword, a family joke that summed up Alexandra Prokofievna's 'system'. Now and again Olga and her mother would exchange glances and whisper to each other, 'This is the first I seem to have heard of it,' and burst out laughing. But that evening it was far from being a laughing matter; reluctantly turning aside from his pictures, Georgii Maximovich began conscientiously to explain why *Guernica* was a great and famous picture. The guests were perplexed. Georgii Maximovich explained enthusiastically and painstakingly. Most of them gradually bowed to his authority and at least pretended to understand what Picasso had tried to express, but Alexandra Prokofievna obstinately stuck to her guns.

'No, I find your arguments unconvincing. I can see nothing there except some broken skulls and scraps of newspaper.'

'Mother, this is your personal problem,' said Sergei's sister.

'I'll work on her; she'll straighten herself out and see reason, don't worry,' said Sergei.

Alexandra Prokofievna answered her son quite sharply, and suddenly she received some unexpected support from Uncle Petya, who was already several drinks ahead of the others.

'You're absolutely right, my dear,' he declared, raising a didactic forefinger. 'They gave you a bashing for formalism, Georgii, but it seems you haven't learned your lesson. Why do you hang that junk in your studio?'

Alexandra Prokofievna went on: 'You yourself are a realistic painter, Georgii Maximovich. When you paint a woman, it's a woman. A head is a head, a leg is a leg, and so on.' As she spoke, Alexandra Prokofievna boldly pointed at the drawing of Olga's mother in the nude. 'Everything in your pictures is in its right place. So why do you preach one thing and practise another?'

Georgii Maximovich was in an awkward situation. He turned

pale, took out a large violet-coloured handkerchief and blew his nose. What could he explain to the guests in the five short minutes before the food, the vodka, and the toasts? Could he tell them the story of his life? Olga began to feel sorry for him, but before she could open her mouth to come to her stepfather's rescue, her mother flung herself into the breach.

'Petya, my dear,' she said, 'you have spent all your life making machine tools, haven't you? What would you have said if Georgii had taken it into his head to teach you how to build machine tools?'

'What would I have said? I'd have ground him into powder.' Uncle Petya roared with laughter, shaking his curly grey head. 'I'd have made mincemeat out of him. I'd have chopped him into shreds, like sauerkraut, if he'd had the cheek to tell me how to do my job.'

Everybody laughed surreptitiously, glancing as they did at Alexandra Prokofievna. Then Sergei's sister said, 'Still, I think life would be very boring if nobody ever gave an opinion except about his own work.'

On that, it seemed, the discussion ended, and at last came the solemn moment for which they had all been invited into the studio, when Georgii Maximovich produced from the storage area a large painting in a heavy gilded frame – his wedding present to the bride and bridegroom. It was an original by the French artist Duvernois, a view of old St Petersburg. Later, when they were in financial difficulties, they more than once cast mercenary glances at the Duvernois; one day they even called in an appraiser from the state auctioneers, but, disappointed by the low figure he quoted (it was not a small amount, but considerably less than the figure which for years they had cherished in their thoughts), they decided not to sell it, and it hung there still.

As the guests were filing out of the studio, politely elbowing one another into the hall, Alexandra Prokofievna remarked in a low voice to Georgii Maximovich (her tone was triumphant, and as Olga overheard it her heart missed a beat): 'You may say what you like, my dear man, but I can't agree with you . . .'

That night, as they washed the dishes in the communal kitchen, trying not to make a noise, Georgii Maximovich whispered to Olga, 'That mother-in-law of yours – oy-oy-oy! Quite a character . . . It's lucky for you you're going to start your married life living here.' Then, after a few moments' silence, he added magnanimously: 'She has an interesting face.

It would be a challenge to paint her.' He and Alexandra Prokofievna were totally different people, sprung from different strata of the earth.

The only occasion on which Georgii Maximovich showed intransigence and reminded everyone that he was the 'responsible leaseholder' of the apartment was in May: the fate of Irinka was decided then.

It was the first spring of their married life. Nothing had yet become fixed, everything was fluid and precarious. Olga was still working as a teacher but was looking for another job. The work in school was hard and the daily journey to get there was a long one. Some university friends of hers had promised to find her something better, but nothing had materialised, and so she still got up every morning at half-past six to trek across to the other side of Moscow.

Having managed to get on bad terms with the director of the museum, Sergei was also thinking of changing jobs. Money was tight. And then it turned out that Olga was pregnant. They did not tell their mothers. They decided to take urgent measures, because to have a child in their circumstances was simply unthinkable. They knew no doctors who did that sort of thing; in fact they knew no medical people at all except Vlad, and they had not seen him for six months. He had already qualified and was now a houseman in a hospital.

Sergei didn't like asking Vlad. Olga hesitated too, but since she had always regarded Vlad as one of the world's goodies – a very faithful, old, tried and tested goody – she made up her mind to ignore Sergei's reluctance (she herself had no scruples; she even had an obscure feeling that Vlad would actually be pleased), and called up her old friend. To her astonishment Vlad, far from being pleased, sounded upset and confused, but then he went zealously and rapidly into action. They went over to his place and he gave her an injection. Sergei stood beside the couch, holding her hand and looking away.

He later confessed that at a certain moment he felt hatred for their friend: Vlad should have refused to do it. But Vlad, with his dogged conscientiousness . . . The injection did no good. Vlad recommended a doctor of his acquaintance, an old man who was prepared to do abortions even though it was illegal in those days. It would have to be done at home, behind closed doors and drawn curtains.

They had to tell Olga's mother, who told Georgii Maximovich – there was no hiding it any longer, and her mother was terrified and helpless. She had never had an abortion. She thought of the

34

operation as utterly shameful, criminal, and probably fatal. She stared at Olga with eyes full of panic, tearful, and whispered, 'Oh, my little girl, what are we going to do?'

In many things she remained naïve to the end of her days, even when she had turned into an old woman. In later years Olga had several abortions, both at home and in a hospital, and realised that it was not the worst pain in the world, if only because it was a pain that came to an end.

But back then, in that May, she knew none of this. Georgii Maximovich suddenly stunned everybody by saying, 'As the responsible leaseholder, I forbid it . . .' They never did discover whether he was really afraid of breaking the law or whether he just gave in to her mother's mood of panic.

In any event, Irinka came into the world thanks to Georgii Maximovich's phrase, 'As the responsible leaseholder . . .' Later there were times when Olga was tormented by unbearable memories. Her daughter never knew that she had been unwanted. Everybody managed to forget it – Sergei, her mother, Georgii Maximovich, and, no doubt, Vlad. But Olga knew and remembered it. And when on a slushy day in the autumn she was hurrying along Gogol Boulevard towards the Arbat, to go to a shop, and suddenly felt such a violent pain in her belly that she staggered and would have fallen had not a passer-by helped her to a bench on the boulevard, she at once thought, 'This is my punishment for . . .'

Irinka was born at seven months. When they had just come from the maternity hospital, Sergei wanted to look at the baby and Olga shrieked, screening the child with her body, 'Don't look! Don't look! Later! Go away!' She couldn't bear having him see such a miserable, puny little creature. Only after three days did she show him the little body, which had begun to look like a real baby. Now Irinka was the tallest girl in her class. And Sergei was no longer on this earth.

How quickly it had all passed.

Their life together had, after all, been long, far beyond the power of memory to recall in full – why had it passed so quickly? Everything was muddled. It had been both quick and short. Times that had gone slowly now seemed like a moment, while the present moment dragged on without end and without meaning.

In December, soon after the day that had smashed their life into fragments, she said to her daughter – it was a moment of despair, Irinka was the person closest to her, and Olga wanted only one little drop of comfort although it was foolish to expect that comfort from a child (what's more, she said it more for herself and for someone who couldn't hear) – 'What a good life we had when your father was alive.'

Not all was truth, of course, in that sigh. There was falsehood in it too. Her point was that mere life itself – not matter whether it was good, bad, or horrible – meant everything. There was life and there was nonlife; there was nothing in between. Everything in the world belonged to one or the other, and therein alone, perhaps, lay hidden not only the source of Olga's suffering but also of her hope. She had not understood this at the time; even now she could but guess at it, and then only vaguely.

The girl sensed the falsity in the remark, spoken as it was 'for someone who couldn't hear', and looking askance, she said, 'It wasn't all that good.'

Olga was crushed by this retort. She couldn't think what to say in reply. Faïna, a most intelligent woman, who had been her friend since their childhood days before the war, said, 'Of course she's an incredibly selfish child – thanks to you and Sergei, and especially to Sergei's mother. But that's not the point. She's worried about you; she's warning you not to live in the past: "It wasn't all that good." '

Faïna thought Olga should start looking for another husband at once: 'Don't be a fool. You can't bring Sergei back, and you're destroying yourself. Bear in mind that you don't have much time – a year or two, and after that you can forget it.' Less than two months after that, Faïna invited her to a party, but Olga refused to go: Why should she go to parties when meeting strangers only made her depression worse? When Faïna invited her to Novgorod for Christmas, Olga again refused; instead she and Irinka went to stay in a *pension*, but there too she felt miserable and fled away, leaving Irinka with the other young people who were staying there. Faïna, however, would not give up; she was an obstinate girl, or rather forty-three-year-old woman – abandoned by her husband, her son in the army, her mother in a home for the aged. She invited Olga to a New Year's party given by some friends of hers who were architects – charming, intelligent people: 'Don't be afraid, you fool; no one's going to make a grab for you or anything like that. You can just relax and listen to the music.' But Olga didn't care whether they were charming or rude, intelligent or stupid; she just didn't want to see anyone.

Not for any good reason, not because it was against her principles; she simply didn't feel like it.

After Irinka's cruel remark, Faïna too, having hesitated a

little, also uttered some of the unpalatable truth, no doubt thinking that although the medicine she was administering was very bitter, it was necessary: 'Do you really believe that life with Sergei was so good?' Olga answered, 'Yes.' What else could she say? 'I don't know'? 'Wasn't it obvious'?

There was a vendor's stall on the corner of Chekhov Street and Sadovaya where she and Faïna loved to buy fresh rolls. They had been on sale there even before the war, at six kopecks apiece, and the physical memory of that childhood pleasure had persisted: one of the thrills of street life was to push a coin into the little square window and from the delicious-smelling depths a kindly hand was thrust out with a soft, puffy, crusty roll, newly born as from the womb. Then, chewing and savouring life, to stroll along Sadovaya towards Samotechnaya, then to Tsvetnoi Boulevard with its crowds and bustle, the circus, the market, taxis, gypsies, the secondhand shop, a cinema – whatever one's heart desired. And the Narva Restaurant nearby. Whenever they felt the need for mutual comfort, for a frank heart-to-heart talk (Faïna in those days lived on Krasnogvardeiskaya in a communal flat that was like an ant heap, in which she shared one room with her mother, her son, her husband, and an aged, stale-smelling female relative who never spoke), they would go to Tsvetnoi Boulevard, down the hill past the cinema or to the market to stare and jostle, to buy fruit, picking out the sweetest pears or a watermelon, or just a glassful of fried sunflower seeds, and then wander up and down the boulevard, complaining to each other of their misfortunes – and life grew more bearable.

The long years of closeness with this woman — her best friend, her best counsellor, her closest rival, the best-informed spy on her short-lived triumphs and disasters – had taught her that the most important rule when dealing with Faïna was to put oneself in her place and try to see everything from Faïna's point of view. Faïna, of course, was profoundly unhappy; compared with her, Olga always regarded herself as shamefully, disgracefully lucky. At times it seemed to Olga that there was a constant overflow of surplus goodness, prosperity, and blatant female satisfaction pouring from her as if from one vessel into another – or rather, to be more precise, she felt this was what it must seem like to other people, and above all to poor Faïna.

It now turned out that Faïna had always seen everything quite differently, and thanks to these unexpected and hitherto carefully concealed powers of insight, she was even daring to cheer Olga up. This was too much! How could she say their married life hadn't been happy? *Their life* had been a complete, living, pulsating organism that had now vanished from the face of the earth. It had had a heart, like a live creature; it had had lungs, genitals, sense organs, and it had developed, flourished, sickened, and worn out; it had died from neither old age nor illness but because the element that powered its bloodstream had disappeared. What a strange creature 'their life' had been. No one else had been able to understand exactly what it was like. Other people could only guess, imagine various shapes in the air, fantasise, make vague assumptions that 'their life' looked like this or that, consisted of this or that. And they themselves . . . they themselves had never been able to define it in words. Sometimes Olga thought quite sincerely that their life was good, sometimes it depressed her, and at other times – which lasted for hours, sometimes days on end – she thought it was terrible.

Now she simply could not believe that such thoughts had ever entered her head, that she had sometimes hated *their life*.

But she had, she had! Like that winter (they were still living in her mother's flat) when she was tormented by the red-haired Zika, Vasin's wife. It had ended in Olga's humiliation and was now almost forgotten; memory had repressed the suffering and shame she had felt. But it had happened – fourteen years ago – and it had also been part of *their life*. She had realised that Sergei was not unaware of Zika's charms. The fact that Zika flirted with him and probably made a serious attempt to seduce him was natural. Women were attracted to him; she knew this and it upset her. But she also knew that he was indolent and hard to arouse, that he was bored by stupid, flirtatious women and greatly preferred male talk over vodka and gherkins to female company. Once, when she was trying to get him to say whether he might ever be unfaithful to her, he said with a sigh, 'Remember what Hemingway said? "If only one didn't have to talk to them . . ." '

Zika was young and robust, with long arms and legs and muscular buttocks. The sculptors on the first floor were always asking her to pose for allegorical statues, such as discus throwers or collective-farm peasant women with baskets on their shoulders personifying abundance. Zika's powerful physique frightened Olga Vasilievna; she felt that Sergei was attracted to this type, that it reminded him of the forgotten Brünnhilde. Zika had an unremarkable face, round, fresh-complexioned, always wearing a faint smile, framed in reddish-blonde curls: the face of a simpleton. She worked as an illustrator for a publisher of children's books, for whom she turned out feeble, unimaginative water colours. Vasin, by contrast, was frail, ugly, and old, at least he seemed old to Olga at the time; he must have been in his early forties, twice Zika's age. It all began with a friendly exchange of invitations, tea parties or drinks around the tape recorder – a pastime just becoming fashionable in those days. Vasin had bought a Dnieper tape recorder, a huge, clumsy thing that felt as heavy as a suitcase full of scrap iron, and he recorded everybody, telling them to sing, talk, or recite poetry, after which they would eagerly listen to all the nonsense as he played it back.

Vasin earned a great deal by painting official portraits, which he did jointly with his partner Arkasha. They would mark off the canvas in squares and paint rapidly and skilfully, as if it were a production-line job in a factory. Sometimes Zika helped them. Apart from potboiling in this way, Vasin also did some serious painting on his own. He would quote Sasha Chërny's poem that says that every artist needs two muses: the shopgirl for the needs of the body and the lady dentist for the good of the soul. 'All next week,' he would say, 'I'm going to work for the shopgirl.' Or: 'I spent this afternoon with my lady dentist. She's so sweet, it was delightful.' This meant that he had travelled out into the countryside on a commuter train with his sketchbook and had enjoyed himself all day painting, wet through and freezing. He painted landscapes, which were remarkably good. Georgii Maximovich thought he was gifted but dissolute and used to say that 'artists like him never amount to a row of beans'. Vasin was a drunkard.

Altogether Olga felt sad about Valerii Vasin; eventually abandoned by Zika, he had drunk himself to death while still in his fifties. He was a true artist; he lived as though in a dream, did his potboiling as though in a dream, and awakened only when he was at his easel and doing the real painting that he loved. Indifferent to visitors, he would have been quite happy to live alone, to drink alone, but Zika was easily bored and forced him to lead a social life. He loved Zika very much and did everything she wanted.

And Zika was cunning: she played up to Olga, flattered her, insinuated herself into her favour. 'Would you like me to take the baby out? Do you need any milk? I'm going to the shop . . .' And it was always said casually, naturally, like a real friend. One day she lent them some money. At first Olga acquiesced and accepted it; then she realised that it had been done with an ulterior motive. She began finding excuses to duck out of Zika's invitations and refused to let Sergei go to the Vasins'.

Sergei took offence. Why not? She could not explain, and he

failed to guess that it was a case of wretched jealousy – so wretched and seemingly so unfounded that she felt ashamed to talk about it, but she could not fight it. 'What's the matter? Why don't you want me to go and see Valerii?' 'I don't want you to – and that's all.' 'I will not be dictated to.' He flared up and ran out to the Vasins' apartment. He had always dreaded being turned into a henpecked husband. All this happened at the time when he had left the museum without first getting another job, and he was touchy and irritable. She was teaching at school all day, while Sergei stayed at home, helped Olga's mother look after Irinka, went shopping in the market, hauled buckets of water – the water was kept in the kitchen and in the hallway, and the supply had to be replenished three times a day.

The domestic chores, the idleness, the lack of money and, above all, the uncertainty about his professional future continued to make Sergei depressed in the evenings. He would loaf around not knowing what to do with himself. It was this that made him easy prey for the tall, muscular Zika. The only puzzle was: Why did she need him?

Now he was dead and no one needed him.

One day Olga went into Vasin's studio and saw Sergei sitting at the table; a grubby cotton towel was draped around his neck, as though he were wearing a napkin in a restaurant, and Zika was cutting his hair. 'What does this mean?' Olga enquired. The reply was a burst of laughter. Vasin and another man, one of his friends, were seized with such a paroxysm of laughter that they were speechless. It transpired that Sergei had bet his hair playing poker and had lost. In a thoroughly natural, cheerful tone of voice, Zika assured Olga, 'Don't worry, Olga dear, I'll only snip off a tiny bit. Purely symbolic. It will even improve his looks.'

Olga was amazed that Sergei was sitting there as obedient as a lamb.

She never knew whether there really was anything between them. Perhaps there was. And then perhaps there wasn't. Olga stopped speaking to Zika; she became an enemy. The change from close friendship to fierce hostility took place with unusual rapidity, in the space of two or three months. Today she had no recollection of how this quarrel had developed, or whether she had had any arguments with Zika before that encounter in the empty corridor. By the spring Olga had already begun to feel afraid of Zika. She would glare fixedly at Olga, and whenever they happened to meet in the kitchen or in the hallway she never made way for Olga but always walked straight towards her and tried to jostle her. At some point Olga must have made some very telling remark about Zika, and the other women must have passed it on; the hatred between them had probably begun with that. All the details had long since faded from her memory, but a vague recollection of that dispute with Sergei about the wretched Zika had remained. It was a dispute about nothing, a pure foolishness on her part; yet at the time it had seemed to Olga that her life depended on its outcome. Did he love her enough to give up – if she begged him to – the minor pleasure of a gossip over a glass of vodka in Vasin's studio? How she suffered – and how convinced she was that she was in the right. She thought: 'What could be clearer? If he loves me, he'll give it up. If he doesn't love me, he'll keep on going to the Vasins'.' An infallible test. But Sergei somehow didn't see it quite so clearly. He wanted proof. He demanded that she show him a warrant for his arrest, as it were.

'For the thousandth time: Why? Are you jealous of Zika – is that it? You must be crazy.'

'I'm simply asking you,' she would say, almost in tears. 'I'm just asking, that's all. I beg you on my knees.' And one day she really did fall on her knees, which so unnerved him that he promised to do whatever she asked. All right, he wouldn't go to the Vasins' any more. She loved him very much at such moments because they revealed an aspect of him that she longed to see. But an hour and a half later – it happened at dawn, after a sleepless night – he was insisting again: 'No, it's the purest insanity, it's impossible. You're demanding obedience and blind faith, like the fathers of the church . . . *Credo, quia absurdum est* . . .' And her wave of joy was followed by misery, because she had browbeaten him with tears and sleepless nights into making a futile little concession. All that effort – just to stop him from going to see Vasin! And what about the future? Would she have to fall on her knees and sob every time? She might have much more important things to ask and he would be unmoved, like a rock.

She was also distressed by the thought that they were quarrelling so desperately, to the point of tears, over a stupid, empty-headed woman who wasn't worth even a contemptuous glance. How Zika would have rejoiced if she had known what discord she aroused! Of course the whole thing was idiotic, and Olga had been stupid; unable to see what was important and what wasn't. She had caused herself agonies over nothing at all . . .

Sergei continued to visit Vasin, doing so now out of obstinacy, as a matter of principle.

At the same time both of them were trying to prepare each other for their future life together. There were grim days when Olga longed to be alone with her mother, wanted to divorce Sergei; it was at such moments that she hated *their life*, when it had only just begun. She had completely forgotten whatever had preceded the encounter in the corridor with which the whole business had culminated. Maybe she had been careless enough to say something unnecessary, to pass on a bit of the gossip about Zika that was going around. Some people stopped seeing the Vasins. Everyone in the house knew of the enmity between Zika and Olga, which naturally extended to Olga's mother and Georgii Maximovich. As a member of an art-purchasing commission, Georgii Maximovich vetoed the purchase of two of Vasin's pictures. Vasin got drunk, stood outside their flat, abd shouted rude remarks through the door. Olga saw Zika on the street with a tear-stained face. It seemed impossible that Sergei should continue to see the Vasins.

She was walking down the big hall when Zika appeared around the corner. They were alone. Zika did not turn aside but headed straight towards Olga until they were staring at each other, eye to eye. She just had time to think, 'The eyes of a madwoman . . .' before Zika came closer to her and with white lips said, 'I know everything, you mean little bitch. You're killing your husband. But to hell with him; just leave Valerii and me alone or I'll destroy you! Got it?' And she took a swing with her powerful arm.

Olga ran down the empty hall, fear gripping her entire body. It was too painful to remember.

Faïna said that Olga should go immediately to the District Prosecutor's office and at the same time to Zika's place of work, where she turned out her messy little water colours. Faïna had a friend who was a journalist, whom they immediately rang up, then and there on the boulevard, from a phone box, to ask him whether he could get a news item or a feature story printed about Zika's attack. Olga seethed with a passionate desire for revenge, wanting to take Zika to court and have her jailed for at least a couple of years for assault.

But when she returned home late that evening she felt nothing but a headache and a sort of jaded exhaustion all over her body, as though she had just survived a serious illness. She decided not to tell anyone else about the incident after all, because she felt so unbearably sorry for Sergei: what he would have suffered if she had told him about it. So in effect the whole affair never went beyond the walls of that empty hallway. And her mother never found out.

She must stop thinking about it. From then on, Olga couldn't bear the thought of seeing the Vasins, of meeting Zika in the hall again or in the communal kitchen. Zika, fortunately, began avoiding Olga – she never looked her in the eye any more and evaded any contact with her. Soon after the affair, Olga and Sergei moved over to live with his mother in Shabolovka Street, where the old lady had been alone since the death of her daughter. Sergei asked Olga if she would make the move and she agreed with relief: there would be no more long corridors smelling of oil paint and turpentine, no more noisy gatherings in the evening to argue about colour values, the French school, or suprematism, no hectic activity throughout the house on the days when the art purchasing commission was at work, no communal bathroom with a concrete floor and a notice on the wall that said: 'It is categorically forbidden to wash paintbrushes in the bathtub!', no shared kitchen with four tables and four stoves, no mother, no Georgii Maximovich forever hoping to astound, if not the world, then the neighbours, no Vasin and no Zika. On the other hand, there would be her mother-in-law.

Faïna said, 'If only you hadn't had to live with your mother-in-law, Sergei might be alive now.'

That was not true, because living with his mother had not been nearly such an ordeal for him as for her. If the cause had lain with the old woman, Olga would have been the one to have a heart attack, not Sergei, though of course Alexandra Prokofievna's presence and her perpetual lecturing were an extra strain on top of something more fundamental. When men pass the age of forty, strange things start happening to them: they understand something about themselves of which they were previously unaware. There are some who come to terms with it and settle down forever, while others are gripped by a restlessness of the spirit. Sergei was one who fell under the spell of this unease.

It began imperceptibly after Praskukhin had arranged for his transfer to the institute. The job at the museum had been undemanding, badly paid and a dead end, but it had the advantage of being extremely peaceful, whereas at the institute things started happening; promises, hopes, plans, passions, cliques, dangers at every step – Praskukhin against Demchenko, Demchenko against Kislovsky, and then there was Klimuk, then the whole business about changing the topic of his dissertation. He dashed around, first to one thing, then to another, then to a third: at one moment it was the history of the streets of Moscow, next a subject so remote as scarcely to qualify history. This constant restlessness was his undoing. At first he would be full of enthusiasm; then inevitably his interest would cool and he would fling himself into some new project. A perpetually restless failure, a 'grasshopper mind'.

But so what? She never reproached him, never demanded the unattainable. If they couldn't afford Yalta, they would spend their holiday with Aunty Pasha in Vasilkovo. When they hadn't enough for a TV set, they listened to the radio. Never once in their life together had she said to him, 'Look at So-and-So, he's made it, and you're nowhere.' She had never urged him to make an impossible effort or to strain himself; other people's success never worried her. On the contrary, she used to say to him, 'We don't need your dissertation. We need you in good health. Stay a junior research fellow, but whatever happens don't kill yourself, don't push yourself too hard, don't try to knock down walls with your forehead – your head's not meant for that.'

It was her mother-in-law who suffered most from the fact that her son's career was not flourishing as others' were. Alexandra Prokofievna greatly disliked certain of Sergei's friends from his schooldays who had made something of themselves, and she treated them coldly whenever they came to visit. In her view Sergei was exceptional and deserved a better fate, whereas Olga was unaffected by vanity or envy. She was worried by something else. Those seven years at the museum had been totally wasted. Of course, the fact that he had nothing to show for them, nothing in return, no reputation built, was his own fault: he had spent his time daydreaming, constantly chasing will-o'-the-wisps. But his colleagues were guilty too, and viciously so: they had not tried to prevent the waste of his talents, like wheels turning, racing endlessly to no effect.

Seven years! The years in which others of his age had made feverish efforts, displayed spurts of energy that got them further and further ahead while he had lived as though he had ninety years in which to prove himself. There had been plans of sorts: he had done archival research and had reached the stage of having talks with a publisher about the topic 'Moscow in 1918'. Someone named Ilya Vladimirovich had made promises and tried to push the plan forward a bit, but in the end it had all come to nothing. After countless meetings, telephone calls, discussions over meals and cups of tea, Ilya Vladimirovich had turned out to be a total nonentity. Alexandra Prokofievna asked Sergei indignantly, 'Why do you get mixed up with such trash?' As was

44

his habit, Sergei made excuses and defended those who had falsely raised his hopes: 'But Ilya Vladimirovich doesn't run the publishing house – he's just another client, like me.'

Those were the years in which Irinka reached the age when she started school; when the household moved to a new flat – the new place was completely renovated and had parquet flooring installed – and Olga was first promoted to senior research fellow and then put in charge of her own laboratory at the All-Union Institute of Scientific Research. Yet all Sergei's work of those years, all the lengthy fuss about his 'Moscow in 1918' ended in failure and the book was never published. Admittedly some of the material from it was used for the first version of his dissertation, but then that version was abandoned. New topics were found: the February Revolution, the tsarist secret police, and so on. But here too Sergei found himself up a blind alley, faced with an impenetrable wall. And there were other troubles: his quarrel with Klimuk, his sudden interest in that house on the embankment and everything connected with it, and Klimuk's treachery . . .

How well Olga knew all the expressions of his face, his walk, the way his voice changed when the next disaster overwhelmed him or some new, fascinating but chimerical project floated into view.

When she had first met him, of course, he had been different.

Year after year of disappointments gradually wore him down, drained his strength; he began to stoop and to weaken; yet some central core remained untouched, like a thin steel rod that bent but did not break. And that was the root of the trouble: he refused to change his innermost nature. This meant that although he suffered agonies as a result of his many failures, lost faith in himself, frittered away his energies in enthusiasms so absurd they made people think he had taken leave of his senses, although he strained his poor heart with the fury of his despair and self-reproach, he still refused to break that invisible, steely core within himself. And despite it all she loved him, forgave him, and never demanded anything of him.

It was two weeks after the funeral that Bezyazichny appeared. Olga had never met him before but had heard of his name from Sergei – in what connection she had forgotten He had apparently taken part of the investigation of Sergei's 'case', but Olga could not remember what his attitude had been. The people at the institute had been divided, according to Sergei, into three groups: the few absolute scoundrels, the few middle-of-the-roaders, and some who behaved impeccably. Olga felt nervous because she didn't know to which category Bezyazichny belonged and, consequently, how she should treat him. He came accompanied by an elderly woman named Sorokina.

'Do forgive me – I've just been to the delicatessen next door,' said Sorokina, smiling guiltily and ingratiatingly as she showed Olga her shopping bag full of food.

For two or three seconds her eyes flickered around in search of a place to put down her bag, and she could find nowhere better than the shoebox. Silently Olga picked up the bag and transferred it to the little table under the telephone.

'What a marvellous delicatessen you have. They have "doctor's" sausage and little Dutch cheeses, which we hardly ever see in the shops around us, even though our delicatessen is supposed to supply foods for special diets . . .'

As she twittered away, the woman looked at Olga with great feeling and gave her voice an expression of profound compassion, as though the fact that Olga was lucky enough to live near such a good delicatessen might help in some little way to relieve her grief. When she realised that Olga was not interested in talking about the delicatessen, Sorokina took off her raincoat and hat and for a while uttered nothing more than an occasional sigh.

Olga had for some time been dreading this visit from Sergei's colleagues. They could only bring her pain. Everyone who had known Sergei, even if only slightly, caused her pain. Clearly, though, she had to put up with this visit, and the sooner they came and went, the better for her. Both these people were from the institute's trade union committee and, as far as Olga understood it, they were fulfilling some formal obligation. The funeral was over, the urn had been buried and the funeral committee had been dissolved; these two, however, belonged to the social affairs committee or something of the sort. They did not intend to stay for long. If the conversation dragged on, the food might go cold, but Olga did not propose to do anything about it. She was incapable of making any special effort for the occasion. Bezyazichny wiped his feet on the doormat and glanced round him, making vague mooing noises. Olga could not understand what he wanted until he suddenly took off his shoes and stood there in his socks. Aha, it was wet in the street and he did not want to mess up the floor. As though she cared about the floors at a moment like this.

Why didn't these people understand anything? She had to give him Sergei's slippers, which were lying near the door for all to see. She found it painful and tactless of him to take them.

Her mother-in-law was doing something in the kitchen when Olga went in to put on the kettle for tea; she had to make some gesture of hospitality. Alexandra Prokofievna refused to go out and meet them.

'I don't want to see anyone from the institute,' said the old woman. 'First they persecute him, then they come and express their sympathy. I have nothing to say to them.'

The implication was that Olga could talk to them because she and they had somehow been engaged in the same activity – persecuting Sergei. She wanted to pretend she hadn't noticed but couldn't help saying, 'Don't talk nonsense. These people didn't persecute Sergei. They haven't done anything wrong; they have simply come to express the usual official condolences. Nobody persecuted Sergei.'

'Yes they did,' said Alexandra Prokofievna and went out of the kitchen.

Olga sat down on a stool and for a minute was motionless – her heart was beating very hard. Sergei had not been persecuted. The harm done to him had not been intentional; it had simply happened because certain people had been pursuing their own ends. That was a different matter. She heard Alexandra Prokofievna go into her room and lock the door.

Olga felt awkward in front of these strangers. Still, let them come – it meant nothing. She stood up, went into the living room carrying something in a little bowl. The two from the trade union committee were sitting at the table, frozen in attitudes of profound dejection. The woman was just perceptibly nodding her head and staring at the floor. Probably she imagined that this pose and the faint nodding expressed sincere sympathy. 'What a fool she is,' thought Olga. Bezyazichny immediately leaped to his feet and began to say that they had come literally only for a minute, she shouldn't have gone to the trouble of making tea for them. He had short legs, a rosy complexion, a robust, young-looking face, grey hair in a short crew cut. It was impossible to tell his exact age; he was perhaps around fifty. He wore a black suit, the jacket crumpled, with disproportionately broad, padded shoulders. 'He put it on specially to visit a widow,' she thought with indifference. 'Black. Out of mothballs.'

'Here are a few articles that belonged to Sergei Afanasievich.' He took out of his briefcase a tin box that had once held Czech cigarettes and in which something rattled; a ruler; a folding hunter's knife that had obviously been used for opening cans and pulling corks during the parties that took place fairly frequently in Sergei's department; three tattered books; a comb with a long handle; a soccer calendar for 1969; a copy of *Foreign Literature*; and an old notebook full of telephone numbers with dogeared pages. He took out each object and placed it on the table with as much care as if it had been made of glass.

With a fixed stare, Olga gazed at this trivial, random collection of junk which for some reason they had brought to her, and thought: 'Don't they realise that it must be painful to have to look at my dead husband's possessions? Why are they doing it?' She wanted to pick it all up and throw it away. Instead she gathered up the things and carried them over to the windowsill.

Bezyazichny said something and handed her an envelope. She thanked him and began to pour out the tea. Some money from the committee, no doubt. Drinking his tea in noiseless sips, Bezyazichny told her how everyone in the department grieved for Sergei and how much they missed him, because many people there had liked him. This remark stung Olga and brought her to life. Why did he say '*many people*' had liked him? According to the rules of this game he should have said 'everybody liked him', or 'people liked him at the institute', or at least 'he was liked'. But he had said '*many people* liked him', which implied that there had been – and still were, now that he was dead – *a few people* who hadn't liked him and still didn't. Of course there were such people. Olga had no doubts about the existence of those *few people*, but it was rather strange to hint about them to his widow in the very first minutes of this visit.

She looked hard at Bezyazichny, trying once again to recall what Sergei had said about him, but nothing came to mind.

'You talk as though Sergei Afanasievich had been working in peace and concord with everyone right up to the very last day. As though he hadn't submitted his request to resign,' said Olga. 'He practically regarded himself as already dismissed.'

'But that's not so. You are profoundly mistaken.' Bezyazichny clasped a hand to his chest. 'I know about his request. But first, the matter remained undecided up to, so to speak, the tragic day . . . The director was on holiday. And Gennadii Vitalevich Klimuk most definitely didn't want to make the decision.'

'Gennadii Vitalevich didn't want to? Don't talk to me about Gennadii Vitalevich. More than any of the others he wanted to get rid of Sergei – but only if someone else would actually do it.'

'I assure you – you're mistaken.'

This man had had an ulterior motive in saying 'many people liked him'. He had shown his hand. It was now clear that he was one of Sergei's enemies, or perhaps sympathised with his enemies. Had they really sunk so low as to send this person on a visit that required such tact?

'Sergei Afanasievich was working in the same field as we do,' said the woman in a quavering voice. Taking off her spectacles and pressing her fleshy chin into her chest, she began to polish the spectacles with a handkerchief. Her face took on a lachrymose expression and her voice was scarcely audible. 'The revolution and the civil war . . . He and I worked together for six years. He was a fine man, extremely kind and responsive . . . a good man.'

The fleshy chin quivered. Olga gave the woman a cold look. 'It would be interesting to know how both of you voted at the hearing of Sergei's notorious "case",' she said.

The woman started; her eyes widened and described a momentary revolving movement. Olga had, of course, put the question rudely and no doubt placed her visitors in an awkward situation, but then they were making things just as awkward for her by simply sitting there, drinking tea and talking about Sergei.

'I didn't vote at all, because I was out of Moscow at the time. I was in Poland, on official business,' said Bezyazichny with a contemptuous wave of the hand. 'In any case, you know . . .' His gesture and tone of voice implied, 'Is it really worth resurrecting all that nonsense?'

Sorokina said, 'I, as it happens, voted for the whole thing to be brought out into the open.' She blushed. 'In the circumstances it was the only proper way . . .'

At that moment Irinka entered – or rather burst in unceremoniously, as she always did – and asked for a rouble and a half before the shop closed. Having fired off this request, she noticed the visitors and said, 'Oh, hello!'

Olga introduced her daughter, who smiled a very charming, welcoming smile, in the way she always did whenever she needed to wheedle money out of somebody.

Olga fumbled in her purse, looking for silver and copper.

'Oh, look!' Irinka shrieked with delight, rushing over to the windowsill. 'I've been looking for it everywhere. How did it get here?'

She seized the long-handled comb.

'They brought it from your father's office. There's a rouble fifty for you.'

'Oh . . .' Hesitating, Irinka put the comb back on the windowsill, then asked, 'Mother, can I have it, please? You did buy it for me, remember?'

'Take it,' said Olga.

Irinka ran out. Someone was obviously waiting for her in the hall; there was whispering, and then the door slammed. There was no more to talk about. It seemed the right moment for them to get up and go, but Bezyazichny started talking about Sergei's unfinished dissertation. The academic council, it seemed, was of the opinion – no decision had been taken yet, but the word was going around – that the institute should undertake the job of completing the dissertation and then publish a monograph. They would assign some special people to it. It would be incorporated into the official schedule, so the whole department would be involved. They would have to process a certain amount of unused source material and find what was still left in Sergei's papers in his desk. They were all counting on Olga Vasilievna's help. She felt irritation beginning to boil up inside her.

'I'll do it when I have the time and the energy,' she said. 'Right now I don't intend to go looking for anything.'

'Of course, of course,' mumbled Sorokina. 'Only when Olga Vasilievna feels she is able to . . .'

'It will be entirely in Olga Vasilievna's own interest,' said Bezyazichny.

Out in the foyer Bezyazichny said unexpectedly to Sorokina as he was helping her into her coat, 'Excuse me, Paulina Ivanovna, but I won't be able to see you out. There is a little matter I have to discuss with Olga Vasilievna . . .'

They went back into the living room. Olga did not want to carry on the conversation in the hall, right outside her mother-in-law's door. She sensed that something unpleasant was impending. Bezyazichny said that he found it embarrassing to mention this, but he had no alternative because it was an official matter. He was chairman of the institute's staff credit union. Sergei Afanasievich had borrowed a hundred and sixty roubles with an undertaking to repay it within six months, but almost two years had passed, the money had not been paid back, and now a complication had arisen: the fund was empty, several requests for small loans were outstanding and they could not be met. The board of management had come to a unanimous decision . . . they felt . . . they were worried . . . the situation was . . .

Olga listened, stunned. The words reached her through a dense fog.

50

'I don't have that much money,' she said.

'The fact of the matter is . . . You see, we haven't the right . . . If there were a general meeting of all the union's shareholders . . . but on the other hand if you were to make a voluntary . . .' Bezyazichny mumbled on, his heavy red face twitching as though he were sneezing, which no doubt indicated his extreme state of embarrassment. 'Believe me, I find it very distasteful. But I am only carrying out . . .'

Olga said that there were a hundred roubles in Sergei's savings account, but it would be some time before she could get that money – not until the court had granted probate, in fact. As for the hundred and sixty roubles borrowed from the credit union, this was the first she had ever heard of it.

'When did he borrow this money?'

Bezyazichny produced a notebook from his pocket, leafed through it, and found the entry: the money had been advanced on March 5, 1971.

Where on earth had it all gone? Why had he needed so much? 'A woman.' This was the first thought that came into her head, and it made her temperature climb. Nevertheless she replied very calmly, 'This is really the first I have heard of it. He usually told me everything about his expenses, his debts.' This was not the complete truth, but it was true enough in broad terms.

'In that case it makes it even more embarrassing for me. I am sorry.'

After a pause he said, 'I'll do everything I can to persuade the members of the board of management, in view of the circumstances . . . You might perhaps care to write a statement. I'll do what I can.' He clasped his hands to his chest and bowed his head. 'Most of his colleagues were on good terms with him, so I hope . . . I'll have a preliminary word with one or two people . . .'

He went on muttering in this vein, pressing his hands to his chest and bowing, while he moved out of the room and into the hall. Everything had apparently been said. It was over for the time being. Why had they given her money in that envelope he gave her if they then demanded it back from her? It was all so confusing. Olga stared at this short, stocky, grizzled little man in his crumpled, old-fashioned black suit dating from the fifties and made some mechanical, meaningless remark.

As he was leaving he said, 'So they'll phone you about the monograph. Do have a look around and collect whatever material you can find. The folder I mentioned is the one tied with pink ribbon.'

In the past, whenever sudden troubles had arisen and she hadn't known what to do, she had always asked Sergei's advice – usually at night, before they went to sleep, when Irinka was already asleep and her mother-in-law had shut herself in her room. Although he was never very successful in solving his own problems, he always gave her sensible advice. He was good at soothing her when something had upset her. But now – who was there? Her mother-in-law mustn't know, because she would feel nothing but malicious satisfaction. She would regard it as confirmation of her belief that Olga and Sergei had never been really close and that he had led a separate life.

Olga was oppressed by a feeling that was not jealousy but something else, an emotion of a different quality – the burned-out remains of jealousy. It was as if she had been handed an urn containing these strange ashes, the ashes of a jealousy that was dead but whose remains she was holding in her hands, clutching them to her heart.

She was convinced that a woman was mixed up in this somewhere. Ashes, ashes, nothing but ashes. Yet her hands were trembling. In her own savings account she had two hundred and eighty roubles, which she and Sergei had put aside for a specific purpose – to buy a television set. To take money out of that account to pay off some questionable debt would be stupid.

Sergei used to say, 'Don't fuss, old lady.'

It was his favourite catch phrase, which he repeated ten times a day, in and out of season. Really, what a way to behave: to ask a widow to settle an unpaid debt with her husband not a month dead. But one thing she knew for certain: she and Sergei had been truly close. No other person was closer to him. So her mother-in-law could shut up. In recent years he had stopped sharing his thoughts with his mother, and had concealed all kinds of problems from her. 'There are things I can't explain to her,' he used to say.

There was a great deal that his mother had been incapable of understanding, and her lack of comprehension infuriated him. But no such gap in understanding had existed between him and Olga. She had fully understood everything that worried him, recognising the significance of his slightest sigh. And even if he had been seeing another woman, it meant nothing.

With these thoughts she tried to persuade herself there was no cause for worry, trying to remain calm and imperturbable, but in reality she felt no calm. And there was no one to help her. It was no good telling Faïna, because although she was her best friend she would interpret it in her own way, and wrongly. No doubt she would also secretly rejoice, because the situation tended to favour her own admitted objective, which was to pull Olga out of her comatose state. This required the casting of mild aspersions on Sergei; but Olga didn't believe, refused to believe that Sergei might have been at fault. There was some kind of mystery about this business, and thinking about it was giving her a splitting headache. Olga put on her coat, took up her handbag, and went out.

There was a slight but steady drizzle of rain. The last customers were hurrying into the delicatessen; it was twenty minutes to closing time. Olga went in to buy butter, yogurt and something for Irinka to have with her tea. The cleaning woman was swishing her mop, muttering with bad-tempered irritation as she made the customers step back from the counter. Olga stood in a short queue at the cashier's desk, then went over to the dairy counter, thinking of how many people she knew: she had plenty of acquaintances, several women she counted as her friends, but there was no one to whom she was truly close – and that meant there was no one to whom she could turn. The worst thing that lay in store for her was loneliness. Death and grief were a mere prelude to the worst. How was she to go on living when there was no one to give her advice, no one to whom she could tell everything? The other people standing in the queue had vacant, abstracted looks, as if they were there by mistake – late evening customers, their thoughts far away. Indeed, most of them were late getting home; at this hour they were usually sitting in front of the TV wearing their slippers, or washing their underclothes in the bathroom, or ironing a school uniform in the kitchen, having spread on the table an old flannel blanket marked with yellow scorch marks from the iron. All this still remained to be done; yet they did not hurry. The salesgirls moved slowly about their work, the tiredness of the day lying on their faces like a thick coating of make-up.

Olga heard a familiar voice behind her and looked around – it was Irinka! Her daughter was standing beside one of the tall tables at which people drank coffee and ate cakes, but now it was too late for coffee and cakes. The snack bar was closed; she was standing there with two of her girl friends, and all three were talking and chewing something. Irinka's long, thin legs in dark stockings, the skimpy little overcoat that she had grown out of (she ought to have a new one – every time she looked at that pathetic little coat Olga felt an inward twinge, a momentary stab of guilt; but she never brought up the subject of buying a new one, and Irinka tactfully refrained from mentioning it too: it would somehow last through the autumn, and for the winter there was a quite presentable fur coat) – her daughter's round-shouldered, lanky figure with her fashionably long, straggly hair produced in Olga a convulsive upsurge of tenderness. It was so strong that she almost ran over to her. 'My poor little orphan,' she thought, almost in tears. 'She doesn't understand yet what that means. But I know!'

Olga took a few steps towards the girls, conscious that the tallest of the three, the most poorly dressed, the prettiest and the nicest one – her daughter – was the one person close to her. She could talk to her about anything. No one was closer to her now than this young girl. As she approached the table, one of the girls – Irinka's best friend Dasha, a pretty little oriental girl, always extremely pale, with long eyes rimmed with eyeliner – noticed Olga, stopped twittering and smiling, and looked frightened.

'So this is where you fritter your life away,' said Olga. 'I wonder what you were talking about?'

'We were talking about tomorrow's sociology class, Olga Vasilievna, when there'll be a very interesting discussion on the individual and society. We were wondering about the best way to prepare for it.' The look of fright on Dasha's pretty little face gave way to an expression of triumphant sarcasm.

The other little girl burst into giggles. Irinka gave Dasha a sullen, warning look that was mixed with a gleam of delight; the sullen glance referred to the appearance of her mother, while the delight, of course, was for Dasha's benefit. Olga didn't like Dasha, whom she regarded as insincere, affected, and, worst of all, precociously grown-up. From certain careless remarks dropped by Irinka she gathered that Dasha had a somewhat complicated private life, and that somewhere in it was a much older man whom she called her 'friend'. No one seemed to know quite how far that friendship went. Olga had made some cautious attempts to find out, but Irinka refused to be drawn into it. One could hope it was nothing serious – after all, the girls were not yet seventeen and Olga herself at that age had had nothing on her mind but her studies. The sixth form – a lot of responsibility!

'By the way, I gave you that money for things you needed at the department store, not to spend here,' said Olga. Dasha's impertinence irritated her. The stupid little creature would not take her eyes off her. 'But I see you just squander it on cakes and cigarettes. Now, girls, why do you smoke?'

They mumbled in chorus something completely and purposely

unintelligible but which to them was funny and sarcastic. Olga knew her presence was making them uncomfortable. Irinka, stupidly embarrassed, was not even looking at her mother; yet she was hanging on her friends' every word and laughing unnaturally loudly. The third of the trio, Lena Kukshina, was a limp, anaemic, fat girl from a very well-off family; she was wearing a suede overcoat, and on one small puffy finger was a ring set with a stone. (Disgraceful! In Olga's day no schoolgirl would have dared wear a ring.) An extremely elegant folding Japanese umbrella lay on the table beside her; one of Olga's friends had a similar one, so she knew how expensive they were. The Kukshina girl exuded an aroma of prosperity and wealth, in the same way that men who have just been to the barber reek of cheap scent. It was an aroma that Olga found hard to tolerate. Irinka, however, always insisted that Kukshina was a nice girl, even though she didn't like the way Kukshina grovelled for Dasha's favour. This Dasha, in fact, was the absolute uncrowned queen among them; she wielded enormous authority despite her diminutive size.

Olga said sternly, 'Come on, Irinka, let's go home. It's dinner time,' and took her arm above the elbow. Not because she intended to pull her away from the table, but simply because she wanted to touch her. 'It's time, dear, let's go.'

'Mama, I'll come home when I want to,' Irinka snapped with sudden hostility.

'What do you mean – when you want to?'

'I mean what I say: I'll come when I want to.'

'No, you're coming with me now.'

'No, I won't.'

Olga felt a kind of helpless fury welling up inside her. 'How could you . . . treat me . . . at a time like this . . .' she stuttered, breathless.

'And how could *you?* I have my problems too. I need to talk to my friends.'

'*You* have problems!' Olga shouted. 'You little . . .'

She turned around and walked out of the shop. One of the girls ran after her and seized her arm from behind.

'Olga Vasilievna! Stop!'

It was Dasha. Again the look of fear in those gorgeous dark-brown eyes.

'It's true, Irinka's been having problems with a boy – you know, Boris – and we really do need to talk a bit more, about another ten minutes. They'll chase us out anyway, because it's closing time. We'll just walk a little way up the boulevard.'

'She's just a little piece of trash,' said Olga.

As the lift in the block of flats was going up to the eighth floor, she thought: '*This* is the truth. Alone in a closed steel box. You can read the graffiti, scratched on the walls with nails. But there's no one to tell how much your heart aches. No one will hear. In solitude we creep higher and higher up the shaft or lower and lower downward – the direction is immaterial, it merely depends on which you regard as the top and which the bottom.'

'No one can hear!' she said aloud.

'Hullo! What's that? Speak louder!' a hollow, terrifying voice barked out just above her ear. She jumped: it was the lift watchman, answering her through the loudspeaker of the emergency call system. Normally, when you really needed him you could never get through to him, but this time he had heard. It was a sign: it meant that one must speak, one must shout, even if there are only bare walls all around. Somebody *will* hear.

It was not ten minutes but an hour later that Irinka came home. Olga had already forgiven her, and when she opened the door and saw her, head bowed and sniffing – naturally she was frozen after walking for a whole hour up and down the boulevard in that thin little coat – she also saw the childishly guilty look on her face and was again overcome by a wave of warmth and sympathy. 'How could I? Why did I bark at her?' she said to herself, her mind suffused with pity. 'The wretched child is an orphan, she has no father, no one to protect her. If I don't, who will . . .?'

Without a word she stroked her daughter's hair. The girl suddenly darted forward, embraced her mother, pushed her wet-nosed, puppyish little face into Olga's cheek, into her ear, whispering something in a miserable voice. And Olga whispered too. Neither heard what the other was saying. It all happened in two seconds, and suddenly both softened in each other's embrace; barely holding back their tears, they went into the kitchen to be alone together for a little while, just the two of them, without Grandma, because no person was closer to either of them than the other. No one on earth was closer. They sat there for a long time, drinking tea, while Irinka told about Boris. Secretive by nature, she rarely shared her troubles and fought her life's little battles in silence. This meant, though, that when she reached the limit of her strength, as she had now, she really needed help. Boris had stopped calling for her, and in school he wouldn't come near her any more. She guessed it was because of a girl he had met on his holiday in the South. Dasha had promised to find out. Boris was a boy from a parallel class. He was even rather ugly – Irinka had never been particularly taken by his looks – but the wretched girl appeared to be in a state of genuine distress.

Olga whispered some soothing nonsense. Irinka calmed down and went to the bathroom to wash her hair. Olga began to clear away the table and put the dirty dishes into the sink; at that late hour the hot water was unreliable and tonight it wasn't hot enough, and she did not want to heat water in the kettle. She decided to leave it all until tomorrow: she would get up at seven o'clock. At that moment the phone rang. It was the woman who had come with Bezyazichny.

'Excuse me for calling you so late. It takes me so long to get out to Kuzminki, where I live, and then there are so many things to do . . . Let me tell you why I'm calling, Olga Vasilievna. I imagine that Bezyazichny tried to frighten you with the business of your husband's debt to the credit union, didn't he? Well, you've no cause to worry – the debt will be written off. The decision, in fact, has already been made. Do you see? And please – don't hand over a single folder or a single sheet of notes. I shouldn't be telling you all of this, of course, but it's simply because I greatly liked and respected Sergei Afanasievich. Please excuse me, dear Olga Vasilievna, for bothering you at this late hour. Good luck!'

This strange conversation, that 'Good luck!' perplexed Olga, but not sufficiently to divert the flow of her thoughts. At night she could only think of the past, never of the future.

She should have done something about it long ago but had lacked the strength. All his folders, notepads, notebooks thick and thin, newspaper clippings clumsily glued into scrapbooks, pages ripped out of journals, heaps of scribbled-over paper, were scattered all over the flat – some things were in the drawers of his desk, others on the lower shelves of bookcases, some folders lay gathering dust on top shelves of cupboards, just below the ceiling, where no duster had reached for months; whenever she had a clean-up Olga angrily demanded that Sergei remove all his 'junk' and put it somewhere else, preferably into the dustbin. She called it 'junk' on the grounds that if it had been of any value he wouldn't have kept it lying around, covered with dust, on the tops of wardrobes and cupboards. Some of his papers had even found their way out onto the landing during the last spring cleaning. But the papers were still, as it were, his flesh; his smell, the emanation of his physical being was still upon them, and she could not bring herself to touch them. She knew that sooner or later this feeling would pass, but so far she could not do it. She was equally unable to look at or touch his clothes in the wardrobe. Faïna told her she should sell them; she said all widows did that, to remove one of the sources of pain and grief, and she promised to find a buyer for them. Louisa, Fedya Praskukhin's wife, who had been widowed eight years ago, said that she sold Fedya's clothes right after his death, all at one time, but Olga lacked such resolve.

In any case, there was no time to spare for such things. Louisa didn't have a job at the time (lately, though, she had started to work as an insurance agent) and had nothing to do but sit at home with the children. What's more, she had someone to help with the children, and her mother lived with her. If Olga had stayed at home, she would have gone out of her mind.

There was something else that was unbearable: photographs. Hanging on the wall was one particularly good snap-shot of Sergei, taken when he was younger; he was smiling gently and pensively, a blade of grass in the corner of his mouth. Olga loved that photograph. She had hung it there long ago, in Sergei's lifetime, and had grown accustomed to it. Now, though, whenever Olga came into the room she tried not to look at it, or at the most only fleetingly, for a second. As for their family album, she had hidden it as far away as possible. Every contact with the past meant pain. Yet life is made up of such contacts, for the threads to the past are a thousandfold and each one must be wrenched out of the living flesh, out of the wound. At first she had thought that repose would come when all those threads, down to the tiniest and thinnest, were broken. It now appeared, however, that this would never be, because the number of threads was countless. Every object, every familiar person, every thought, every word – every single thing in the world was linked by some thread to him. Would it last all her life? Yesterday her work had taken her to Novo-Basmannaya Street; she had got out of the metro at Lermontovskaya station, and immediately she had felt a stab at her heart as she remembered how last winter, in bitter cold, they had run from this station down Sadovaya Street to visit some friends. Seven months, and it wasn't getting any easier to bear. People said that five years had to pass, but Louisa had said this was untrue, and she ought to know, having been widowed for longer than that.

She had chanced recently to meet Louisa on the street. They had both been delighted to see each other; there was so much they wanted to say, so much to ask: How are you? How do you feel? What's happening to you? Is it getting . . . even just a tiny bit?

Louisa looked at her with grey, desolate eyes: 'I don't know how to measure it. There's no such instrument . . .'

Olga also wanted to ask her, 'Have you found someone else?' but she did not dare. In this battle, each one fought alone. Louisa looked well in her old fur coat, although cleaning had lightened its brown colour and given it a rather vulgar pinkish tinge.

Olga asked, 'How are the children?'

'Just fine,' Louisa replied. She answered 'Just fine' to every question.

Eight years ago, early one morning in September – so early that Irinka had not yet left for school – the doorbell had rung long and loud. When she opened the door, Olga was amazed to see Gennadii Klimuk – then still known familiarly as 'Gena', their old friend – who at that hour should have been doing his morning gymnastics before breakfast on the pebbly beach at Koktebel. Klimuk's face was covered with purple blotches. Without even saying good morning he asked, 'Where's Sergei?' Then he stepped into the foyer and collapsed sideways against the wall. Sergei came out of the bathroom, his face lathered with shaving soap.

'Sergei, you must tell her . . . I can't . . . I don't have the strength . . .' This huge boy, with his round, prematurely old-looking face, swayed, and his legs crumpled as he gently slid down the wall to the floor. He did not quite fall, but somehow ended up sitting on his haunches, where he stayed for two or three seconds, breathing heavily.

Two days earlier, Klimuk and Fedya Praskukhin had driven south together for a week's holiday. Fedya had just bought a new Moskvich. They sometimes organised bachelor outings – or, as Klimuk liked to say with conscious archaism 'sorties' – to which they tried to entice Sergei, but Olga did everything in her power to dissuade him from joining these excursions. It might have been that she was jealous of this male friendship, or that she was worried about his morals in the company of old friends, who had still not lost the freewheeling habits of their student days (whenever the three of them got together, these usually dormant habits were somehow galvanised back into life: they would start to play the fool, to brag, and to egg each other on to God knows what lunacy); or maybe she was worried about his health, because wherever Klimuk was, there was hard drinking. The plain fact was that she didn't like it when Sergei disappeared out of her sight. He should always be alongside, nearby, best of all in the same room with her. This was, no doubt, the greatest failing in her character, but she could not change herself and indeed had never even tried to.

She always did everything possible to counteract the wiles of Klimuk or Fedya or anyone else who attempted to take Sergei away from her. Sometimes she would skilfully find genuine reasons, sometimes invent plausible excuses – pleading, for instance, some ailment of hers that demanded his uninterrupted presence – and sometimes she would appeal flagrantly and directly to his conscience or his innate kindness. It was, in effect, the clash of two brands of egotism. He loved these stag outings, which were a change from everyday tedium, from work, from home, and he specially enjoyed the 'sorties' to see Fyodorov, his old friend from the museum, or going anywhere with Fedya Praskukhin in his car, even just to the Sevan bar; she knew he liked it, and that for a number of reasons he needed it, but she couldn't help herself: whenever he disappeared, she almost became ill. Sometimes she even started to develop a nervous rash. Sergei, however, was relentless in his struggle for independence and rarely gave in to her. That rare occasion was in September. The institute was being redecorated, work had stopped, everyone was loafing around at home; Fedya and Klimuk took it into their heads to go South for a week's fresh air and tried to persuade Sergei to come too. There was such chaos at the institute that no one would notice they had gone. In any case, who was there to notice? As academic secretary, Fedya Praskukhin himself was the boss.

Sergei very much wanted to go, but some instinct prompted Olga not to let him go on any account. Hell, no, it wasn't instinct at all; she was simply annoyed at the thought of his leaving her behind while he went South, where he would have fun, fool around, and, of course, drink. She pointed out that they were broke, that none of his projects were getting anywhere – his dissertation, the book he was supposed to be getting published with the help of that fraud Ilya Vladimirovich – and how it was all right for Fedya Praskukhin and Gena Klimuk to fritter away their time and energy – they had tenured jobs – but he couldn't afford to behave like that.

'The thirty roubles that I can give you for the trip won't go far; you'll just be sponging off the others. Doesn't that worry you?'

No, he said, it did not. The three of them, he said, had a healthy male attitude about these things, not like the miserable female habit of counting every kopeck they spent between them.

He even went so far as to say, 'It's something you'll never understand.'

Poor man, how wrong he was. Olga said that if he went with them, she would divorce him. Someone rang up, it might have been Louisa or it might have been the stupid Mara Klimuk, prompted by the men, to try to persuade her to relent and let Sergei go. But she was adamant. If he went – it was divorce. Sure, go if you like, no one's stopping you, but when you come back I won't be here, that's all – I'm going back to mother. Can it have been that she was prompted by a voice of prescience from those unearthly regions into which Sergei was later to descend and where his own destruction awaited him? Sergei was furious and refused to speak to her for several days, but he did not dare go. At dawn, on the Simferopol road south of Kharkov, a deaf old man who couldn't hear their horn had started to cross the road in front of them; Fedya could not slow down in time; he swerved to the left and was hit by an oncoming lorry. Fedya had died in the local hospital without regaining consciousness, while Klimuk had escaped with nothing more than bruises. He had somehow managed to brace himself with his arms against the sides of the car – he had strong arms – and although the car turned over twice, he had survived intact.

Now, his lips white, he could barely whisper, 'Fedya's body is being brought back by bus . . . I paid a hundred and twenty roubles . . .'

He begged Sergei to go to Louisa and break the news to her. Sergei went. He knew how to be a friend. That was why 'many people liked him', flew to him whenever things were going badly – and undoubtedly they exploited this quality of his.

That night she could not restrain herself – she should never have said it, but the words just broke through – and said quietly into his ear, 'Sergei, I saved your life. See what a good prophet I was?'

Without saying a word he pushed her away and turned over towards the wall.

She immediately realised that she had said the wrong thing, but the inner pressures prompting her to speak had been very strong indeed; terror, pity for Fedya, of whom she had been fond; and some strange, irrepressible inward feeling of secret self-satisfaction. No doubt, she thought, people experienced the same feeling in war when their comrades were killed beside them while they themselves somehow stayed alive and unharmed. She should not have said it. In the very instant that the thought was given utterance it inexorably turned false.

After a silence he said, 'I was hoping that you might bite your tongue off rather than say it. But no, you had to . . .'

Of course she shouldn't have said it, but he shouldn't have been so angry with her, either. Because it was true: she *had* saved his life. He talked about Fedya, about how he was the best friend he would ever have in his life. True, they had been friends; all three – Sergei, Fedya, and Gena Klimuk – had been at university together. But so what? She was always amazed at this childish attachment to friends from school or university days. Sergei always managed to overlook their failings, never saw what was ridiculous or unpleasant about them. For him the labels 'schoolmate' and 'classmate' were the highest possible forms of recommendation and a guarantee of all the virtues. It was friendship not by choice but by force of circumstance: if someone happened to share a school desk with me, I am therefore his friend. All men, what's more, shared this peculiarity: they couldn't live without their old pals. Yet Olga managed very well without female friends, and when Sergei was alive she could go for months without seeing Faïna or anyone else. She needed no one but him. Well, she saw Louisa and Mara now and again, but only because their husbands loved doing things 'all together': 'Let's go, all together!' or 'Why haven't we all been together for such a long time?'

Now they were linked by their common interest in the institute and everything that went on there. Gena Klimuk used to joke, saying with a wink, 'Let's set up our own little group, our own clique, our own cosy little gang.'

Fedya, however, did not just chatter; he got things done. He was really helpful: he bent over backwards to get Sergei into the institute, helped his progress in every possible way, got him a higher salary, persuaded Ivan Demchenko, the popeyed director of the institute, to change his mind and accept an alteration in the topic of Sergei's dissertation, and pacified Sergei's supervisor, Professor Vyatkin, who was by no means pleased with the change of topic. None of this was easy, but Fedya did it. If Fedya had not been killed in the car crash and had remained academic secretary, he, of course, would never have countenanced the disgraceful way Sergei had been treated, which was the fault of his old friend Klimuk and his 'little gang'.

Gena took over the post of academic secretary so quickly and with such readiness that one might have thought he had arranged the accident on purpose, like the diabolical Woland in Bulgakov's *The Master and Margarita*.

It was after Klimuk's appointment to the job that things imperceptibly began to deteriorate. For a long time Olga did not notice anything. Whenever Gena called up, he was as cheerfully friendly with her as ever; sometimes Mara called, to give Olga the latest tips on knitwear and cosmetics (she had a very enviable job, in an exclusive shop on the Petrovka near the Arcade), but several months went by before it occurred to Olga that she wasn't actually seeing either Gena or Mara any longer and that their contact was limited to phone calls. It was a long time since Gena's joyous catch phrase 'Let's go, all together!' had rung out. Once aware of the situation, Olga put it down to Fedya's death. It was, after all, most often at Fedya's place that they had all met. Apart from the three couples, there were other friends of Fedya's – a physicist, Shchupakov, with a Bulgarian wife named Krasina, a couple by the name of Luzhsky who were both doctors, she a radiologist, he a psychiatrist; in fact, it was because of the Luzhskys that Olga had first started visiting Fedya and Louisa because she was very much interested in medicine and loved talking with doctors.

But after Fedya's death Louisa stopped inviting friends; they had forgathered only after Fedya's funeral and then once again on the sixth anniversary of his death. Even in the old days Gena Klimuk had never been very hospitable; he was always renovating, redecorating, repairing, or changing flats, inexorably enlarging his living space and moving into ever more fashionable districts. Now, it appeared, he had made it to the New Arbat, in the skyscraper above the Melodia record shop.

At some point Sergei had said with a chuckle, 'Our Gena has really become a big wheel. He makes it rather obvious, too. When Fedya had that job, I somehow never noticed . . .'

She asked what characteristics of big-wheeldom were showing in Gena. Sergei grinned and said nothing. She knew, however, that he would be unable to keep it to himself for long, and he did tell her a few days later. The committee of the institute's staff association had been given a number of travel vouchers for a trip to France of eleven days, six in Paris and five in Marseilles, Nice, and so on – the dream of a lifetime, and costing a tidy sum. Since there were only four of these vouchers, the staff association decided not to advertise them but to distribute them, as the saying goes, on the sly. Sergei learned about this quite by chance, and not from his friend Gena but from the director's secretary, who had a soft spot for Sergei. Many people wanted to go on the trip. At first the committee intended to draw lots, but then Klimuk showed caution, saying that drawing lots would introduce an improper element of chance and a dangerous lack of control by giving the vouchers to people who had no *need* to go to France at all, while passing over others for whom it was a genuine *necessity*. In fact, this argument was perfectly reasonable and logical, as was every position that Klimuk adopted. But the catch was: Who would decide who needed to go and who didn't? At one point Sergei told Klimuk to his face that he needed to go to Paris not for sightseeing or amusement – there was a touch of hypocrisy in this, of course – but to look for research material that was essential for his work. Everyone knew – and naturally Klimuk was well aware of this too – that in studying the tsarist secret police the historian would inevitably be led to France, to the Russian political émigrés who had gone there and the police agents whose job was to spy on them. The point was quite easy to explain by rational discussion, because Sergei was right and had an entirely lawful ground for claiming one of the vouchers, but Klimuk merely gave a sort of grunt, cross-questioned him, demanded specific evidence – although what was there to grunt about when the claim was absolutely justified? – and Sergei, losing patience, said something rude and personal, something like: 'Stop being such a bore!' or, 'Lay off the bullshit, Gena!'

Klimuk shrugged and replied coldly, 'Submit your claim in writing. The three-man committee will decide. Do try to understand – the matter isn't as simple as it looks.'

'Do try to understand' was the only human, friendly remark he made during the whole conversation.

Sergei became very depressed as he told the story.

Olga decided that Sergei might be exaggerating, that he was too easily offended by trifles, especially the main trifle: the fact that Klimuk had talked to him like a boss. But what could one do? One had to come to terms with it. He *is* the boss, you *are* the subordinate. It's something you have to live with. Without telling him, when Sergei was out of the house, she rang up Mara simply as one friend to another – why haven't you rung, what's become of you, how are things with you, and so on. She realised that she had to act. Sergei was already despondent, even though nothing was decided yet; what would he be like if he really didn't get the trip? She wanted him to go. A little 'escape' to Paris might give him new strength and become a turning point. When one failure after another hits a man, or doesn't even hit him but simply settles on him softly and habitually like birds settling on a tree, he starts to grow wooden, loses all feeling and gradually turns into a tree himself. The trip would cost a great deal of money, and they didn't have any, so they devised a plan. He would raise half of it by selling his eight-volume collected works of Stefan Zweig to an acquaintance who was a secondhand book dealer; published by Vremya, it was a magnificent edition in very choice bindings with red leather spines, for which he had originally paid fifteen hundred old roubles; Olga would ask her mother to lend them the other half.

So she called up Mara and chattered to her in a voice of phony, cheerful friendliness, not knowing exactly where the conversation might lead. The aim was to sound her out, but Olga's probing revealed nothing; Mara prattled on in her affected, would-be amiable voice, passed on bits of silly gossip, laughed out of place – in other words she was unbearable, but there was nothing new in that, so Olga, feeling slightly relieved, decided that all was normal and Sergei was getting into a panic over nothing. Mara, however, was too dense and lacked the subtlety to react to indirect suggestion; to find out anything useful meant talking to Klimuk himself, so to her own surprise Olga invited Mara and Gena to visit them at the *dacha*, out in the country at Vasilkovo. It was early summer, a lovely time of year; they could swim, sunbathe, wander through the woods . . . how about it, then? Why don't we all get together soon, without planning too far ahead, on Saturday, or even Friday – whenever you like. Mara said she herself would love to come, but she would have to check with Gena. He was working terribly hard; they never went anywhere nowadays and had grown quite unsociable. Gena was in the next room. He asked Mara to say hello for him and promised they would come as soon as they could make it.

Sergei grumbled, 'It looks a bit weird: I see him practically every day and don't invite him, while you never see him – and you invite him.'

On balance, though, Sergei was pleased. There is nothing so touchy as a friendship that is cracking up.

Every evening she would ask him, 'Did you see Klimuk? Are they going to come?'

'I saw him, but I didn't ask . . . I didn't want to push it . . .'

What had once been easy and natural to do had turned into a problem. His tongue wouldn't form the words needed to ask the simple question: 'When are you coming to see us, Gena?' One day, however, he came back from the institute in some excitement and announced that Klimuk had himself come into Sergei's room and said that if the invitation to Vasilkovo still held good, then they would like to come for a short while on Saturday.

'For a short while?' asked Olga.

'Well, I don't know. That's what he said.'

On Friday they bought food, two bottles of vodka, two bottles of white wine, a few bottles of beer, and took a taxi out to Vasilkovo. Irinka and Sergei's mother had been there all that week, with Aunty Pasha, the old peasant woman from whom they rented the *dacha*. Getting out to the *dacha* on weekends was always rather a struggle: it was a long way from the station, it meant getting away from work early, and the train journey lasted nearly an hour. Even so, whenever she did manage to get away early enough and stepped out onto the platform, however exhausted she was by the long ride, the pushing and shoving and standing in queues in the shops, however heavy her cartload of packages, paper bags, loaves of bread, cans, and books, stuffed into string bags and baskets, she felt immediately refreshed by the cool forest air. She would take deep, deep breaths, of the kind one never once took in a whole day in the city, and she was pleasurably aware of the tiredness slowly ebbing away as her whole being was filled with new strength. It was so lovely! Where did that strength come from, after an exhausting, grinding, relentless day? From the sky? From the woods? From the fact that Sergei was walking beside her and carrying the bags, humming to himself, or bringing her up to date on the news from the village as he puffed at a cigarette? Aunty Pasha had bought some sour cream from the village shop . . . Ginger, the dog, had been chasing the neighbours' chickens again . . .

There were fixed days on which he had to attend the institute, but on other days – sometimes three or four in a row – he could work out at the *dacha*. He would meet her on the platform and pick up the bags for her. At first they followed the same road as the crowd of other weekenders; past a green hedge, they would turn off through a little oak wood where the other people usually dispersed, group by group, to their cottages; then, leaving the wood behind them, they crossed a field, after which they were on the road leading into Vasilkovo village, and by now they were generally alone. The weekenders tended to live near the station, while the people who lived in Vasilkovo did not take the trains from Moscow. The field they had to cross was enormous and rose to a knoll at the far end. The village lay beyond it, at the bottom of a steep slope, as though it had fallen over the edge of the field and tumbled down into the valley below. There the scattered cottage roofs peeped up, with their long protruding television aerials; willow trees clustered like piles of tarnished silver along the banks of an invisible river; a boy in a red shirt rode a bicycle along the path that cut across the field; and the silence was disturbed only by the puttering of a distant tractor. The clear sky was so bright that it made you want to look up. In the city no one ever noticed the sky or felt the urge to look upwards.

It was a two-mile walk to the village. Back in town Olga would think longingly: just let me go the distance, hauling the bags, then have a quick bite to eat, drink a cup of tea – and sit down exhausted in Aunt Pasha's big living room, which smelled of fresh hay and thyme, bunches of which were stuffed into crannies of the woodwork to stop draughts and scent the air. Yet every time what happened was quite different: after tea they would go walking in the woods with Irinka; at ten they would put her to bed and afterwards Olga and Sergei would take another long walk by themselves. If Alexandra Prokofievna joined them they would go only a short distance and soon return, but the old lady didn't often do this; even she realised that husband and wife needed to be alone together. Or else they would bathe in the deep water at a bend in the river, where they would sit on the bank and gossip with neighbours, all the while absorbing new strength from some mysterious source and not feeling tired at all.

There were, of course, days when it was wet and cold, when the path across the field turned into an impassable quagmire – and then came the onset of the Great Boredom of country life. Alexandra Prokofievna wrote interminable letters, Irinka whined and complained first of earache, then of tummy-ache, sending Sergei running through the rain to fetch Agnia, the district nurse.

Klimuk arrived in his old Pobeda, bringing with him another visitor – Kislovsky, the deputy director of the institute. No one had expected Kislovsky. Olga noticed that as Kislovsky stepped out of the car Sergei cringed for a second and his face took on the expression she knew so well, which meant: 'Oh, hell!' With Klimuk was Mara, wearing a stunning dark-green trouser suit – it was when trouser suits were just becoming fashionable and were being imported – white sandals, white handbag, and white earrings; a dazzlingly chic figure, her hair transformed by henna into a deep auburn. Everything about Mara was new and unrecognisable and took Olga's breath away. It was not exactly a pleasant surprise: you're sitting at home with an apron over your drab workaday clothes and suddenly the woman you thought of as a friend turns up in all this gorgeous plumage . . . But it wasn't Mara who struck the jarring note. She couldn't help the fact that she simply oozed stupidity; poor thing, if only she had the good sense to sit in silence and smile thoughtfully as she held a cigarette in her thin fingers, she would be irresistible, but she would insist on butting into every conversation. She even tried to argue with Olga about biology. No, Mara was hopeless but harmless; it wasn't she who spoiled the atmosphere for Olga.

The trouble lay elsewhere: the woman who had come with Kislovsky. Although she had long since forgotten her name, Olga disliked this young creature on sight – a dark, loose-jointed gypsyish creature, thin and affected. She was adorned with masses of jangling silver bracelets and beads; her jewellery was, in fact, beautiful and expensive, but it was absurd to festoon oneself like that for a day in the country, and it showed her lack of taste.

As soon as possible, seizing a convenient moment, Olga whispered to Mara, 'What does Kislovsky's wife do?' To which Mara, as Olga had guessed she might, replied, 'If she's his wife, then I'm your grandmother.'

In other words, it was one of Klimuk's usual bits of effrontery. Once he had produced some dubious-looking girls who, he claimed, worked in TV; what's more, he had brought them, without asking or phoning, to their flat in Moscow. Sergei, always ready to bend over backwards to humour a friend, was just about to offer them biscuits and the last vestiges of some French brandy when Olga came home from work; rapidly sizing up the situation, she firmly put a stop to it all and escorted the uninvited guests off the premises. Klimuk was furious. Now, however, he felt he was the boss – and the invitation had been so pressing. Besides, this time Mara was with him.

'We've only come for a moment . . . we're on the way to the reservoir. Just thought we'd drop in for a second or two,' they said as though apologising for descending like this and bringing these strangers with them; at the same time their remarks implied more than a touch of condescension, because they made it clear that the visit was a quick one, a mere drop-in and therefore did not count as a real visit.

Olga rushed about trying to cope with the extra numbers, but Irinka helped, and Aunty Pasha lent a hand by clambering down to the cellar for sauerkraut, gherkins, and pickled mushrooms, and sending her son Kolka off to the village for bread – he roared away on his motorbike, in joyful anticipation of the drinking to come – and only Alexandra Prokofievna stayed out of the kitchen, touched not a piece of crockery, and instead retired behind a screen on the veranda to continue her endless letter writing. She answered readers' letters for some newspaper, which ran a column entitled 'Consult Our Lawyer'. Long ago she had been a defence counsel in the courts. Olga could not believe that her mother-in-law had ever been a good or successful advocate; but although she felt convinced of this, she never discussed it with Sergei.

They had lunch in the garden behind the house. The day was hot, the air under the apple trees sultry. Most of all they drank ice-cold well water, which Kolka brought by the bucketful. The water in Vasilkovo was truly delicious; Olga had never drunk water that was so sweet and so cool. It was even better than the water in Yerevan, which the Armenians boasted was quite special . . . But what good was nostalgia? Something was depressing her; she was irritated by the girl who had come with Kislovsky, annoyed by the way she was giving Sergei the glad eye and flirting with him under the pretext of asking questions, to which he reacted by putting on a stupid frown and mumbling in embarrassment. She was irritated, too, by Mara's brainless chatter, worried that there wasn't enough food and wine to go round, that Sergei wouldn't find an opportunity to talk to Klimuk about the trip to France, and perplexed over how to treat Kislovsky, a smarmy, rubbery man who had the look of a double-jointed acrobat in a circus. Yet despite it all there was such a feeling in the air of something genuine, young, summery, unique – well, of what? – well, of happiness, she supposed . . . Yes, for a little while they were happy in that country garden, where it smelled of a mixture of earth and manure and sweet, lush June greenery. From behind them came a grunting sound and much scrabbling and stamping as Matilda, the sow, pushed the creaking gate open and lumbered into her sty, while Aunty Pasha, slightly drunk, fiercely shook her little brown fist: 'Now she's in paradise, God bless her, the lazy brute.' By now the visitors' 'second' had long since flown, the whole day had flown and evening had come, and they were all still sitting there, drinking, laughing and chattering; the bottles were almost empty, and Kolka had roared off again on his motorbike to get some home-made vodka from an old woman at the other end of the village.

Olga was just going into the bedroom when she saw Kislovsky clasping his friend around the waist, trying to push her onto the big double bed. Her silver ajangle, the girl was resisting.

Olga went out into the garden and sidled up to Sergei,

who was talking to Klimuk about something trivial and inessential, and whispered into his ear that she had just seen some rather tasteless goings-on in their bedroom.

'Suppose it's love?' he asked, giving her a glazed look. He was not, in fact, as drunk as he made out. His expression was one of submission to fate.

'Well, there are special places for that sort of love,' said Olga, 'and not Aunty Pasha's cottage.'

Aunty Pasha, not understanding what they were talking about but hearing her name, bristled aggressively: 'What's that about Aunty Pasha? You leave Aunty Pasha alone! I'll give you "Aunty Pasha". I'll show you all up.' And she wagged her finger. 'I'll unravel all your secrets. You tell 'em, Kolka . . .'

Kolka was an auxiliary policeman, which he bragged about a great deal, telling it to everyone as a great secret. His real job was being a carpenter on a state farm. Short, thin, with a consumptive pallor on a soft, girlish face, he wore his hair as long as a seminarist at Zagorsk, played the guitar rather badly and was, it seemed, besieged by girls every evening. Aunty Pasha was annoyed with him for not getting married and for 'just frittering his strength away'. Kolka had been rejected by the army as physically unfit because of a weak heart, and he was forbidden to drink – at any rate forbidden to drink more than one glass of vodka a day, as he said, quoting the doctor; this annoyed him, but at the same time he told it with a certain pride, as proving the special peculiarity of his organism. Needless to say, the prohibition was violated almost daily.

Alexandra Prokofievna kept a sharp eye on Kolka's health; she always scolded him when she saw him drunk, and she was, it must be said, the only person to whom he paid any attention. This was typical of the strange effect the old woman had on people: her relatives completely ignored her – and with reason, for they knew her character only too well – yet outsiders respected her and were even slightly awed by her. Evidently this was the result of her compulsive need to domineer, to which simple souls of limited intellect naturally submitted, while thinking people instinctively resisted it.

That same evening, when they all went for a walk in the woods after their greatly extended lunch – Kislovsky could be enticed out of the bedroom only with difficulty – Alexandra Prokofievna started up a carping, tactless conversation (more like a courtroom cross-examination) with Klimuk, whom she always treated with scant respect. She remembered him when he used to come to visit as a very young student, dirty, thin and hungry, from the student hostel ('Whenever he came he was always hungry, he would eat whatever was put in front of him and more – five, eight, twelve large meatballs, fantastic quantities'). Sergei would invite him to stay over for the night. They would play chess till midnight, smoke endless cigarettes, swot up for exams together, quarrel and make up. She called him Gesha and thought he was a nice boy but not too bright. Sergei had to coach him for his exams in Russian and dialectical materialism – and now he had shot so far ahead that he was Sergei's boss. She noticed how her son's relationship with Gennadii Klimuk had changed, unnoticed by anybody, even by Olga; Alexandra Prokofievna, however, had been a witness of that relationship from its very beginning, when they were boys in lumber jackets drinking tea in the kitchen, spreading apple jam on enormous hunks of bread; and there had been a third boy who talked in a deep bass voice, who acquired a wife and son well ahead of the others – the unfortunate Fedya, of whom she had been very fond. Nowadays, she noticed, her son behaved towards this stupid Gesha with a sort of stiff embarrassment and even a certain shyness, in the way that a subordinate is supposed to act in the presence of a superior; she found this intolerable, and felt offended on Sergei's behalf. If Klimuk's head had swollen and he had turned into one of those self-important Soviet bureaucrats she had derided as long ago as the twenties, then Sergei had no business to play up to this style of behaviour; instead, this lanky young upstart should be taken down a peg or two and taught sense. So Alexandra Prokofievna made a point of patronising Klimuk whenever she talked to him, called him Gesha as she did in the old days, and did everything she could to deflate his ego.

'I seem to have forgotten; my memory has started to play tricks on me,' she said. 'It's strange, because I always prided myself on my memory when I was a schoolgirl . . . What year was it, Gesha, when your brother came from Kremenchug? He stayed with us and I found him a lawyer. He was in some sort of trouble, something to do with embezzlement . . .'

'Alexandra Prokofievna, what's the point in digging up ancient history?' Olga put in, sensing that Klimuk was irritated and starting to sulk, which was not going to make the forthcoming conversation any easier.

'No, I well remember I called up Elizaveta Markovna at the Moscow College of Advocates, and if it was Elizaveta Markovna that means it was embezzlement. She liked those cases – or rather she didn't particularly like them, but she knew how to handle them because she had studied accounting. After all, what is important in such cases? The precise amount that was embezzled. It must be established, down to the last kopeck.'

The old woman's force of character was such that the drunken guests quietened down and sobered up slightly as they listened to the story. Her complaints about her memory were completely unfounded: she remembered it all perfectly. Klimuk scowled in an effort of self-control, then suddenly burst into laughter:

'But this is the theatre of the absurd! Pure Grand Guignol! My God, what on earth is the point of bringing all this up; what use is it to me, to you, to anybody? There's such a thing as historical expediency, you know. Do you know who my brother is now?'

Laughing and bragging, he told a story about his brother, at which for some reason everyone else started to laugh. And so, shrieking with pointless laughter, they all walked down to the bend in the river where there was a sandy beach, the bathing place. By day it was seething with children, the weekenders lay sunbathing, the village boys would be diving in off the iron jetty, but now it was deserted, scraps of newspaper glowed white in the twilight of the grey sand. The water was cold and smelled of mud. The men went swimming; the women sat down on the grassy slope and talked, but sitting on the grass and chatting was too feminine and too petty-bourgeois an occupation for Alexandra Prokofievna; she announced that she would bathe, away from the men and farther still from the women, and asked them all not to go past the alder tree. About twenty minutes later a cry of help came from beyond the alder tree: Alexandra Prokofievna could not climb out of the water up the slippery clay slope and asked Sergei to give her a hand.

Imperceptive though she was, Mara had grasped a certain amount of what was going on and whispered to Olga: 'You have my sympathy.'

That evening was memorable, however, for something else. Sergei latched on to Klimuk's words about historical expediency. It was obviously a sore point with him. They started off with a friendly slanging-match in the water as they fooled around and splashed each other like boys; then the dispute got really serious and on the way back to the village they were arguing hammer and tongs. After their dip in cold water all their drunkenness had vanished and the remarks started to get personal and Kislovsky joined in. It was something to do with

Sergei's work and someone else's work, and with a view of history in general.

It may be that it was on that drunken evening in Vasilkovo – in fact it was probably earlier, but that evening impressed itself on Olga's mind as the beginning – that there began the long feud between Sergei, Klimuk and all the rest, which caused him such pain and ended so tragically.

By the time they arrived back at the cottage and sat down on the veranda to drink tea, Sergei and Klimuk were shouting at each other in real animosity. Olga had no idea that Klimuk was capable of being so angry.

She knew, of course, that when Sergei got into an argument he was gripped by a kind of frenzy; he forgot about the rules of propriety and lost all sense of fairness and generosity. He wanted one thing only – to prove his point.

'In Aunty Pasha's bedroom there's an antique clock in a wooden case. Where did it come from, Aunty Pasha?' shouted Klimuk, thrusting out his right hand as though speaking from a rostrum.

'How do I know? Father brought it from somewhere. He exchanged it for food, he told me, during the famine in twenty-one.'

'He exchanged it, he brought it – it's all the same now. Whichever it was, it doesn't *matter* now. What does matter is that the clock keeps good time and plays Strauss every half hour. Am I right, Aunty Pasha?'

Aunty Pasha pursed her lips primly: 'Right or not, young man, I did not give you permission to call me Aunty Pasha.'

'Well said. Nothing matters and nothing has any meaning except historical expediency – remember that Aunty Pasha, and pour me some more tea, please. My mother, by the way, is another Aunty Pasha just like you, except she's called Aunty Paulina and she lives near Shebekinsk, Belgorod province . . .'

'This historical expediency that you keep talking about,' said Sergei, 'is something vague and treacherous, like a swamp . . .'

'It's the only solid thing that's worth hanging on to.'

'I wonder who decides what's expedient and what isn't? The academic council – by a majority vote?'

Sergei was now so carried away that he had forgotten that Kislovsky was chairman of the academic council. Olga hoped that people who had spent the whole day drinking and talking nonsense would forget who had said what, but it turned out later that they remembered Sergei's outbursts only too well. It is not the meaning of what is said that offends people but the intonation, because the intonation reveals another meaning – the hidden real meaning.

When Sergei had asked jokingly, 'The academic council – by a majority vote?' – and grinned sarcastically, his sarcasm had been more offensive than his words. And Kislovsky, if no one else, was unlikely to forget it. Sergei was talkative, indiscreet, and careless, and he had made enemies – a host of them, thanks to his jokes, his arguments, his venomous remarks, his inability to stop himself in time and think twice. A typical example was the nickname he had made up for Klimuk at the time when they were not yet out-and-out enemies but were moving towards it: he took Klimuk's name and patronymic, which were Gennadii Vitalich, and ran them together to make the hilarious but somewhat indecent combination of 'Genitalich'. People in the institute seized on it with delight. But why did Sergei have to do it? Why be so offensive?

It was late, but none of them showed any signs of going. The men were still arguing at the tops of their voices, smoking, drinking the last of the alcohol – Kolka had again been dispatched for another consignment of home-brew – while the women were nodding off and Irinka had long since been sent to bed. Olga was yawning and visibly exhausted, and from high in a midnight-blue sky the moon gazed down through the open windows.

And still they refused to go. The visitors, too, were yawning, stretching, giving every indication that they were dead tired and wanted to lay down their heads and curl up for the night. Then a conversation took place between Sergei and Klimuk while the men made their way to the outdoor privy at the end of the yard, and when they returned the visitors immediately started to depart. Olga realised that something had happened between the two of them: after the evening's second round of drinking both had relapsed into gloomy sobriety. Kislovsky was heaved into the car in a state of lethargy. Mara took the wheel, having purposely refrained from drinking so that the men could let themselves go. It was strange: Olga found herself thinking that the feather-brained Mara was in fact the only normal human being among the four of them. As she gave Olga a farewell kiss on the cheek, she whispered, gratified: 'Sergei was right not to let those two stay here. Really. And to think who they are.'

Kolka blew his police whistle, waved his arms in front of the car's headlights and shouted: 'Hey, what's all this – driving after drinking? Who's responsible? Out you get: this car's not going anywhere.'

Later, Sergei told Olga that Klimuk had asked if Kislovsky and his girl friend could stay for the night. This was, in fact, the reason why they had come. Sergei lost his temper at this and refused. Klimuk tried by every possible means to persuade him to change his mind:

'You invited Mara and me to spend the night here, so I have a claim to sleeping room for two in your *dacha*. Well, I'm merely giving up those places to my friends.' Then he switched to threats: 'You're acting very stupidly, old man. You'll have only yourself to blame for any consequences.' Finally, almost with tears in his voice he begged: 'Do it for my sake, old man. I promised him. On your word. How am I going to look if I let him down?'

Sergei told Klimuk that he felt a sudden and insurmountable aversion to the whole thing. Describing this, he said: 'I suddenly realised that the man I work under was a cheap little wheeler-dealer. Our *dacha* was a consignment of goods in some deal he was fixing. He had promised this to Kislovsky, who had promised him something else in return, and now, thanks to me, the deal was off. He threw a fit of hysterics. He positively hissed and boiled with rage. "You're no friend; no one can rely on you. You simply hate other people." And all this quite genuine fury was not because he sympathised with his friend Kislovsky but because someone was taking something away from *him*. I had robbed him, you see.'

Why, though, couldn't the couple have been allowed to stay over for the night? Granted that the gypsy-like girl was fairly loathsome, but since Kislovsky was such an important figure and Klimuk had asked . . . They could have given them the bedroom, and Olga and Sergei could have slept out on the veranda. Even in serious matters that could affect his career, Sergei's attitude to everything, however, was based on a peculiar criterion of taste. He did what pleased him and he didn't do what displeased him. Herein, incidentally, lay a fundamental cause of the constant trouble in which he found himself.

'I suddenly felt that I was a cheap little fixer too, and I was taking part in some squalid and protracted trade-off. I felt nauseated, and I refused, using you as an excuse: I said you had very strict moral standards . . . Anyway, to hell with him.'

God, it was obvious now what a chain of absurdities and pathetic subterfuges it had been. She shouldn't have invited them to the *dacha* in the first place. Once having invited them, he shouldn't have argued in such a pigheaded way and offended them. And both shouldn't have been so desperate about that trip to la belle France. At Vasilkovo, of course, Sergei had not said a word to Klimuk about the trip (and he was right not to have done so), but in that case, what was the point of all that frenetic hospitality?

Two days passed, and Sergei went to the institute. Returning that evening to the Moscow flat, he described with joyful excitement how Gena had been unusually affable and friendly, how he had made kind enquiries about Olga, her mother-in-law, Irinka, Aunty Pasha and Kolka and hoped that the guests hadn't done anything stupid while they were drunk. In the same half-joking tone Sergei had said, 'Did Kislovsky say anything? About the shortage of beds in the hotel?'

No, he hadn't said anything, because he had been in no fit state to talk: he hadn't made a sound all the way back to Moscow. Only as they reached the city did he utter his first words in a hoarse voice. For some reason he had asked: 'Have they brought it?' They never did find out what he meant.

Standing in the corridor as they talked, Sergei and Klimuk had laughed and parted. And what about France? So far, vagueness, although Klimuk had promised to say a word in the right quarter.

'Don't fuss, old lady! Gena will fix it, no problem.'

At that moment he seemed sincerely to believe it.

The problem was to find the money. As a first move, Olga had secretly spoken to her mother, who often used to help her out by lending or giving her small amounts, but this time her mother hesitated: she was shocked by the amount Olga asked for. She simply didn't have that sort of money: Georgii Maximovich gave her money every month but it was only enough for housekeeping expenses.

'Is this trip really so necessary?' Olga's mother tried feebly to resist. 'There's so much that needs doing to your flat. You need a fur coat; Irinka has grown out of everything. And then – if you were both going it would be different.'

Olga explained that it was quite impossible for them to go together; in any case, such a suggestion had never been made. In every sense, it was Sergei who would benefit from the trip. Olga's mother could not quite understand what was meant by 'in every sense'; this was difficult to explain, because it was a matter of certain rather vague, intangible factors – such as intellectual stimulus, self-affirmation – but she believed Olga. In the end her mother always believed her. She promised to talk to Georgii Maximovich. Next day she rang up to say that Georgii Maximovich had asked Sergei to go and see him.

They were certain that 'go and see him' simply meant to go and collect the money. All three of them went together on Saturday. For the past three years Olga's mother and Georgii Maximovich had been living in a new flat, not far from the old one in Sushchevskaya Street, where Georgii Maximovich still kept his studio. His affairs were now prospering; he had some appointed position, was in charge of something or other, did some teaching and no longer worked so hard. His doctors had forbidden him to work too much, but he still liked going to the studio every morning, and even if he wasn't drawing or painting he would quietly busy himself with his pictures, knock nails into frames with a little hammer, sort out his prints, and touch up a painting without straining his eyes; or he would invite a friend from the second or third floor and they would make tea on the stove, discuss their work and reminisce about the past while they inspected Georgii Maximovich's enormous collection of reproductions that he kept in huge portfolios.

Sergei got on rather well with Georgii Maximovich; he regarded him as a decent, honest man and felt something like gratitude towards him – not because of his creations on canvas or paper, but because he was such a good stepfather to Olga. One day, though, he said to Olga:

'There is a certain kind of picture they make for children: look at them through a piece of pink cellophane and you see one picture; look at them through a strip of blue cellophane and you see quite a different picture. Forgive me, but your stepfather reminds me of one of those pictures: now I see him as an artist, a real artist, who has sacrificed everything for art – and then I see him simply as a businessman, grubbing around for commissions.'

Olga did not like this; it degraded her mother, who could never have loved a businessman. The man she had fallen in love with was an unfortunate, unrecognised, hungry, poor but honest artist. And what sort of people prospered in the conditions of wartime evacuation? If he had really had a business sense, he would have prospered. He was incapable of working simply to make money; he couldn't do anything, in fact, except slap a brush on paper. One morning he had tied string around his only pair of boots – large black boots with square, squashed toe-caps (Olga remembered them well) – because the soles were coming away. It was later, years, decades later, that his fortunes improved and he started to earn good money for his work.

Olga's mother had once whispered to her that Georgii Maximovich had quite a lot of money in his savings account. Olga was glad, of course: she was assured that her mother would be taken care of, and it meant that she herself had somewhere to turn if she ever needed to be helped over a rough patch.

But that Saturday, Sergei did not want to go to see his father-in-law; it was as if he had a foreboding of something unpleasant.

'You go by yourself,' he begged Olga. 'Please . . .'

'No, I'd feel too embarrassed. You're the one who's asking for the money for your trip. If you don't come, they'll think it incredibly rude of you. You hardly ever go and see them, anyway.'

'Tell them I'm ill. I really don't feel too good.'

'No, if you don't go, I'm not going either. Then he'll withdraw his offer.'

His unwillingness to see his relatives struck Olga as extremely hurtful. They had made a noble gesture: who else would lend them such a large sum of money? Their friends? Like hell they would! And in return for this generosity Sergei was merely being asked to show the absolute minimum of courtesy – to sit and drink a cup of tea, to talk to the old folks for a while. And, of course, to say 'thank you' or 'I'm most grateful', just a word or two as a token of his gratitude. Surely that wasn't so difficult, was it? No, it wasn't difficult; he even enjoyed chatting with Georgii Maximovich, who had such a vast fund of experience and who had actually lived in Paris himself, in the rue de Mouftard, but . . .

'Hell, what's the use of talking? If it isn't immediately obvious to you why I don't want to go, then there's no point in trying to explain. Having to ask people for things is sickening, unbearable, and that is what turns all the tea and talk and visits to relatives into something strained and awkward. Now, once again, I'm in the intolerable position of being a supplicant, and that's why I asked you, if possible, to save me from this ordeal. But if you can't, then by all means let's go . . .'

She should have understood his feelings, but she didn't, because she was preoccupied with thoughts of her mother, who had also been placed in an awkward, perhaps, too, an intolerable position; but she had managed to overcome her distaste and had *asked* Georgii Maximovich.

"There are times when we have to do something unpleasant.' Olga was adamant. 'I know you don't like it. Now make up your mind: Do we go or do we stay at home?'

They took the trip in silence. Olga now had another cause to feel angry: Just why did he think he had the right to be resentful? What, in any case, was there to resent? The fact that he was going to France while she stayed behind? Irinka was silent too. She was very sensitive to arguments and tiffs between her parents, and she reacted in her own way. Unlike the role so often assigned to children in novels and films, she did not try to distract them, cheer them up or make peace between them; she behaved in just the same way as her parents; if they sat in gloomy silence, so did she; if they were snappish and irritable, then she would adopt exactly the same irritable, querulous tone – like a little old woman.

So the bus ride to Sushchevskaya was spent in silence. They walked past the old house, then plunged into a maze of back alleys, where thanks to demolition and rebuilding nothing was any longer recognisable. Strange riddle: Why was Olga in such a glum mood as she approached her mother's house? And why was he? After all, they were both young, healthy, and working at jobs of their choice; he was about to go abroad, while she was planning to use that time to rearrange their flat and was also counting on his bringing a few nice things back from Paris (she had already told him exactly what she wanted). And they were all three together . . . together! It was *their life*.

Yet they were gloomy as they went in the front door, gloomy as they got into the lift. The only remark that Olga made was a stern command to her daughter: 'Don't lean against that dirty wall!'

Her parents' flat was small and comfortable. The hall was decorated with some beautiful Hungarian wallpaper, carmine in colour, while the wallpaper in the living room was a wood-grain pattern. Here Georgii Maximovich had tastefully arranged the remnants of his antique furniture; he had fixed up some shelves, placed bookcases here and there, and everything that in the old house had seemed like junk here acquired a special, expensive look of old-world distinction. In addition there was, of course, a multitude of pictures, engravings and drawings on the walls, not only by Georgii Maximovich but by other artists too; among these trifles were two little studies by Levitan and Korovin, some drawings by other notables, and – the pride of Georgii Maximovich's collection – a wavy pencil sketch by Modigliani, depicting something vaguely erotic. On all the shelves, bookshelves and the big bookcase stood candles: thin candles and fat candles, ornamental candles, candles of unusual shapes and shades that burned with a perfumed aroma, candles bought abroad by friends of Georgii Maximovich – on doctors' orders he himself no longer travelled abroad – and now all these were smoking, flickering, burning and giving off a sweet, delicious smell.

'The illuminations are in your honour, mesdames et monsieur!' With a flourish, Georgii Maximovich invited them into the living room. The words in French were spoken intentionally, and this obviously displeased Sergei: Olga noticed his lips pouting slightly in a familiar grimace. Although the act of generosity – making a loan to his wife's relatives – was being carried out at home, it was being done with ceremony. Georgii Maximovich himself had a ceremonious look: he was dressed in a black velvet artist's jacket (recently made for him in the tailoring workshops of the Moscow Society of Artists), a snow-white shirt, a violet silk foulard at his neck, and trousers in the fashionable shade of charcoal grey, although the effect was a little spoiled by the fact that he was wearing his worn old carpet-slippers.

They began by sitting down to tea and cake. Irinka described her life at school, to which Olga listened with great interest, because at home Irinka never said a word about school; yet as soon as she was in the company of her grand-parents or of other people who were not too close to her but also not absolute strangers, she revealed a genuine talent for descriptive storytelling and delighted in showing it off. Then Olga's mother took Olga and Irinka off to her bedroom and left the men together for a talk.

Georgii Maximovich began by describing his life in Paris, in the rue de Mouftard, which the Russian expatriates in Paris, his friends of those days, called the 'Mouftarka'. Two were from Odessa, one from Elizavetgrad and one from Vitebsk – the one who later became world famous. About the others, though, he now knew very little: one of them, he thought, had gone to America, others had died in obscurity, and one had been killed by the Germans when they occupied Paris. It had all happened so incredibly long ago. It was in the youth of the century, the youth of the epoch, the youth of aeroplanes, films, soccer, modern art – everything that the world was crazy about now – and – coincidence – it was Georgii Maximovich's own youth, too. So there were a lot of girls in his memories – their little jokes, their gestures, the way they took their clothes off and closed their eyes and what they said while they did so; he remembered being hungry; he recalled the cafés; he recollected working furiously, joyously, all through the night on some painting that no one had commissioned and was never going to earn any money. In recounting his memories Georgii Maximovich grew more and more animated, his large, fleshy, big-nosed face grew red; he took a violet silk handkerchief out of his jacket pocket to mop his bald head and his cheeks.

Olga imagined all this very vividly, because Sergei later retold the conversation in much colourful detail, just like an actor, imitating Georgii Maximovich's voice and movements.

'Actually I lived in Paris twice . . . The first time was when I was just a boy, before the first war, but I understood nothing in those days. The second time was in the twenties, I was sent there officially, and then I understood a bit more. How shall I explain it? The second time we lived in the rue Vaugirard. It's the longest street in Paris . . .'

Sergei thought: 'The prologue is taking a very long time. When will he come to the point?' Georgii Maximovich talked for a little longer with fading enthusiasm, sweating and mopping himself with his handkerchief, telling something about his first wife, with whom he had lived in the rue Vaugirard and who had worked as a typist in the Soviet embassy. He had made sketches for a big picture of the Paris Commune – a picture which somehow never got finished.

'Now what can I tell you about Paris?' Georgii Maximovich mumbled in an unexpectedly weary voice. 'Paris, of course, is beautiful. But it's no more beautiful than Odessa or Kiev. It doesn't have the Black Sea or the Dnieper, and the Seine, to be honest, is a rather dull and dirty river. In summer it's so hot and humid, you can hardly breathe.'

Sergei asked whether Georgii Maximovich was implying that there was no point in going to Paris.

Georgii Maximovich shook his head and smiled a sly, meaningful smile. Oh no! Not at all. As an old, experienced gentleman who had seen a lot in his time, Georgii Maximovich was saying that in the past people had gone to Paris for two reasons. Firstly when they were very poor, hoping to cheat fate and make their pile there, and secondly when they were very rich, seeking to buy themselves some pleasure and squander their money. And as for modern tourism, Georgii Maximovich had no idea what it was like and didn't propose to venture an opinion. Sergei laughed. 'I get you. I don't belong either to the first or the second category, and anyway . . .'

'Heavens, my dear boy, I'm not trying to dissuade you from going. In fact, at your mother-in-law's request I've taken out a certain amount of *argent* so that you can –'

A wad of ten-rouble bills appeared from a pocket of the velvet jacket.

'There you are,' said Georgii Maximovich, showing all his plastic teeth as he beamed with pleasure and kindness and handed the wad to Sergei.

'Thank you,' said Sergei. But he did not take the packet of money. As he said later, in that second he felt a strange shift of perception: it was just as if everything suddenly started moving backwards.

Georgii Maximovich put the money on the table alongside Sergei. They went on with their conversation. Georgii Maximovich asked him about his work and how his dissertation was progressing.

His dissertation was going badly. Sergei didn't like talking about it. His answers started to get spasmodic and offhand, and to one of Georgii Maximovich's questions he gave no reply at all, but simply switched off, hummed a tune, and looked out of the window, obviously thinking about something else.

'Couldn't I help you in any way?' asked Georgii Maximovich.

Sergei thanked him and said that no one could help him. What could anyone do to help? He wasn't painting a fence or digging the garden. He gradually became more heated. Georgii Maximovich was showing him sympathy, and sympathy being something he particularly detested, it was then that he finally decided not to take the money.

'Do you know what I used to do whenever my work wasn't going right?' mused the old man, failing to sense that at this moment the tactful thing to do was to say nothing. 'I found the strength in me to scrap what I'd done and start all over again . . .'

'Yes, yes, I understand.' Sergei nodded, smiling.

'You're up a blind alley – isn't that so?' The old man outlined a shape with a vague gesture. 'You need to step back a few paces and start looking – am I right – for some new way, a different approach. One must always be flexible, and then . . .'

'You're absolutely right, *cher maître*. And your work is a perfect example . . . (Olga came into the room at that moment and as she heard these words she groaned inwardly, realising that Sergei was in the last stage of irritation and was about to resort to sarcasm) '. . . but please don't worry, Georgii Maximovich. Everything will work out all right, I promise you.'

Seeing Olga, he said hastily, 'Come on, we've already stayed too long. Time to go home.'

Georgii Maximovich exclaimed, 'Wait, you've forgotten something! Take it!' He waved the bundle of money over his head like a flag.

The word 'something' produced a new burst of sarcasm from Sergei:

'Not "something" but a certain sum of money, which you, Georgii Maximovich, have very kindly . . . and so on. I am extremely grateful to you, but I can manage without it, thank you. Thank you very much.'

Out on the street, after a long silence, he told Olga that she shouldn't talk to her parents or to anyone else about his problems with the dissertation – or about any of his affairs for that matter. The presence of Irinka restrained him somewhat, but Olga could see that he was seething. He hissed a series of short, cryptic remarks whose meaning Irinka could not understand, but she could see that her parents were quarrelling and that it was her father who was on the attack, so she took Olga protectively by the arm and stared angrily at Sergei. She was eleven years old at the time, and already quite able to join in grown-up conversations. He was saying that he found any sort of sympathetic enquiries, advice, and recommendations drawn from other people's experience not merely useless but – oh, they could all go to hell! For a long time Olga kept herself in check as she could see that he was abnormally wound up, but when he said something that was an obvious slander – 'I've warned you more than once not to tell anyone about my affairs, but you just can't help shooting your mouth off about them, can you?' – she could restrain herself no longer and retorted that this was a lie: she never indulged in indiscreet chatter, and there was no need to take out his bad temper on her.

'Then how does Georgii Maximovich know about them in such detail?'

'You told him yourself!'

'Anyway, why can't you write a dissertation?' shouted Irinka.

'You keep out of this.' He slapped his daughter on the top of her head. 'Shut up!'

Irinka ran ahead of them, shouting and leaping up and down in time to her words:

'You're no good! You're no good! Can't write a dissertation! Can't write a dissertation!'

Irinka's silly outburst had an unexpected effect on Sergei: he laughed aloud, then fell silent and did not utter another word until they were home.

But what was happening to him? She could not understand. It was not that she was too preoccupied with her own work at the laboratory or with the complex relationships that existed as much in her professional world as everywhere else – she had, in fact, a talent for getting on well with people and was not afraid of the complexities – but because his subject, history, seemed to her such a baffling fusion of simplicity and mystery. What could be simpler, one might think, than describing *what had already happened*? All the exact sciences were concerned with advance, with moving forward, with constructing something new, creating what had never existed before, and only Sergei's discipline, history, was devoted to restructuring what was old, recreating the past. Olga had a mental image of history as a vast, endless sequence in which epochs, nations, great men, kings, generals, and revolutionaries stood in line one behind the other; to her, the historian's job was rather like that of the policeman who was stationed outside the entrance of the local cinema to keep order whenever the premiere of a film was being shown: to ensure, in other words, that the epochs and the nations didn't get mixed up or change places, that the great men didn't try pushing ahead in the queue, didn't quarrel, and didn't try to get a ticket to immortality out of turn.

This simple policemanlike activity, however, caused Sergei a great deal of frustration and distress – and herein lay the mystery that her mind could not grasp. Why couldn't he just sit diligently in the archives for a month, or two months, or five months, or however long was necessary, and extract from that gigantic queue everything that concerned the czarist secret police in Moscow in the period immediately before the February Revolution, and then carefully work up all this material into presentable form? After all, the historian didn't have to create something totally new. He didn't have the problems that faced her and her colleague Andrei Ivanovich in their work on BSCC – biological stimulation of cell compatibility; they were trying to create something that had never before existed – not in America, not in Japan, nor in Ancient Greece, nor in Egypt, nowhere in the world. Sergei sat in the archives from morning till night. He had filled thirty-six notebooks with transcribed material. Thirty-six! She had recently counted them. And yet he still felt that something was missing, some final bit of information, some ultimate insight; or perhaps the missing factor was his own lack of dedication, of will power.

Being, in fact, prone to a sudden fading of interest, or to be more exact, to the development of an interest in something else, he had decided against the trip to France. He suddenly announced that he had lost all desire to go: 'I can't spare the time right now.' They called him up from the committee to tell him that the size of the party had been reduced and that he, unfortunately, would not be going. He listened with indifference and in a languid voice – as though out of mere politeness – he murmured a few words in response: 'Oh, really? What a pity . . .' The committee members no doubt thought he was exhibiting amazing self-control while actually being overcome with disappointment. But Olga saw that his indifference was genuine: he had simply lost interest.

He said to her, 'What's the point of going to France? Everything that I need can be found here.'

At first he needed a very great deal of material. Not being fully aware of the nature and scope of the work he had planned to do, she felt with increasing frequency that he had taken on something that was too big, even perhaps boundless. She cited as an example Andrei Ivanovich's dissertation – a doctoral, not a master's dissertation – on biological stimulators, written with amazing terseness and economy, without a single superfluous detail. The whole thing worked, as it were, by springs; it was as simple and dynamic as a Yale lock, of which the spring was the central idea – Andrei Ivanovich's single insight of genius into the diffusional structure of stimulators. It was this that made Olga ask Sergei: 'And what is *your* idea? Do you have in your mind some all-embracing concept that will weld all your notebooks, transcripts, facts and quotations into one integral whole?'

It was not said as a reproach, but from a desire to help. Sergei, however, never talked seriously to her about his work – or rather he never finished saying what was on his mind. She felt he always left some thoughts stored in the cellar, like some emergency reserve. But suppose . . . suppose it turned out that there was no reserve there at all, and all his evasions had just been a bluff, or more precisely that he had been *bluffing himself*? Gena Klimuk had hinted at this when he came to see Olga one day – still at the beginning of his career as an academic administrator – for a confidential talk about Sergei.

She had found it difficult to understand what Klimuk had wanted; it had not been clear then and was now even less so, since the details had been forgotten. He had suddenly appeared on a day when Sergei was in Leningrad; he was carrying a bunch of mimosa, wearing a red shirt and red socks just as if he were a student again. He embraced Olga and even gave her one of his pecks on her cheek. She said, 'Genitalich!' Threatening him with her finger, she added: 'You're only supposed to kiss your friends' wives when their husbands are there.'

He told her not to use that idiotic nickname, because ladies were frightened by it.

For a moment a look of cunning flickered across his ageing little boy's features, and Olga felt – in her heart, as usual when it was something to do with Sergei – that the cunning was only a mask for feelings of bitter animosity. What did he want? He droned tediously on about a 'false position', about some 'obligations', about the institute's having accepted Sergei on certain conditions but that Sergei had managed – with Fedya's help – to get the topic of his dissertation changed and this was, for some reason, a bad thing. She couldn't understand why it was bad; apparently it spoiled the institute's plans or something of the sort.

'We met him halfway,' he said in a tone of increasing severity. 'We agreed to his request to our own detriment.'

He was not talking like a friend but like an official. This startled her. For the first few minutes her attitude towards him was familiar and very slightly scornful, because she was aware that from having been a friend he was now changing for the worse, and she wanted to teach him a lesson, but after a while his language and the tone of his voice so stunned her that quite involuntarily and out of sheer perplexity she began responding to him as though she were a subordinate.

'All right,' she said, 'I'll tell him. I'll give him the message.'

One thing was clear: The institute officials could, if they wanted to, prevent the submission of his dissertation.

The whole diatribe was dressed up in the guise of concern for Sergei – how he was destroying himself, how he had taken the wrong direction and was rummaging around amid the debris of history and had lost the guiding thread.

'Sergei is horribly obstinate, you know that' – he suddenly interrupted his pompous speech with this one human remark – 'and if he's not stopped in time, he'll ruin himself.'

She couldn't decide whether to tell Sergei or to keep it from him for a while. He came back from Leningrad tired and angry: everything there had been terrible – the weather, the hotel; his colleagues had been disrespectful and failed to show him sufficient attention, and worst of all, he had failed to find what he had been looking for in the archives. But she told him all the same. To her amazement, he took the news calmly and was even able to dismiss it with a condescending laugh:

'Poor fools, they're terrified that I'll defend Brosov . . .' Tolya Brosov was a researcher whom Klimuk was trying to hound out of the institute.

That was not, however, the real matter at issue: Brosov, it transpired, had nothing to do with the case, and two years later, when Sergei's own 'case' was being investigated, Brosov and Klimuk joined forces to mount a concerted attack on Sergei. They objected to the method that he insisted on using and that he called half-jokingly, half-seriously 'grave-robbery'. The letters 'GR' were written on the covers of many of his notebooks, the metaphor describing his quest for the threads that link the recent past with the distant past and with the future.

From remarks that he made at various times she managed to piece together his guiding principle, which was that the individual is the thread stretching through time, the super-sensitive nerve of history that can be teased out and separated – and from which one can then learn a great deal. Man, he used to say, is never reconciled with death, because implanted in him is a sense that the thread of which he forms a part is endless. It is not God who rewards man with immortality, nor is the concept of immortality instilled into him by religion, but by that innate, genetically coded awareness of being a link in an infinite chain. She used to smile when she listened to him holding forth in this vein at dinner or in bed, at moments when he would suddenly feel the urge to smoke and philosophise. Did he expect her, a biologist and a materialist, to put forward a refutation of these theories of his? If only she could refashion her cast of mind, even if only for a moment, but unfortunately it was not within her power. The only thing she knew firmly was that everything began and ended with chemistry: in all the universe, and beyond its bounds, there was nothing that could not be expressed in chemical formulae. Several times he had asked her quite seriously:

'You don't really think, do you, that we disappear from the world without a trace? That I will disappear?'

And she had replied with genuine amazement: 'Do *you* really think that we won't?'

To this his answer was that no matter how he might rack his brains or strain his imagination, he could not conceive . . .

And now he had disappeared. He was nowhere; he had merged with the infinite, which he had once discussed so lightly while smoking a cigarette. My God, though, if everything begins and ends with chemistry, why was there such pain? Because that sort of pain wasn't chemistry, was it? And *their life*, which had suddenly been extinguished like a burned-out light bulb – had that simply been a combination of formulae? A person departs from the world, his departure is accompanied by an emanation in the form of pain; then the pain will fade and at some point – when those who feel the pain themselves leave the world – it will vanish completely. Completely, completely. Nothing but chemistry . . . Chemistry and pain – that is all that death and life consist of.

For Sergei, what he called 'grave-robbery' (but was more precisely his way of trying to make contact with that endless thread) began with his own family, with the thread of which he himself was a particle. He started with his father, for whose faint memory he felt a great love. He thought of his father as a great man, which was no doubt an exaggeration and, in a certain sense, arrogance. It derived in large measure from his mother, who had worshipped her husband and had placed him in a private hierarchy of the great, the sequence of which ran approximately thus: Gorky; Lunacharsky, the first People's Commissar for Education; Nadezhda Krupskaya, Lenin's wife; and her husband, Afanasy Dementievich Troitsky. After the civil war, Afanasy Dementievich had held some post in the field of education. In 1917, after the February Revolution, while still a student at Moscow University, he had worked in the commission investigating the archives of the czarist gendarmerie. The commission had revealed the names of the secret informers who had worked for the police. When Sergei discovered this fact – his father's participation in the work of this commission – he had begun burrowing in the archives and became fascinated with the whole story. From there – in an attempt to find out why his father had undertaken this work and what were his origins – he began studying his father's family, then his grandfather's family as far back as his great-grandfather, for which purpose he travelled to Penza.

Olga guessed that he had somehow ventured too far and too deeply into this research. It was all very interesting, entertaining even, but – what was it for? It was like the occasion when someone had given them an address at which, if they wanted to, they could meet the grandson of a famous poet, and he had seized on the idea with enthusiasm.

'Yes, we must go!'

The invitation came from a woman who worked with Olga. The poet's grandson, she said, would not have much time to spare; he would drink a cup of tea, stay for perhaps half an hour and then leave not later than five o'clock. The meeting took place in one of the high, slablike blocks of flats in the new suburb of Cheryomushki. Everything in that totally anonymous, standardised little room seemed to consist of fragments salvaged from the wreckage of the past. Around the table, covered with a plain tablecloth – the hostess pulled back a corner of it and showed them the carefully polished inlaid antique tabletop – alongside the usual hideous mass-produced chairs stood two simple, elegant chairs of the early nineteenth century with gilded sphinx-heads on their high backs, while the party drank tea out of antique cups that were made in the Kuznetsov and Gardner factories and were, of course, also fragments of long-scattered tea services.

The poet's grandson was middle-aged, ash-blond, with a wrinkled face and fashionably close-cropped hair. He wore a blue jacket adorned with several little medallions and badges. He clinked his teaspoon against the side of his cup, drummed his fingers on the table and monopolised the conversation with a long, breathless, wordy yet incoherent story about his attempt to exchange flats. Now and again he repeated the phrase 'with regard to'. Olga stared wide-eyed at the grandson and felt shy at first, not knowing what to say to him: Sergei, too, said nothing and sat looking sulky, but then Olga began discussing the business of changing flats and gave the grandson some advice, as she and Sergei themselves had recently completed a satisfactory exchange of flats.

'With regard to the fact,' muttered the grandson, 'that we are approaching the centenary of Lenin's birth . . . With regard to that I have composed a letter . . . Academician Veleglasov has promised to sign it, and Sanin, the actor, has already signed it . . .'

The old ladies talked to each other in French. Soon the grandson hastily took his leave, pecked one of the old ladies on the cheek, kissed the hands of the others and said, as he wrapped a sandwich in a table napkin: 'There's nowhere to get anything to eat there; it's an awful place with regard to that.'

One of the old ladies asked: 'Where are you going today, Alexis?'

'Oh, a long way away, *ma tante*.'

The grandson made a sibilant, whistling noise when he talked. 'But transportation for getting there is excellent: by metro to Sokolniki and then a five-minute bus ride . . .'

When he had gone the old ladies explained that on Sunday

afternoons he refereed soccer matches. What else could he do? He was an engineer, his salary was low, and he had a sick wife and two children . . .

Olga and Sergei walked along the dark boulevard. He was gloomy. 'It would have been better not to have come . . . One of two things: either there is some untapped mystery hidden inside that blockhead or the famous poet had something wrong "with regard to" his head.'

Sergei thought that the thread of human continuity should function as a channel through which certain indestructible elements were transmitted between the generations. The concept had more to do with biology than with history. Now that he was engaged in a detailed study of the Moscow secret police on the eve of the February Revolution and was using documents to compile lists of secret informers together with their professional 'achievements' and their 'services to their country' (a tedious job, which took no less than two years of painstaking work, although it was only one part of his dissertation), what interested him as much as anything was the same thing that had driven him to meet the poet's grandson: the search for those elusive threads. It seemed to Sergei that something extremely important was concealed behind all this. At times he worked with furious enthusiasm. He would come home from the library or the archives with a face the colour of putty, he could hardly stand and could not sit down to dinner straightaway: he would have to lie down for several minutes to rest his heart. For the last two years before his death he had become so weakened that he even stopped drinking. If they were invited out, he refused. His work absorbed him so much that he put into it much more than he should have, more than it could absorb.

One day he came home looking as if he had been drinking. He had an odd smile on his face. She was frightened, because if he had been drinking it meant that something terrible had happened.

'Have you been drinking?' she asked.

'No. Just one on the way home.'

He kept smiling that strange smile. She could see that there was some reason for it.

His mother sensed something, too, and hovered around the kitchen, where Olga was cooking dinner. She knew that he was not always prepared to speak frankly in front of his mother, so Olga refrained from asking Sergei any questions as long as his mother was in the kitchen. Meanwhile Sergei sat with his legs crossed, like a stranger who didn't belong there, wagging the toe of his shoe and staring out of the window. As soon as her mother-in-law had left the room, Olga said quietly:

'Tell me about it . . . I can see something's happened.'

He nodded and said nothing. When his omelette was ready, he prodded it with his fork and left it uneaten. His mother came back into the kitchen, ears cocked to catch every word, so Olga purposely started telling him some trivial piece of gossip that she had heard at work. Then he drank some tea, after which his pallor left him and he looked visibly better. They went to their bedroom (now, since exchanging their flat, Irinka had her own room, Alexandra Prokofievna had hers, and Olga and Sergei had a shared room in which *their life* took place); he shut the door firmly, took Olga by the hand and said:

'Well, they've really given me a bashing this time. My supervisory committee discussed my dissertation in front of the academic council and they shot so many holes in it that I'll have to do two more years' work on it, if not longer, before I can submit it. Only don't tell mother!'

He said it all in a voice of utter gloom, but his final remark – 'Only don't tell mother!' – was spoken with a nervous intensity that betrayed something like real fear. At all costs his mother mustn't know. Olga couldn't decide whether his motivation in this was genuine concern for his mother's peace of mind or – which, if true, was appalling – his perpetual dependence on the old woman's opinion and moods, his compulsion to explain and justify himself to her.

The news, of course, was bad. She knew what it meant when a dissertation failed at the preliminary discussion: she had been anxiously waiting for this to happen, but he had concealed the fact that the discussion was being held today. What extraordinary people he and his mother both were. They were always having to stress that they were loners, that they could manage on their own, that they would somehow always cope. He had gone to the discussion without telling anyone, just as eight years ago his mother went to hospital for a dangerous operation without letting them know. 'Grandma went out this morning and said she would be late getting home,' Irinka had said. The old lady had called up that evening to announce that she was in hospital and that it was all over – but *what* was all over, for God's sake?! – and she would be coming home next day.

Olga was overwhelmed by Sergei's news. She was also annoyed by the remark, made with real fear in his voice: 'Only don't tell mother!' She said it was a stupid thing to say and this wasn't the moment to be worrying about his mother's feelings.

He asked, 'Well, what should I be worrying about?'

'Worry about the real problem – how to get out of trouble – and not about domestic trivia.'

Of course she shouldn't have let her irritation show. Was he anxious about his reputation as a model son? She knew, of course, that he wasn't a model son at all, and therefore it annoyed her even more when he suddenly insisted on acting as if he were. She had to bite her tongue until it hurt, in order to prevent herself from shouting it out; because he really was in trouble and you don't hit a man when he's down. Yet a demon egged her on, and in a half whisper (afraid that her mother-in-law might knock or even walk in without knocking), with unusual venom in her voice she said: 'Instead of worrying so much about your dear mama, you should have shown the same amount of concern for your dissertation.'

Looking exhausted and resigned, like a man prepared to accept anything, he asked, 'What do you mean?'

'You should have prepared the ground. Talked to people. Talked to everybody whose influence counts. But you with your usual sloppiness just let everything take its course. It's your own fault. That's not the way things are done.'

He shrugged. 'But I thought they would . . .'

'Why did you think that? Why should they? What are you to them?' and more advice in the same shrill, schoolmarmish vein. Sergei said nothing, looking at her with a glazed stare; he had the same look whenever he was suddenly plunged into thought.

Then he asked, 'Do you seriously mean it?'

As she continued her lecture, irritation brought her basest feelings boiling to the surface. He gestured defensively and went out, to return a minute later with a suitcase. At first she didn't realise that he was intending to go away, but when he said he was going to spend a few days in the country at Aunt Pasha's cottage (which was absurd: no one had invited him to Vasilkovo; there was no room for him to stay there, because now that the summer was over Pasha's relatives had all moved back into the cottage from their summertime shacks), she lost her temper and her self-control, shouting at him that he was running away like a coward and that if he went to the country now she would wash her hands of all responsibility for his health and well-being, and furthermore, she would give him no money. She yelled incoherently, shamefully, in the way people yell only in the grip of furious anger. The shouting brought her mother-in-law and Irinka running in from their rooms. And Sergei immediately told his mother about the discussion, about the savage criticism of his dissertation and the news that its submission was postponed by at least two more years. Olga found it incomprehensible: at one moment he was ordering her not to tell his mother – and at the next he himself was explaining it to her in detail.

It was, of course, a blow to his mother, but not such a blow as it was to Olga. The old woman always assumed an air of dignified authority at difficult moments, whenever she felt that a display of wisdom and sang-froid was called for. At such times she liked to think of herself as indispensable.

'Keep calm, comrades, there's no need to panic. Whatever we do, let's not panic,' she declared in the tones of a commissar encouraging the troops. 'What, precisely, has happened? You've been given a reprimand? Good. The more criticism you get, the better, because then the quality of your finished work will be higher. I really don't see why you're being so weak-kneed about it, Sergei . . .'

'No one's being weak-kneed. It's just that I don't like the whole disgusting business.'

'You're not meant to like it. How could anyone like it? But you can't just . . . When your father . . . If it had been your father . . .' As she tried to calm him down, her tone gradually changed from commissar to kind old granny; she finally even patted him on the cheek. This gesture struck Olga as false. She talked to him as if he were a ten-year-old boy, and he played up to it. Olga said that there was, in fact, no panic; what Sergei had to do was to think it all over calmly, to take note of the adverse comments, to revise whatever was necessary and whatever, in his own view, was genuinely in need of revision – in other words, to roll up his sleeves and get down to the job but *not* to give way to weakness. Sergei wanted to go to the country, which was wrong: that was simply running away from the problem.

Essentially right though it might have been, Olga's view was mistimed at that particular moment. She should not have used the word 'weakness'. Sergei listened to her gloomily and went on tossing things into the suitcase.

'No, you're wrong, Olga,' said Alexandra Prokofievna, switching back from her grandmotherly tone to one of metallic, commissar-like firmness. 'You're profoundly mistaken. If he feels he ought to go to Vasilkovo, then let him go. He can take his books and his notebooks and work in peace.'

'But he *won't* work! He'll drink vodka with Kolka. And at night he'll feel bad.'

'Papa, Mama doesn't want you to go, so don't go!' said Irinka as she went up to the suitcase and started throwing her father's clothes out of it.

He slapped her and she ran away, clutching some of his underwear and his electric razor. The argument about whether he should go lasted until ten o'clock that night, without any decision being reached. By then it was too late to go. Alexandra Prokofievna continued to act out her self-chosen role of family arbiter, full of nobility and justice:

'I don't understand why you both look so miserable. The submission is postponed, so Sergei's rise in pay is postponed too – is that what's worrying you? Forget it. You'll survive. At your age we never thought about money at all. Who bothered about money? Private traders, grasping peasants, and people who had lost their property at the revolution. But we had no time for that sort of thing. We were too absorbed in life, work, friends, events. Yes, events! Don't smile, Irinka. At your age I was up to date on all the political news, I knew what was happening at the front, I cut clippings from the papers, but all you can think about is films and ice cream. In the twenties, Sergei's father had a very modest salary, the furniture in our flat was supplied by the government. We needed nothing except books – and even books Afanasy Dementievich borrowed from libraries. He never owned a suit, he never wore a tie. Don't worry, Sergei, if necessary I'll help you out if money gets really tight. You've got to work without worrying about anything.'

Two days later he went to Vasilkovo.

What hurt Olga was the fact that whenever things were going badly for him his instinct was to go away somewhere, and not with her but alone. This implied that she was no support to him. His mother thought this, which was unfair and dishonest – as dishonest as her suggestion to him that the only reason why Olga was worried about the failure of his dissertation was that they would lose the extra money that would accrue when he got his master's degree. She didn't think about money! The thought of money never entered her head. In fact, apart from Irinka, who saved money in a piggy bank to buy a new record or perhaps a three-rouble necklace, no one in their family thought about money. There was no need to be so self-righteous about being 'above' such considerations. What really hurt Olga – and was the reason why she had exploded and shouted at him so disgracefully – was that his instant reaction was *to go away from her*. As though she were the cause of all the trouble, as though without her he would be saved. After a while, though, when she had calmed down a little, she became reconciled to the idea, and

Sergei, also having cooled down and thinking things over, decided not to go to Vasilkovo. But the arrival of Klimuk upset everything again.

Klimuk came on the day after the discussion. He and Sergei went out for a walk. It lasted a long time – so long, in fact, that Olga started to worry. Sergei returned at half-past eleven.

'That's it!' he said. '*Finita la commedia!* After a row like that, Gennadii and I are through. He's hopeless.'

There was no regret in his voice. The inevitable had happened. She only asked, 'What was the reason?'

'Huh!' He gestured dismissively. 'Everything . . .'

His expression was distracted, as though he didn't want to tell her what had happened and it wasn't worth the trouble. But soon afterwards he told her everything. They made love. Somehow she had a particularly vivid memory of their lovemaking that night, when he first told her about Kislovsky. Usually he fell asleep immediately afterwards; making love affected him like a sleeping pill, whereas Olga, on the contrary, stayed awake for a long time, and the more intense their lovemaking the longer it took her to go to sleep. That night, however, he was keyed up and wanted to talk; he told her that Klimuk had tried to persuade him to hand some research material over to Kislovsky, who needed it for his doctoral dissertation. He had refused, saying that he didn't want to lose such valuable material, which was not to be found even in the archives and of which he possessed the only copy. Klimuk said it was better to lose the material than to lose one's dissertation. This really started the swearing match. The question of this material was, it seems, a long-standing bone of contention between them. Klimuk called Sergei an idiot, and he said to Klimuk: 'You're a shit!'

What was this material? She could only remember that when Sergei acquired it – which happened unexpectedly, by sheer chance – he had been excited beyond all measure. It was the lists of names of the secret informers working for the Moscow division of the czarist police during the period from 1910 right up to the February Revolution of 1917. The material was, of course, priceless, because all the records of the czarist secret police had been destroyed. Somehow or other he had managed to acquire these lists. He had found a man, who may have been an alcoholic or a crook, or maybe just a seedy old tramp (Olga never saw him, he had an odd name – Selifon or Selivan, or something of the sort) who sold the lists to Sergei for thirty roubles. Apparently his grandfather had been a minor official in the czarist police and had kept the lists in order to extract money from people by blackmail. For a time Sergei had been very interested in this man's story, which was quite fantastic. Some of the people at the institute didn't believe Sergei and said that Selifon had fooled him, that the lists were forgeries, that someone had fabricated them, if not recently then in the twenties, though they might well have used them for blackmail. In particular there was a certain Professor Vyatkin at the institute who hotly contested the authenticity of the lists. It was during his dispute with Vyatkin that Sergei had conceived the idea of going to Gorodets. And of course it was these lists – in the folder tied with pink ribbon – that Bezyazichny and now Klimuk were so keen to have Olga hand over.

Why should she? Kislovsky wasn't in the institute any longer. She would never give them up; she could see no reason why she should help Klimuk in any way.

When Sergei went away alone to Vasilkovo – by then it was the last week in September – her sufferings began. A day, another day, a third passed. At first she fought against her feelings. She tried to conquer the nagging unease, the awareness of missing him, worrying about him – which was nothing other than *deadly, humiliating dependence on him*, and she adjured herself not to think, not to remember him, to load herself with work. He didn't want her to go and join him. He needed to be alone – and she understood that need, she truly understood it. But disquiet, or longing, or God knows what else it was – a sort of merciless, corrosive anxiety – grew inexorably within her, and she knew that sooner or later she would go to him; it was only a question of finding a pretext. And at that very moment along came a letter bearing the official seal of the institute, containing the formal notification and results of the assessment of Sergei's dissertation: the discussion had taken place, such-and-such modifications had been suggested (here followed a long list), and the date of submission for the completed dissertation was postponed until such-and-such a month of the following year. Without even waiting until the weekend, Olga took a day off from work on Friday and went, armed with the letter.

Vasilkovo had been part of *their life* for a long time. Irinka was about four of five; their tenancy of a *dacha* on the Klyazma River had ended, and they were in a hurry to find a new one. They were advised to try the countryside to the north of Moscow, and one day they just took the train, without any address, and got off after a fifty-minute journey – they simply liked the deserted platform, the clumps of trees, the expanse of meadows – and walked towards the little village on the horizon.

Aunt Pasha's cottage was distinguished by a wooden plaque on which hung an axe. It was this that made them stop. Why a hatchet? What was the reason for it? As they stood discussing it with Irinka, Pasha came out into the yard and they asked her about it '. . . because our little girl is curious to know.' Aunt Pasha explained that when there was a fire in the village, a hatchet was always needed. Other cottages had plaques with other implements – one had a bucket, another a grapling hook. So they stayed, and arranged to rent the house from Aunt Pasha, the 'house with the hatchet'. Years later, after they had spent several hot, or cloudy, or damp, or sunny summers with Aunt Pasha (her husband Vanya, or Ivan Panteleimonovich, to give him his full name, was a quiet, insignificant little man, a carpenter who travelled the countryside with his cooperative team of carpenters, so that he was never at home in summer and no one regarded him as the head of the household: that was unmistakably Pasha and only Pasha, a tall, powerfully built, hard-working, loud-mouthed but kind-hearted woman) and Sergei had come to know her and her family thoroughly well, he would often revert in conversation to their first discovery of the house, to the hatchet. He was particularly fond of talking about it when he was a little drunk: 'The house with the hatchet! There's a hidden meaning in it. It's a symbol . . . full of significance . . .'

Sometimes he would seem to philosophise on it quite seriously, and at other times, when neighbouring weekenders dropped in for a cup of tea or to borrow some pickled mushrooms – such as Lev Semyonovich, a physicist, or the charming old Goryansky, a retired music hall actor – he would gabble endless nonsense about the hatchet, fooling around and assuming a high-falutin', old-regime style of language: 'Are you aware, gentlemen, of the name of this dwelling in which you are drinking your vodka? It is the house with the hatchet. So you must be careful . . .' It seemed now as if he had played the fool once too often and brought disaster on himself as a result.

The day was crisp and clear, but already there was a chill in the air; the sky was cloudless; the path through the woods smelled of fallen leaves, a favourite smell of Olga's, like the smell of soured wine – and she hastened onwards, noticing nothing around her, breathing in that smell and growing intoxicated by it. She was hurrying to see him as if they had not seen each other for years. Yet only four days had passed. He was sitting on the porch with a book and when he saw her he said: 'Oh, it's you . . .'

He didn't smile, didn't jump from his chair, didn't kiss her and didn't even relieve her of the weight of the heavy bags she was carrying, full of food in cans and packages, and two bottles of Egri Bikaver, the red Hungarian wine (their shared fondness for dry red wine, which began countless years ago, still persisted, although nowadays it was more of a tradition, an echo of better times; Olga, in particular, especially cherished the memory of red wine, and the fact that she had carried two bottles of it all the way from town meant a great deal in their language); he only sketched a limp movement with one hand which might have been either a half-hearted greeting or a gesture meaning 'It's no good; I'm all washed up', and went indoors. Despite this lukewarm welcome, she had decided to forgive him for everything. She picked up the book he had been reading: Pushkin. It was somewhat tattered and dirty, and no doubt it came from Kolka's bookshelf.

Olga sat down on the porch, not knowing where he had gone and why. She put her bags down on the floor.

After a short while he came back, and asked with an angry look, 'Why did you come?'

She should have said that she simply couldn't bear life without him, that she hadn't the strength for such an ordeal; it was absurd, because they were not having a quarrel; they had parted on good terms, and she understood that he needed to spend some time alone. But what could she do if she hadn't the strength? Instead, she waved the letter from the institute at him, speaking some banal-sounding nonsense. He shouted, 'Why did you come?' And shook his two fists in front of his face.

Afraid that he was about to burst into tears and fall down, she ran indoors, calling for Aunty Pasha. The house was empty. She scooped up a mug of water from the bucket and ran back out to the porch. Sergei was lying on a folding cot, facing the window. She sat down beside him, stroked his hair and said in a low voice that she had been worried about him because he had left home in such a bad mood. They were all worried – his mother and Irinka too. The mention of his mother and daughter should have had a calming effect on him, but instead he shouted: 'Don't lie! Don't try and drag Irinka and mother into this.'

She tried to explain, but he refused to listen.

'Don't lie! Don't lie, I tell you,' he repeated. 'You came of your own will, and of course only because you are imagining the most idiotic suspicions . . .'

'Nothing of the sort! What nonsense!'

Her denial was sincere, because she never admitted to herself the suspicions that did, in fact, plague her. It seemed to her that what upset her was something else. Therefore her suspicions did not, as it were, exist, so she could deny the accusation with an honest expression of anger on her face. But, God, how relieved she had suddenly felt when she saw him sitting alone on the porch and reading a book.

'What are you talking about? What suspicions? Forget it, my dear; we're past it at our age. You've missed that boat by now, and so have I for that matter . . .'

She was thirty-nine at the time. And he was forty. But she never lost an opportunity to remind him that his days of philandering were over. It always amused her whenever he sat down in the metro and began staring at some girl sitting opposite. She would sometimes tease him on this subject and he would get angry . . . She started talking again about the letter from the institute, which she was still holding in her hand. He snatched the letter away from her, crumpled it and threw it into the bushes.

'I don't want to read it, I know it already . . . to hell with it,' he muttered. 'Brilliant, aren't you? There's only one way to treat that crap: Forget it! But you, as if on purpose . . . I need that letter like I need a hole in the head!'

She wanted to help him, but she didn't know how to. Pasha and her husband, Ivan Panteleimonovich, came back from digging potatoes in some distant field. They were delighted when they saw her:

'Lord! It's you, Olga Vasilievna! Your man has been quite down in the mouth without you.'

Everything was confused, because these people didn't understand what was happening between her and Sergei. She felt extremely sorry for him and wanted to help. What had driven him out here, to this age-blackened wooden house and its old-fashioned country porch, with strings of onions hanging from the rafters, with a jumble of cans and sacks piled on the floor? Aunty Pasha's hands, as she cooked supper, smelled of earth. Ivan Panteleimonovich twiddled the knobs on his transistor radio and talked to Sergei about the American president and the Suez Canal, while Pasha with warm interest enquired about Irinka and Alexandra Prokofievna, also about Olga's mother and Georgii Maximovich, who made occasional visits to Vasilkovo. Georgii Maximovich used to say that Pasha had 'an interesting face' and induced her to pose for him. Then Pasha and Ivan Panteleimonovich complained that the potatoes this year were small and the crop poor, that it was almost too late to try digging them now; there was no hope of borrowing a horse and cart, it was a long way to carry sacks of potatoes on your back, and the potato field was now 'on the poles': that is, it lay across the path of a new high-voltage power line; a trench had been dug right across the middle of it and planted with poles. As Olga listened, looking at Aunty Pasha and Ivan Panteleimonovich she thought to herself: 'They're old, Pasha is over sixty and he is nearly seventy, but they still toil away with all their strength, dig the soil, carry sacks of potatoes and do countless other sorts of hard work day in and day out; yet they don't think their life is particularly hard.' Suddenly she said on impulse, for a joke:

'Sergei, you sit here reading a book while these old folk break their backs digging potatoes. You should get up and help them . . .'

Pasha turned on her, while Ivan Panteleimonovich simply waved the suggestion aside: 'Why should he? The very idea. Let him rest. And let's not hear another word about it.'

From outside came the roar of a motorcycle: Kolka had arrived. Both he and his father were short and thin, with pale, finely moulded features, blue-eyed, fair-haired (although the old man's hair was mostly grey); both had a trick of twisting their lips into a look of cunning whenever they smiled, while in conversation Kolka still lowered his eyes bashfully, like a girl. Only after a few drinks did he become bold and talkative.

As he spooned up his cabbage soup, with which he ate first a slice of brown bread and then a sausage – he had brought home a huge sackful of sausages, from which Pasha immediately took a dozen and fried them; she was very pleased with Kolka's booty. He told how the timber store at Istomino (the same village at which he had been so lucky with the sausages) had got in a stock of fence rails, laths and squared beams, just what they needed to repair the gate, and how he had tried to make a deal but for some reason the old man in charge of the store had refused to accept his offer. As he said all this, Kolka seemed strangely embarrassed and would not look at Olga. She had long ago noticed that the young man was shy in her presence. One day she could not help mentioning this to Sergei:

'You know, I think Kolka . . .'

'Well, what?'

'I think he rather fancies me.'

He looked at her in amazement: 'Why do you tell me that?'

He purposely assumed a façade of coldness and indifference whenever there was the hint of a cause for him to feel jealous.

What causes could there be? There were none. Sometimes she would invent something just to tease him, to provoke him into showing some interest, but he grew used to her tricks; and when he knew she was making it up he paid no attention. With Kolka, however, it was something like the truth. She sensed it; perhaps Sergei sensed it too, but just didn't care. His mind was preoccupied. Gradually he became reconciled to her arrival, and towards the end of the day – after they had taken a walk down to the river – he even admitted that he was glad she had come. That night was good together. They did not sleep until early morning. He told her absolutely everything about his work, down to the smallest detail. He asked her advice: What should he do? The chief problem was that he had irrevocably ruined his relationships with the people at the institute. He had been rude to Klimuk and made an enemy of him; he had said the most offensive things to him in front of other people, for which Klimuk would never forgive him. But he and Klimuk had been heading for a breakup anyway; there was a certain inevitability about their clash; but did Sergei have to be offensive to Professor Vyatkin, an influential man? That was *not* very clever, was it? And what about Kislovsky? What about that cunning, rubbery, devious creature, whom Olga imagined to be a dangerous, ruthless man? To hell with those damn lists, for which Sergei had paid thirty roubles: he should have handed them over to Kislovsky and the whole business would have been finished and forgotten. Unfortunately, in saving thirty roubles, the chances for his dissertation were ruined.

It was now obvious to Olga that the whole of Sergei's strange family had something in common which doomed them to failure in life: his father had once been an outstandingly able man; yet he had never made it to the top; his mother was a non-practising lawyer with principles and high standards – and Sergei was similar in nature to both of them. His sister, too, was cast in the same mould. She had died an old maid, whose misfortunes, unhappiness and depression had all contributed to her final illness; it was said that a man had loved her very much and might have made her happy, but she had spent her whole life in love with another, wretched, insignificant man whom she had known since their schooldays. Some kind of emotional ineptitude and a compulsion to do only what pleased them had destroyed this family.

That night he suddenly said: 'Do you know why everything I do seems to go so wrong?' Barely audibily, he whispered: 'Because the threads which stretch out from the past . . . don't you see? They are fraught . . . They are fraught. Do you see what I mean?'

'Fraught . . . with what?'

'But it's obvious.' He laughed. She felt a sudden sickening awareness that he was going out of his mind. 'Nothing, you see, breaks off without leaving a trace of some kind. There is no such thing as a total break with the past. Don't you understand? There has to be continuity, there must be. It's so obvious . . .'

She looked at him and turned cold with horror.

Madness! She had always been afraid of it, knowing how highly strung and unstable he could be. She embraced him with her bare arm, pressed his head to her breast and stroked his hair. He gave a little snort of laughter, which made her shudder.

'I expect you think I've gone off my head, don't you? Nonsense, I'm perfectly all right. But you know my theory about the unbroken thread running from generation to generation . . . If one can dig deeper and deeper, and farther backwards then it must be equally possible to trace the thread leading forward . . .'

It was not madness – or rather, up to a point it might have been madness, and to some degree a joke, but to a greater degree he was quite serious. Mad and serious – it was all one. Olga burst into tears as she listened to his incoherent babbling. She had the feeling that he was finally cracking up. He rambled on with some confused story about his own ancestors, runaway serfs and religious dissenters whose branch of the family tree eventually led to an unfrocked priest at Penza, from him to some political deportees who had lived in a commune at Saratov, thence to a teacher in the depths of the Turan swamp land, who was in turn the father of a future St Petersburg student who thirsted for justice and social change: common to all of them was a seething, bubbling urge to dissent. There was some trait in them that had never been eradicated by the sword, by the lash, or by time, something innate in the genetic stem . . . Suddenly the impression of nonsensical raving stopped, and what he was saying seemed rational and coherent, maybe even highly intelligent; yet even so Olga was nagged by the fear that he really was going out of his mind. Whatever connection could there possibly be between an unfrocked priest in Penza a hundred and twenty years ago and the problems that Sergei was having with his dissertation? He said there was a connection. It was that night that he made up his mind to go to Gorodets.

Professor Vyatkin had doubted the authenticity of the lists, which Sergei had acquired by not entirely orthodox means.

Quite recently she had dug out the folder tied with pink ribbon, buried under a pile of other folders on the bottom shelf of the big bookcase; the folder was made of the shiny, marbled, yellow cardboard that was much in vogue in the years before the revolution. She read the contents, although without fully understanding them; the letters danced around in front of her eyes, because reading these lists made her realise bitterly how much of life is made up of irreparable gaps. What an enormous part of Sergei's nature had remained unknown to her. She had thought she knew quite enough, indeed more than enough about him; yet she found all the material in this folder totally uninteresting. It was hopeless. She turned over the brittle, thin, musty-smelling sheets of paper and tried desperately to force her brain to make sense of them, only to realise with despair that their meaning eluded her: empty and lifeless, they refused to yield up their secret.

To her they were just a series of names, dates, villages, counties, towns, code names, occupations, addresses. Many of them had several code names. What could anyone do with it all? She did not understand. Anguish gripped her heart. Before putting the sheets back in the folder, tying the ribbon in a bow and shoving the folder under a heap of other, thicker and heavier folders, she noticed in one list the name of Yevgenii Alexeyevich Koshelkov, peasant, born 1891 in the village of Gorodets, Moscow Province, by trade a tailor, employed at the Jacques menswear shop in Petrovka Street, Moscow.

The name Koshelkov was linked with one distinct memory: a misty September morning, the silence of a deserted pathway, already a touch of overnight frost on the ground, the yellow rustling leaves of the birch trees, the smell of mushrooms. As she and Sergei walked along the path through the woods, they were not hurrying but not dawdling either, because they had a long way to go. Sergei was in a wonderful, cheerful mood; he joked, played the fool and held her hand, making their arms swing as if they were a couple of teenagers in love. He even said words backwards. He had suddenly become what he had once been long ago, and Olga thought: 'Is this, I wonder, what's called happiness? A bright morning, a path through the woods in the autumn?' No, Irinka was missing. Once they had gone to Vasilkovo in March, during the winter break between Irinka's school terms, and went skiing in the woods. Sergei was far ahead; Irinka could hardly keep going. Evening was coming on, the light through the tree trunks was reddish-yellow, and the late afternoon glare from the snow was blinding. Irinka asked:

'Mama, happiness – what is it?' She was ten years old, and one had to give serious answers to all her questions; Olga thought how to answer briefly and comprehensibly but could think of nothing really suitable, so she just said, 'An evening like this in the forest, the three of us on skis – that's happiness. Do you see? That's what it is.' Irinka, of course, didn't understand. And in fact Olga herself, having said it, didn't really understand either. *Their life* had yet to come to an end.

When they set out from Vasilkovo to the station that September morning, she was afraid of getting sore feet. Her new shoes were not suitable for long walks, and they felt tight. But in the end all was well. They were going to the village of Gorodets in the hope of finding some trace of Yevgenii Koshelkov, once an informer for the czarist secret police under the code names of 'Tamara' and 'Phil'. Sergei said that of course there would be no surviving relatives or offspring after so many years and so many changes and upheavals, but at least some trace must have survived, some fragments of the thread, a few sparks that could be struck in someone's memory. If only one scrap of evidence could be found – such as an entry recording birth and baptism in the parish register of the local church – it would mean that the list was genuine. They had chosen Gorodets because it was the point nearest to Vasilkovo – a distance of twenty-eight kilometres.

First they took the train, then a bus. The village had grown into a town. Around the old garment factory, built by a French industrialist in the nineteenth century, had grown up an ugly clutter of four-storey, slablike blocks of flats with clusters of TV aerials sprouting from the roofs; when they crossed the bridge over the slimy, weed-choked little river called the Voprya, to the left rose a steep hillside dotted with old black rotting shacks and squalid little wooden houses. It was not clear whether they were still inhabited or whether they had been preserved as a historic relic of prerevolutionary poverty and social inequality. In front of a single-storey building – the sign said 'Grocery and Vegetables' – stood a few men whose expressions had that look of slackness and lethargy which was the unmistakable sign of enforced idleness and the lack of something they all needed at that moment. Sergei walked over to them to make enquiries. A quarter of an hour later he was still leaning up against the brick wall of the building with a group of three of them, drinking vodka out of paper cups and eating tomatoes. By now Olga was feeling nervous and uncomfortable. The men were joking; Sergei seemed very relaxed and cheerful. It was a gorgeous blue-gold day. They wandered around the little town, which in places still seemed just a village, went in to several houses, talked over fences where it smelled of apples. Towards the end of the day they found an old man, very rosy-cheeked and fit-looking, but who could walk only with slow, short, little steps on legs clad in black felt boots: he had had a stroke the year before and had thought he was going to die, but recovered. Smiling with his handsome mouthful of white teeth the old man said:

'The Indian summer has finally come.'

It was none other than Yevgenii Alexeyevich Koshelkov.

When Olga returned home from a trip to Leningrad in March (she flew back by plane, because she missed Irinka so badly) the first sounds to meet her ears were complaints from both her daughter and her mother-in-law. Irinka said that Grandma had kept her under martial law, had refused to give her any money, wouldn't allow her to go anywhere and had behaved horribly to Irinka's friends who came to visit. She had thrown them out of the house, when it wasn't late at all – well, eleven-thirty at the latest. The girls went, and Irinka went too, to see them home, and came back an hour later to find Grandma in hysterics, having called up each of the girl's homes in succession – Dasha, Tamara and Bella. Everyone had gone to bed by then, so she had woken them. She had gone completely insane.

'After that, I didn't talk to her for three days.'

'But perhaps you weren't entirely in the right.'

'What did I do wrong?'

'Well, why did you spend so long seeing your friends off? You stayed out far too late in my opinion. She was worried about you.'

'But why did she have to be rude to them? There was no need for that at all.'

The conversation had started immediately on her return, before she had had a chance to change clothes or unpack her suitcase, in which lay the few modest presents she had bought in Leningrad. Her mood had not yet had time to turn sour. As she listened to her daughter and mildly reproached her, she stroked Irinka along her bony spine: her shoulder blades protruded, and her blue, short-sleeved blouse was noticeably too small for her and wouldn't last the summer.

A quarter of an hour later Olga, having changed into a dressing-gown, went into the bathroom, turned on the hot water and started to scrub the bath furiously with scouring powder and an old loofah. Soon she was humming a tune half-aloud – something she hadn't done for a long time, perhaps six months. She seemed to have lost the habit; now she was doing it unconsciously, and if she had suddenly realised she was humming, she would no doubt have stopped it at once. When the door of the bathroom creaked she heard Alexandra Prokofievna's voice:

'Don't leave Irinka in my charge again. I can't cope with her any more; she's a big girl now and she can do what she likes, but don't expect me to control her.'

'All right, let's talk about it later,' said Olga.

'Or else you can try staying at home a bit more often and put up with the boredom for a change. I have my own work and I must get it done.'

The old woman was very proud of her pathetic 'work' – running the legal advice column on a newspaper – which she had managed to get on a non-retainer basis after many letters and phone-calls; they gave her the job only because they felt sorry for her as a pensioned-off veteran of the law courts. In everyday life, however, after long experience of the cut and thrust of the courtroom, she had an undoubted ability to guess her opponent's sensitive spot and to probe it. So it was now: the words 'put up with the boredom for a change' touched a sore spot, but Olga was still in no mood for a quarrel and answered peaceably:

'Very well, Alexandra Prokofievna, let me take a shower first. We can talk about it later.'

It turned out that Irinka had got wildly out of hand, that she refused to do a single thing that she was asked to do: she wouldn't go out to the shop, or to the laundry, wouldn't even sweep the floor; she answered impertinently and did nothing but make demands, demands, demands all the time. Irinka, who had sidled up to the kitchen door and was listening to her grandmother's accusations with a mocking air, asked:

'What did I ever "demand"?' Her tone of voice most certainly was cheeky and rude.

'I do not wish to talk to you. I am telling your mother about your behaviour; how she deals with you is her problem.'

'Oh, so you don't wish to, do you? I never "demanded" anything from you.'

'Irinka, don't speak to your grandmother in that tone of voice. Go to your room and leave us alone.'

'Oh, so I have to go away while she tells lies about me . . .'

'Did you hear that? "She" . . . "tells lies" . . .'

'Irinka, do as you're told.'

'All right, I'll go, but please don't believe what she says. The only thing I asked for was enough money to go and see *A Taste of Honey* at the Sovremennik Theatre. She wouldn't give it to me, so I borrowed three roubles from Dasha. She promised me a pair of winter shoes, but I knew all the time she wouldn't buy them. Situation normal, in fact.'

'I believe I explained to you why I couldn't give money either for the theatre or for the shoes,' said Alexandra Prokofievna. 'I have never patronised the sort of black-market dealers from whom you wanted me to buy those shoes, and I am not going to start now. I will not support illegal trading. When you see a nice pair of shoes in a shop, then tell me and we'll go and buy them. I have told you that many times. After this display of misbehaviour, however, you can forget about them.'

Olga could feel the pain beginning to bore into her head just above her eyebrows. Irinka went out, while her grandmother continued to recite a catalogue of her sins: she was naughty, malicious, stupid, badly brought up – all of which, of course, was her mother's fault. As this accusation was twisted into an ever-tighter knot, from whose bonds there was absolutely no escape except her oncoming migraine, for which there was no remedy, its effect was to make Olga plunge further and further into a pointless and bad-tempered argument in defence of her daughter:

'You never see any good in her. And she needs kindness and affection – after all, she has lost her father . . .'

'How dare you remind me of that!'

Tears started in the old woman's narrow little eyes, her face turned pale, her lips slackened and began to tremble. This sudden change in Alexandra Prokofievna's features somehow spurred Olga on, and she stood up. Pressing one hand against her forehead as though trying to hold back a pain that was thrusting itself outwards and waving the other hand in front of her – self-control had left her – she said loudly and incoherently: 'Because there's no kindness in you. You're an evil woman! But I won't allow you to . . . I won't let you . . . Because she has no father, you think there's no one to stick up for her, don't you? I . . . I won't let you!' A spasm gripped her throat. 'Why didn't you give her those miserable three roubles? Were you afraid I wouldn't pay them back? The girl has to beg from others, like a pauper. She's not a beggar. As long as she has a mother, she's not a beggar– do you hear? Why did you lie and tempt her with those damned shoes?'

With a look of scorn and disgust, the old woman shook her head and retreated to the door. Her face had turned to stone. Olga could no longer hear her own voice. Suddenly she heard a cry: 'Mama! Stop it!'

She saw her daughter's face distorted with fright. Irinka embraced her and led her off to her room. Then Irinka disappeared. Olga lay in semi-darkness, the curtains drawn, and thought: 'My daughter's grown up. She'll defend me. I can't manage without her. I must tell the old woman once and for all: Don't dare . . .'

It was dark when she got up and had supper alone in the kitchen – Irinka had gone out to the cinema. Her mother-in-law took something out of the refrigerator and silently put it on the stove. Why had Irinka sneaked off to the cinema, knowing that her mother was so upset, knowing that there was a row in progress? What a strange character she had. There was a streak in it of excessive pliancy, of instability, of inconsiderate thoughtlessness – just like her father, in fact. She had the same tendency to disappear and run away from problems. At one moment she could show genuine compassion, revealing a capacity for pity and sympathy, showing – briefly – that she possessed a mind that was perceptive and mature, and then at the next moment she would confound them with some juvenile prank, some childish caprice or some act of such calculated selfishness that it took one's breath away. It was true, of course, that she had been subjected to conflicting influences: her grandmother had said one thing, her father another. For Olga, the most important thing was to teach Irinka to be independent of others. Nothing was more pathetic than a wretched person psychologically dependent on other people. Olga had been like that all her life. That life was now over, and she found herself the victim of another kind of scourge: she was independent – but empty.

For Irinka, despite her spoiled-child behaviour, her outbursts of selfishness and rudeness, had a weakness: she was highly vulnerable to the will of others. The business at the theatre in January during the holidays was typical. In the past, getting theatre tickets had always been Sergei's responsibility. He still had some friends from his student days who were in the theatre world: one had become an actor at the Mossoviet Theatre, another had become a highly placed theatrical manager who wielded a lot of influence. But the problem was to get Sergei to call them up. How he hated asking favours. Olga and Irinka both had to nag him for a whole week. If he managed to get three tickets, they would all three go together; if he could only get two, then Sergei stepped down in favour of his daughter. Irinka loved being taken by her father: he was more generous at the buffet during the intervals. Now she was going to the theatre for the first time since her father's death. Dasha had got the tickets, and as it happened they were for a play at the theatre to which Irinka had been most often with her father – the Mossoviet. Olga was worried that the place might have too many upsetting memories for the girl; she herself would not have gone to that theatre again at any price. Olga spent the whole evening in a state of gnawing unease, and called up Dasha's mother to enquire whether any arrangements had been made to collect the girls from the theatre and bring them home. Dasha's mother seemed amazingly unconcerned. Irinka came home around eleven, looking miserable. She refused supper and ran straight to her room, saying only that she had a headache. A quarter of an hour later Olga looked in, and Irinka was crying. Overcome by a surge of pity, she hugged her daughter, stroked her hair, consoled her and could hardly keep herself from bursting into tears too. When she had calmed down, Irinka told a story that was somewhat unexpected: Dasha, it seems, had invited another girl to the theatre as well and had spent the whole evening talking to her and not to Irinka. During the interval they had strolled around together arm in arm, treating Irinka as if she were a stranger and whispering secrets to each other. This annoyed Irinka so much that after the theatre she ran off home without saying goodbye. Olga was astonished. Irinka had loved her father so much; yet the thing that really upset her was the childish behaviour of a silly little girl. And she very quickyly made it up with Dasha; soon afterwards, she said happily to Olga: 'Dasha says that Maya is stupid! She's not worth talking to – she doesn't like Fellini . . .'

Loud noises, the slamming of doors and footsteps pounding in the hall announced Irinka's return from the cinema at eleven o'clock. Before she had taken her coat off, standing in the middle of the room and unwinding her long woollen scarf, she announced the latest news: tomorrow she wanted to go out of town for a couple of days, to stay with Dasha and some friends at her family's *dacha*. She realised, of course, that this would be a blow to her mother, who had been missing Irinka badly and was looking forward to spending the weekend with her. A look of furtive mischief lurked in Irinka's eyes. Olga tried not to show her annoyance and disappointment.

'First take your coat off.'

Irinka took off her coat and sat down at the table. She could have sat down on the divan alongside her mother, but chose to sit at a distance, which meant that she was preparing to put up a resistance. At that moment Alexandra Prokofievna came in to say that tea was ready. Olga asked Irinka who else was going on this outing to the *dacha*.

There followed a recital of about eight names, several of them unknown to Olga. It was good for her health to get out of town and breathe a little fresh air, wasn't it?

'And does that mean you'll miss school?'

'Well, so what?' She dismissed it with a wave of the hand. 'We only have one lesson on Saturday anyway. Everyone's ill; there's an absolute epidemic of colds in Moscow at the moment.'

'Which subject?'

'Physics.'

'No,' said Olga. 'I don't like you to miss lessons.'

'Oh Mama, why?'

'I don't like it when you miss a lesson.'

'But why, why? Why does it matter so much? It's only one, for heaven's sake.'

'If you don't understand why, I'm not going to explain. I don't like it, that's all.'

It was not only missing school that Olga didn't like; she probably disliked much more the fact that her daughter was so ready to rush off and leave her, having barely seen her again after a ten-day absence. How, for God's sake, could she be so obtuse, so unaware of her mother's feelings? She inherited it from her father; there had been many times when he had been totally insensitive. Her grandmother was standing nearby and listening in silence. She could not, of course, approve of Irinka's adventure, but to say a couple of words in support of Olga was more than she could bring herself to do.

'There are plenty of things you don't like. Maybe there are a few things I don't like, too.' Irinka was sitting bolt upright at the table, her legs crossed, glaring at the tablecloth with a disdainful expression, swinging her right foot up and down. She was, in fact, the very image of that independent personality that Olga so much wanted her to have.

'What don't you like?'

'This and that.'

'For example?'

'Lots of things. For instance, the fact that you go away so often. First you go to Chelyabinsk, then to Leningrad . . .'

'I go, my dear, on official trips that are essential for my work. I am sent, like it or not. ('God, why do I have to justify myself to her?') Do you imagine I go from choice?'

'I know you go because of your work, but you also enjoy getting away from home, having a bit of fun, don't you?'

'What do you mean – fun? What stupid nonsense you talk.'

But it wasn't all nonsense. The blood rushed to Olga's face. Alexandra Prokofievna continued to stand there in silence.

'Whoever gave you the idea that I want to go away "for fun"? Who's been telling you that?' Olga was not looking at her mother-in-law, but she felt her presence with all her being. She had the impression that the old woman was smiling.

'Of course we all find it hard without father,' the girl muttered, 'only Grandma and I can never go away anywhere. But you . . .'

'What about me?'

'Well, you can take a breather every now and again. Maybe I get fed up staying at home all the time and I want a bit of fun for a change. Just for a couple of days.'

'You're such a little fool,' said Olga in a weak voice, wiping her eyes with the palm of her hand. 'I never enjoy these trips; I'm always so longing to get home. I call you up every evening. I count the days until I can see you again, you heartless girl. And you say I go away for fun . . . You're an ungrateful little monster. Go away, I don't want to see you!'

Irinka ran out of the room.

Alexandra Prokofievna announced into empty space: 'She should not, of course, be allowed to go out of town.'

'Why didn't you say that to her face?' asked Olga. 'Or were you trying to be nice?'

After that, Olga washed clothes until midnight. Irinka, idle little devil, had done none of her own laundry. But Olga would have had to wash it all again anyway, because all Irinka ever did was shift the dirt around. Next day, before she left for school, seizing a moment when her grandmother was out of the kitchen, Irinka asked forgiveness. As usual, she gabbled her apology in a perfunctory whine: 'Mother, I am sorry, forgive me please, I won't go if you don't want me to.' Olga, however, felt that this was a significant act of contrition. She forgave her, saying that she would call up Dasha's mother and between them they would come to a decision. But the real reason was that she was once again overcome and reduced to weakness by pity. She glanced sidelong at Irinka and her heart was wrung: an orphan, always alone, alone in her room, no father, her mother always away out of town . . . how could she refuse to let her go? And she let her go.

* * *

The little old man in black felt boots padded noiselessly around the yard without even making the dead leaves rustle, smiling all the time:

'Yes, the Indian summer has come through . . .'

Olga did not like the old man. She thought uneasily: 'My God, but why "come through"?' There was something unsettling in the glorious weather, in the remote overgrown garden, in the old man's lack of memory; she sensed it plainly, yet could not quite pin down where the feeling came from and why. The whole of this search was an unnecessary amusement. Sergei had finally tracked down this mossy old relic, who had once worked in Jacques men's outfitters in Petrovka Street; he had pulled him out of oblivion, like pulling an ace out of a pack of cards – so what next? The old man remembered nothing, wanted nothing, knew nothing, because after his days at Jacques, life had come crashing down on him like a heap of rocks and everything that might have remained alive in his memory was buried and crushed.

'Do you know what Monsieur Jacques was like? Oho! Not like a Frenchman at all.'

'Do you remember the last days of February 1917?'

There was nothing, absolutely nothing to be coaxed, prised or squeezed out of the cavernous depths of old Koshelkov's memory. It was full of wars, hard times, distant lands, icy cold, death and destruction, whereas the peace and quiet of Gorodets with this little garden had only recently come to him, like a patch of bright sky in the evening of his days. And the Lord be praised for small mercies. Sergei took out a notebook and pencil, but he never managed to take any useful notes. The old man's daughter, a stocky, glum-faced peasant woman, invited them out onto the veranda for dinner. Also there was her daughter-in-law, who was a nurse, and her two children. Soon they were joined by the nurse's husband, the old man's grandson, who was called Pantyusha – a name they were to remember.

Pantyusha was round-shouldered and stooping, a head shorter than Sergei, dark, with bushy eyebrows, beneath which two sharp, malevolent little eyes, like rats' eyes, gleamed out from deep eye-sockets. Either he was drunk, or ill, or he was simply endowed by nature with a surfeit of seething malice which threatened to overwhelm him, just as some people suffer from high blood pressure. At first he said nothing and passed the time staring at Sergei's trousers, his shoes, his watch, and his sweater, then with equal intentness inspected Olga's shoes and her suede jacket, which in those days was still new, unstained and very beautiful. He spent a particularly long time looking at the jacket, until it began to make Olga feel uncomfortable. Sergei did not notice Pantyusha's surly, hostile attentions (just as he seldom noticed people's appearance, looks or facial expressions; what interested him were their words) and continued obstinately in his efforts to wring out of the old man some details about his work for the secret police in pre-revolutionary Moscow. Suddenly Pantyusha touched the sleeves of Olga's suede jacket and asked, 'Where do jackets like this come from?'

'It comes from Hungary,' Olga answered.

'Oh, so it's not made here? Look, it's just like velvet.'

'It's suede, that's all,' said the nurse. 'Can't you see?'

'I can see. Course I can see.'

'Well, sit down and shut up. Don't touch it. I'll bet you haven't washed your hands, and the slightest bit of dirt or grease will stick to suede. Oh, dear – I do believe you've stained it already.'

She seized a handkerchief and hastened to wipe the mark off the sleeve of the suede jacket. The children leaped up and clustered around, itching with a desire to touch the exotic garment. Pantyusha ground his teeth. The old man, who had seemed to be absorbed in his conversation with Sergei (and appeared to have great difficulty in hearing him), suddenly interrupted the conversation about the jacket with an entirely pertinent remark:

'What d' you mean – it's not made here? You used to be able to get it at Schultz Brothers' shop in Kamerger Street. "*Gemsleder*" it's called. Gloves, waistcoats . . .'

Pantyusha brushed aside his grandfather's interruption with an impatient gesture.

Boiled potatoes were served in a cast-iron pot. The weather turned suddenly overcast and dark, so they switched on the porch lights. Sergei was still trying to make notes, to extract from old Koshelkov some information about a fire that occurred in February 1917: Who started the fire, who put it out, who was giving the orders. The old man had been an utter little nobody at the time, a speck of dust in a tornado – yet fifty-three years had gone by and by some strange quirk of fortune that little speck had survived, was still dancing in a ray of sunlight, while all else around him had been obliterated, swept away. And Olga understood why Sergei was listening with such avidity to the old man's semi-coherent mumbling. The chief question, which puzzled and tantalised them, was: How did he survive? Hadn't the authorities ever . . . picked him up?

'Picked me up? Of course,' said the old man with a smile. 'They tried to take me off to the war; then they put me in prison. I was lucky, though; being a tailor's a good job, keeps you out of harm's way . . . We made uniforms for the officers, so we always had a crust of bread . . . They tried to order us to be moved to another prison, but our warden, comrade Gravdin, wouldn't let us go. So they even quarrelled over us . . .' And the old man winked gleefully.

Pantyusha, who had gone out somewhere, appeared again at the table. 'Why are you bothering the old man?'

'Your grandfather has had a very long and interesting life,' said Sergei. 'We were talking about his life.'

'And who are you writing it down for?'

'I'm a historian. It's important for the history I'm writing.'

'What history?'

'The history of the February Revolution in 1917. The February Revolution and everything connected with it. It is a complicated period that hasn't yet been fully studied, and every new firsthand witness is valuable. Forgive us for boring you – we're going soon.'

Sergei spoke calmly and patiently, but Pantyusha was in a mood to make trouble. Suddenly he shouted, 'You won't get a thing out of him! That's enough! That's what I think of you historians.' And he thrust a gnarled finger in front of Sergei's face. 'I won't allow it.'

Pantyusha's mother and wife tried to calm him down, but timidly and ineffectually. It was time to go, but Sergei never could leave at the right moment; he always felt that something was still to be finished – the drinking or eating, the explanations, the hurling of the last insult. Now, his neck turning purple, seething with fury, he set about trying to explain to a drunken fool what history was and why it was needed. Pantyusha listened with a sarcastic, hostile sneer, and accompanied his objections with a furiously wagging finger:

'We learned all about history in school. We know it all. Why are you trying to muddle me? History, history . . . forget it. There's only one history, and we don't need any more.'

'Listen, Pantyusha, what's your job? What do you do for a living?'

Whenever Sergei talked to uneducated people, especially when he started to argue with them, for some reason he invariably adopted an unpleasant, condescending tone of voice, which was clearly involuntary, but which irritated them. Pantyusha answered rudely: 'Where I work's no business of yours. Maybe I dig graves at the cemetery for three kopecks a time. Look, are you one of those snoopers from the police or the social security?' This was spoken in a threatening voice, and he no longer shook just a finger but a clenched fist under Sergei's nose. Olga tried to drag Sergei away from the table, but he remained obstinately seated and plunged headlong into the increasingly tense dispute.

'No, listen, I haven't said anything to offend you. I'm simply interested to know why you pitched into me like that.'

'I don't give a damn about your history. Just stop bothering the old man.'

'History isn't *mine* – it belongs to you, too, and to your grandfather. It belongs to everybody. Did you know, for instance, that Gorodets is a very ancient town . . .'

The nurse whispered to Olga that she shouldn't be offended by her husband, he was a bit weak in the head, and whenever he had a drink he always behaved stupidly and pestered people. Because of this he was often getting beaten up, but he had a good job as a mechanic at the grain elevator and was really a decent man at heart.

Old Koshelkov, once an informer for the Moscow section of the czarist secret police – but so long ago that nothing perceptible remained of it except burnt-out ashes – was dozing peacefully, his nodding head crowned with its little circlet of pale hair. Sergei was telling some story about the feudal lords of Gorodets in the Middle Ages and about the Tartars. The children were listening to him. Pantyusha frowned with a glare of manic distrust.

'Suppose I punched you on the back of the neck?' He ground his teeth. 'That would be the end of you and your history.'

It was a long walk to the bus stop and it was in the dark. Olga was shivering, either with fear or with cold. The golden day had changed into an icy autumn evening. She tried to make Sergei hurry, but he could barely walk straight, his legs weakened with vodka and euphoria as he babbled delightedly about his success with the old man. To Olga this was nonsense; what good was it all? Some dogs started barking, and a few particularly fierce ones ran out into the road and chased them; Sergei waved his arms at the dogs and threw stones, which only made them more furious.

'Stop it!' she begged.

Sergei, however, seemed to enjoy his skirmish with the dogs. At any moment men with sticks or pitchforks might emerge from the darkened yards. God, how angry she was with him! It had all been such a stupid, childish escapade – the trip to Gorodets, sitting there till late at night, talking to a senile old man.

'Woof! Woof!' he teased the dogs, laughing as they barked at him.

'My God,' she thought, 'and this man is almost middle-aged, almost a professional historian, almost a scholar . . . No, he'll never make it.' This sudden insight, which came to Olga that evening on a pitch-dark country road, was mingled with fear as her husband fought off the dogs. They were now surrounded by them, ranging from sizable farmyard curs to yapping little mongrels that bounced around them like fleas. Suddenly came salvation – the roar of a motorbike engine that scattered the dogs, dazzling them with its headlight, as it drove up before them and stopped.

'Hop on, Mr History!' rasped Pantyusha. His white motorbiking helmet and white gauntlets shone in the darkness like a police patrolman. 'I'll run you to the railway station at Voronov. It's only seven kilometres, we'll be there in no time!'

Olga hesitated – the man, after all, was crazy, and drunk as well – but Sergei was already pushing her into the sidecar, while he climbed astride the pillion, grasped his recent adversary around the waist as if he were his best friend (men were amazing: alcohol could so easily reconcile and unite them, so quickly enable them to forgive each other), gave a wild whistle, as he had not whistled for years, and – off they went. The journey was short, lasting probably no more than a quarter of an hour, but it was unforgettable. Olga wondered whether they would ever come out of this mad adventure alive. She was thrown around, flung from side to side and bumped so hard that her teeth rattled; she wanted to cry out but could not open her mouth or take a deep enough breath. Worst of all was her fear for Sergei, who insisted on standing up, flinging his arm into the air and shouting in a thunderous, parade-ground voice: 'Hurrah for the glorious workers of Gorodets!' or 'Hurrah for the heroic collective farmers of Baranovka!' Pantyusha clearly approved of these slogans, because he joined in with shouting 'Hurrah!' The road was winding, houses would suddenly rush towards them in the glare of the headlight; signposts flickered by, lit for a moment; vague shadows loomed in the ditch beside the road. 'Hurrah for a lone walker!' roared Sergei, waving his cap at one of the shadows. Although Olga was terrified, at the same time she was laughing so hard that she cried, or perhaps crying from the violence and utter confusion of her emotions. She was both angry with him and full of love for him. That noisy, irrepressible, arrested adolescent had not much time left on earth to shout and misbehave.

Klimuk suddenly demanded that Sergei corroborate the fact that Kislovsky had asked him, Sergei, to give him some documents for his dissertation; in return, Klimuk promised his support when Sergei came to submit *his* dissertation. What Klimuk said of Kislovsky was no doubt true, but Sergei had only heard about it from Klimuk himself, who had acted as go-between, and who now for some reason had made a 180-degree turn and was trying to set a trap to catch Kislovsky. Sergei was incapable of intrigue; it angered and disgusted him, and out of spite he responded to Klimuk by doing the stupidest things. Lord, if only he had allied himself with Klimuk at that moment. How Klimuk begged him. Everything might have turned out differently. He would have stayed alive. He would have lived on in good health, he would have gone on working, telling jokes and skiing; he would have climbed up the career ladder and lived to a ripe old age. But nobody knows why people die. Unexpectedly, something dries up, runs out: *the grace of life*, as Tolstoy put it. The 'grace' of his life endured for a while longer: he still drove himself on, still looked for something, still strove to get somewhere.

He could still meet new people and acquire, as he thought, new friends. Suddenly Darya Mamedovna appeared. It was painful to recall her, but it was equally impossible to avoid thinking about her. This was the woman who for the first time gave Olga a real fright, because it suddenly became a distinct possibility that Sergei was drifting away and might disappear. Later, in fact, he did disappear altogether, for which Darya Mamedovna was distantly responsible, in so far as she was the ill-omened starting point from which was unwound the whole skein of disaster – like the blizzard in Pushkins's *The Captain's Daughter* which develops out of an almost invisible little cloud. During the course of a lifetime, people surround us in clusters, like incrustations: these formations suddenly crystallise around us and then just as suddenly they fall away, in obedience to some obscure laws. Once there had been the friends of their youth, student companions like Vlad – they had vanished without trace; these had been followed by neighbours at the Sushchevskaya studios – artists, old men, drunkards, Valerii Vasin and Zika – they too had sunk beneath the waters of time; then there were friends from the museum, and others, like Ilya Vladimirovich – gone, as if they had never been. Later came colleagues at the institute, neighbours at Vasilkovo – they too had disappeared into oblivion. And now there was Darya Mamedovna.

The first time Olga saw this woman with her tawny-olive complexion, a hint of blue in the whites of her eyes, her smooth black hair without a curl or a wave hugging her snake-like head as though poured over it like water, she sensed with her heart: Trouble! A bit over forty, but with the figure of a twenty-year-old girl. It was not her figure, however, or her dark complexion, or her shapely legs that worried Olga, but her widespread reputation, inflated by sycophants, flatterers and various brands of charlatan, which claimed that she was quite unusually intelligent. What nonsense. Pure invention. Olga had seen her several times, at parties, at the theatre and at the Luzhskys', once even in her own home, and had talked to her on all kinds of subjects, from Darya's favourite, parapsychology, to modern poetry, and she quickly realised that the empress had no clothes. Everything was approximate, superficial, purely for show, but she also had a diabolical self-confidence and a firm, categorical way of expressing herself as though delivering a judgment that was not subject to appeal. A most unpleasant creature. But a lot of fools were taken in by her. Imagine – she had a master's degree, almost a doctorate; it was ridiculous, but people talked of her in a phrase that she herself had probably coined: she was 'five-minutes-to-a-doctor'. Well, in philosophy or psychology or something, she had devoured a mass of books and she had the gift of the gab, but that wasn't everything. You can stuff yourself full of information, but that doesn't make you any more intelligent.

It was the sixth anniversary of Fedya's death, and Louisa his widow had invited a few friends – Boris and Vera Luzhsky, Shchupakov and his wife Krasina, some other people from the institute, and Gena Klimuk and Mara. By now, Sergei and Klimuk were almost outright enemies. Louisa was nervous about this, and she called up Olga to ask her advice. It was impossible not to invite Klimuk. The change in him had come about after Fedya's death; in Fedya's lifetime Klimuk had behaved tolerably well, and Louisa knew him as a decent man, an old friend. Sergei said, 'To hell with him. Of course let her invite him. I won't touch him.'

Louisa was very fond of Sergei and he was her favourite guest – because Fedya had been so fond of him too – but Klimuk had also been Fedya's friend, his companion on his last journey and, apart from that, had organised some financial help from the institute. He had arranged a once-only, non-repayable, *ex gratia* payment (and as Olga was to discover later, the sum was not a small one – twice as big, in fact, as the amount she received), and every summer he sent Fedya's children to the summer camp run by the institute. There were strong reasons, therefore, why she was bound to invite Klimuk.

'I know that many people don't like him and think he's strange, but he's always been kind to me,' she explained to Olga. 'Every New Year he sends a card, and he calls with good wishes on Fedya's birthday, even brings me flowers. And Sergei forgets . . .'

Sergei did indeed forget. There were times when he forgot even Olga's birthday, and he constantly got the day wrong – he would wish her 'Happy birthday' on the third instead of the fourth of June. Klimuk never got anything wrong. For some reason he felt a need to be kind to Louisa. Apparently Louisa was hoping that Klimuk would not want to sit down at the same table with Sergei and drink vodka with him and might therefore make some excuse not to come. But he came. Mara wanted to show off in front of her erstwhile friends, to talk about her new flat, about the blue-tiled Dutch stove, the simulated-oak wallpaper, the amazing intelligence of her spaniel Rudi, and, of course, about her impressions of their trips abroad – so much had happened since they had last seen one another.

It was indeed a long time since their last meeting. In one way or another, all of them had lost some of their lustre, had somehow withered. Shchupakov's wife, Krasina, a beautiful Bulgarian woman, had acquired a yellow tinge to her complexion. Boris Luzhsky, the psychiatrist, with whom Olga so much enjoyed talking, had turned into a wizened, middle-aged little man who wore heavy American spectacles that made him look older than he was. Vera, Boris's wife, had a liver complaint and couldn't eat anything. But the most noticeable change had occurred in Louisa; she had grown much thinner, she had a pronounced stoop and the dress she wore was so appallingly tasteless and cheap that Olga was horrified: the woman had so obviously stopped caring. She felt very sorry for her. Louisa had, of course, made a colossal effort to invite all these people and feed them properly; the table was richly spread, but from the greedy looks of the children and from the way in which they sneaked pieces of ham or cheese from the plates it was obvious that they didn't often eat in such abundance. There were two bottles of vodka. In the old days they would have drained them in a moment and somebody would have gone out for more, but now they barely managed to empty one bottle, and even then without much enthusiasm: one person had hypertension, another had a paper to write that night, Klimuk and Boris Luzhsky were driving. Sergei, of course, did not refuse, but the person who punished the vodka most heavily was Mara. She was, it seemed, the only one who had blossomed during those six years: she had filled out, put on weight and turned into a sleek, well-upholstered lady; reddened with an alcoholic flush, her little round face positively gleamed, expressing complete satisfaction with life. Irritated, Olga felt no wish to talk to her, still less to listen to her tactless bragging.

As soon as Mara started talking about her spaniel, who understood a hundred and forty words, or about her trips abroad: 'Imagine, horrors, there we were in Nice walking down the boulevard . . .' Olga purposely interrupted her in a loud voice, asking her to pass a dish, or switch on the television – anything. Of course it was rude to interrupt, but Olga couldn't help herself: listening to the self-satisfied Mara was intolerable. Both she and Klimuk had apparently managed to forget that Sergei had tried for a long time to get a trip to France, which he needed for his work, but had somehow failed to make it; yet this squawking little parakeet, this nonentity, who did no work of any kind, had already been to Nice, to Paris, to Rome, and to God knows where else. All right, so you were clever enough to play the game and wangle yourself all those goodies, but at least show a little tact and don't shout about it from the rooftops, least of all in front of Sergei.

In fact Sergei appeared not to be listening to Mara's twittering about her experiences abroad and was preoccupied with his own thoughts, but it made Olga furious. People who acquire an ever-thicker skin in proportion to their increasing success and affluence are obnoxious, and she always tried to keep her distance from them. In the past she had treated Mara tolerantly, even amiably. Olga regarded her as a cheerful little birdbrain, remote from the machinations and intrigues to which her husband devoted himself. Now, however, it turned out that she had an insatiable appetite for the fruits of those machinations and intrigues.

'Louisa, darling, everything is so delicious,' said Mara in condescending approval as she ate her way through the contents of the fruit bowl. 'Why don't we get together more often, as we used to do?'

The children watched longingly while one after another of the juicy pears, as if on a conveyor belt, disappeared into the toothy maw of the fat, rosy-cheeked lady in the blue wig.

Klimuk, on the other hand, seemed in a sombre mood, or he

was, perhaps, overconscious of his own importance: he was not his usual talkative self, he didn't tell any jokes, and when Louisa produced a guitar – the famous guitar that had belonged to Fedya, on which he played so wonderfully – and asked him to sing Fedya's favourite song, Klimuk said that he hadn't time for such amusements any more and politely refused, with the excuse that his voice had quite gone.

He was too great a man nowadays to accompany himself on the guitar and sing a risqué little song, like a student in a railway carriage. Of course, if the song had been something like 'My Beloved City, My Golden Moscow', that would have been different. At home, after the party, Sergei sneered as he recalled Klimuk and the changing moods of the evening, which had ended in quarrelling and abuse. It was awful that they had been unable to control themselves and had caused an embarrassing scene on such an occasion. And it was just as much Sergei's fault as Klimuk's. At first all was quiet and peaceful; they were seated at opposite ends of the table and did not talk to each other. Their relationship was not yet one of deadly enmity, as it became later, but their feelings for each other were openly contemptuous: Sergei despised him for his blatant careerism, while Klimuk despised Sergei for his alleged enviousness; he was convinced that Sergei couldn't bear the fact of his, Klimuk's, great success.

Everything might have ended with decorum, especially since the Klimuks had planned to leave early, had it not been for a stout lady from the institute, her black hair streaked with grey (Olga had since forgotten her name), who suddenly began with great fervour to praise Fedya's unselfishness and unworldliness.

'There simply aren't such people any more!' she exclaimed. 'In that respect Fyodor Alexandrovich was absolutely unique. He never used his position to get anything for himself, not even *that* much.'

The lady's voice quavered with emotion. She was, of course, exaggerating; Fedya had been a good man, but by no means such a plaster saint as she was making him out to have been. Someone else spoke up in similar terms, and then everyone began recalling Fedya's kindness, his love of helping others, and at the same time (with a touch of pathos) his improvidence and impracticality, which were indeed his outstanding characteristics. Suddenly Louisa burst into tears and began a litany of complaint: how Fedya had never taken them anywhere except to the Crimea; how he never possessed a decent winter overcoat;

how he had never managed to exchange their flat for a better one, although everyone else seemed able to do it . . . Now there was no hope left for her.

'He always thought last of all about himself, always about other people, always,' Louisa whispered, bowing her head, now noticeably streaked with grey.

Nobody had wanted these tears, these embarrassing complaints. The atmosphere of restraint was broken; everyone began talking at once, seized by a wave of affection for Fedya – so pure, so unlike the common run of humanity (God, it was all so exaggerated, but at that particular moment it felt as if they had perceived the ultimate truth!) – moved by this woman's grief, by the sight of her pathetic little flat with its shabby old furniture, and, no doubt, aggravated by Mara's insensitive prattle about Klimuk's prosperity . . . And Olga wondered how her own flat would look in six year's time.

The praise of Fedya had the unintended result of seeming, by contrast, to condemn Klimuk. Although he, too, added some laudatory remarks about Fedya, he was visibly strained and his voice betrayed his tenseness. The situation was building up to an explosion. The bearded Shchupakov, a friend of Fedya's since their schooldays, and unconnected with the institute, inquired naïvely: 'Does the academic secretary have any special opportunities for feathering his nest?'

The question, in fact, was probably not quite as naïve as Shchupakov tried to make it sound; he just happened to be the first to strike an overt blow. The black-and-grey lady immediately responded: 'What do you think?'

'I don't know. That's why I asked the question.'

'Quite a few opportunities. There's Gennadii Vitalevich sitting opposite you: he will confirm that, I think.'

Klimuk opened his eyes wide in a look of guileless honesty, shook his head and confessed that, with the best will in the world, he could not think what these 'opportunities' were: 'I really can't imagine what you mean.'

'Oh come, come, Gennadii Vitalevich! It's all in your hands!' exclaimed the lady in sincere amazement.

'Exactly *what* is in my hands?' Klimuk laughed. 'I wish I knew.'

'Everything. Absolutely everything.'

The lady laughed too, this time with a hint of flattery in her voice. Klimuk shrugged his shoulders. It might have all dissolved in jokes and inconsequential chatter had not Sergei suddenly remarked in quite a different tone – hard and contemptuous –

that Fedya's talented dissertation had never been published, whereas Klimuk's extremely mediocre piece of work had been published in two editions – in a symposium and as a separate book.

Klimuk pretended not to hear. He did not even look in Sergei's direction. There followed a few irrelevant remarks from other people, after which Klimuk said with a sigh: 'I feel sorry for you, Sergei. How painful it must be for you, always having to be a witness to other people's successes.'

It was said without malice, in a voice of apparent sympathy. Sergei exploded: 'What successes, for God's sake? You make me sick! That's not success – it's crap! –' And more of such comments, spat out in fury. Louisa turned pale. Olga signalled furiously to Sergei to shut up; she was terrified of what he might do next. Squeaking indignantly, Mara rushed to her husband's defence. Several of the institute people – and none more heatedly than the stout lady – rounded on Sergei. Klimuk smiled vengefully. The stout lady exclaimed: 'Unparliamentary language! You have used unparliamentary language!'

Klimuk and Mara left, and soon afterwards the other guests from the institute left too. Their faces, as they said goodbye to Sergei, expressed disapproval. The stout lady – who was, it transpired, an important functionary, and a member of an influential committee – whispered anxiously: 'Sergei Afanasievich, I hate to tell you, but that is what is known as a *casus belli*.'

Sergei laughed unconcernedly: 'Ah, hell . . . who cares?'

His mood had turned cheerful. He became talkative and noisy, he told stories and gave a hilarious description – as only he could – of the trip to Gorodets and the meeting with old Koshelkov. Louisa calmed down, everyone else gradually relaxed, while Shchupakov and Krasina, of course, had always been on Sergei's side. The unpleasantness and the shouting were somehow smoothed over and gave way to a happier atmosphere (the episode could not be forgotten, but they all did their best to forget it) and it was then that the name of Darya Mamedovna came up for the first time. Sergei was saying that his list of czarist police informers included three important people, known only by their code names, whose real names were still undisclosed. The arrests that took place in 1916 were probably connected with these three, or with one of them. He was constantly preoccupied with this topic. Olga even used to make jokes about it:

'What are you – a historian or a private detective?'

A few minutes earlier, Krasina, who was a sweet and kind woman but not too bright, told a story about a peasant woman from a mountain village in southern Bulgaria who had the gift of second sight and other parapsychological talents, which were so amazing that people came to see her from abroad, and a woman of Krasina's acquaintance had been given an exact answer to her question about a friend who had died in mysterious circumstances. Someone then said jokingly that Sergei should find a clairvoyant like that, ask her about the anonymous informers, and perhaps the secret would be revealed. And then, roaring with laughter at the idea, someone else suggested that they ought to hold a spiritualist seance and summon up the spirit of Colonel Martinov – the chief of the Moscow secret police in 1916 – who would surely know all the answers. At this point Boris Luzhsky told them about Darya Mamedovna Nigmatova. He described how she was engaged in serious research into parapsychology and was also interested in all sorts of occultism, oriental magi, pyschic mediums and other obscure matters. She was also a highly educated woman who spoke four languages and gave lectures. Her father came from the Caucasus (hence her unusual patronymic 'Mamedovna'); he had been a homeopathic doctor, very rich, who had died during the war, and Darya's mother was of aristocratic descent.

The fact that Vera referred to Darya Mamedovna somewhat coldly as 'that woman' put Olga even more on her guard. Obviously Vera, too, sensed danger here, and Vera was not a person to be alarmed without reason; she was a rational, intelligent woman. Olga asked her: 'Vera, do you know this Darya Mamedovna?'

'I saw her once. On that same occasion, at the Kostins'.'

'Well, what did you think? – An oriental beauty?'

'No, not exactly . . .' Vera answered hesitantly. 'That is, not unless you like that type. But our Boris definitely *does* like that type. In my opinion, she bowled him over at first sight.'

'Boris – you must introduce me to her at once,' cried Sergei. 'Call yourself a friend? Aren't you ashamed of keeping her away from me?'

'Forget it – you'd never make it with her.'

'I wouldn't make it? And who would – you, I suppose?'

'I am questionable – but still, there is a chance. Because I'm a psychiatrist, which is close to her interests. But you, old boy, with your history of the February Revolution, you haven't a hope . . .'

As they continued to banter in this vein, Olga felt her heart gripped by an evil premonition. Gradually more details about Darya Mamedovna came to light: she was forty or so but still looked marvellous; she was very athletic and swam a lot. She was once married, but her husband had died. A year ago the magazine *Science and Life* had published an article of hers on parapsychology, entitled something like 'The Mysterious World Around Us', and now that issue of the magazine was unobtainable: in libraries, people queued up to borrow a copy. Boris wagged a warning finger at Olga. 'Olga, this husband of yours is really out to make a conquest. You should keep an eye on him.'

Everyone laughed, and Olga made a great effort to smile and reply in the same frivolous tone.

Three months passed, in which nothing more was heard of Darya Mamedovna. Then Olga discovered that Sergei had met her: he mentioned it casually, in passing, as something quite insignificant. Perhaps he really thought it was, or perhaps he was pretending. Describing his visit to an exhibit by an artist called Presnin, he let slip the remark: 'By the way, I met that woman Nigmatova when I was there.'

'Nigmatova? Who's she?'

'You know – Darya Mamedovna. Don't you remember? Boris was talking about her at Louisa's –'

How could she forget! Olga went cold. Presnin, it turned out, had been a friend of this woman's husband, the artist. Had this meeting been arranged in advance? Nothing of the sort – it was pure chance. There was nothing of the *femme fatale* about her. She was rather skinny, sun-tanned, rather like a gypsy to look at. She had said that she was being heavily attacked for her writings, even persecuted. Presnin had arranged a little buffet supper for his close friends after the private viewing, and some people from the Sushchevskaya studios had been there. One of them had told him that Georgii Maximovich was ill . . .

Olga interpreted the reference to her stepfather as a smoke screen and did not pursue the subject. She knew from her mother (with whom she talked almost daily by phone) that Georgii Maximovich had had some tests done and the results were disturbing, that he was weakening and complained of pain, and would probably have to go into hospital. All this was by now common knowledge; Olga felt very sorry for Georgii Maximovich and was worried about her mother. But right now she was amazed to learn that Sergei had been to some buffet supper – without her – where he had met and talked to this creature. At the mention of her name Olga experienced a strange sort of asthmatic irritation, as though she were slightly short of breath. What exactly was Sergei up to? In this state of irritation, gasping for breath a little, she began to scold him for taking unfair advantage of the fact that while she worked to strict hours he had no fixed timetable and so was free to go roaming around on his own – visiting friends, going to art exhibitions, making new acquaintances. Just as if he were a bachelor . . .

It was unfair of her to have such thoughts, and even worse to utter them. As soon as she had spoken, she was ashamed of herself. But it was like a disease, an allergic reaction that made her gasp for breath, unable to control herself.

That winter Aunty Pasha arrived from Vasilkovo in tears; Kolka was under arrest; he was due to appear in court and might get a heavy sentence. The Vasilkovo people had got into a fight in the club with a crowd from the nearby village of Semkovo, and Kolka, as an auxiliary policeman, had tried to separate them and had knocked one of the Semkovo men to the ground. The man had almost died, and was still in hospital, where the doctors had just managed to save his life. Kolka had never seen the man from Semkovo before in his life, and now – this terrible accident. What had Kolka hit him with? An axe. Of course, as a police reservist he had only been trying to separate them, and they, drunken fools, had turned on him and he had lashed out. Alexandra Prokofievna remarked that an axe was an odd sort of weapon for a police reservist.

'Have you forgotten?' said Sergei. 'The house with the hatchet – remember?'

Weeping, Aunty Pasha begged them to help her in hiring a lawyer – it didn't matter how much it cost, she would raise the money somehow. She would sell the cow, sell the motorbike. Although she regarded the case as hopeless, Alexandra Prokofievna went into action. She went out to Vasilkovo and to Ryabtsevo, the district centre, where Kolka was detained under arrest. There she talked to the state prosecutor and the local police chief. When she made the first trip it was in the late autumn, towards the end of November. The weather was horrible, cold and sleety, and everyone tried to persuade her not to go. Sergei shouted at her: 'I forbid you! Don't you dare go. You're an old woman and you should behave like an old woman.' He was seldom as rude as this, and it was a sign that he was really alarmed. She replied: 'I will never behave like an old woman. I made a promise, Pasha is expecting me, so therefore I must go.'

He shouted some more, threatened her and went off to the

institute convinced that his mother was not yet totally out of her mind and would stay at home. Olga went to work, Irinka went to school – and the old woman put on her 1920s hiking rig, took her umbrella, pulled on her rubber boots and set off for the station. When she returned that evening, worn out and soaked to the skin, looking like a weird, pathetic scarecrow, she announced that the facts of the case were not at all as Pasha had told them. They were both worse and better. Sergei was furious with his mother, refused to listen and demonstratively left the table. Since Olga was never the most sympathetic of listeners when the old woman was holding forth, Alexandra Prokofievna started telling the whole story to Irinka. Strangely enough, her voice sounded firm and confident.

She had found out that Kolka, of course, had been as drunk as the rest of them and that the fight had not just been the usual drunken brawl. The cause of all the trouble was a girl called Raisa. The Semkovo boys had been pestering her; they were out for revenge because she had dropped one of them in favour of Kolka. It emerged that Kolka – the apparently shy, sickly and unprepossessing Kolka – was in the habit of sleeping around with lots of girls and was looked upon, for some reason, as a most eligible catch. Raisa claimed she was already pregnant by Kolka, but Pasha insisted that she was lying and that Kolka had no intention of marrying her.

'I persuaded her that they must base Kolka's defence on exactly the opposite standpoint, do you see?' Alexandra Prokofievna explained to Irinka. 'That is our only hope. Kolka must claim that he acted in a fit of jealousy to defend the honour of the mother of his unborn child . . .'

She talked to Irinka as though she were grown up; yet the girl was only fourteen at the time. Olga didn't like it, but to express her disapproval was out of the question: her mother-in-law would have instantly taken offence, resulting in yet another row. Olga patiently endured all the endless discussions, phone calls, telegrams and fuss about Kolka. Alexandra Prokofievna took the case very seriously and did indeed find a lawyer, a tough old war-horse named Lupovzorov. Gradually Olga was more and more amazed: whence all this zeal, why all these exertions in the defence of people who were, after all, outsiders? What were Kolka and Aunty Pasha to her – to all of them, for that matter? Merely the landlords of the *dacha* they happened to rent – and landlords who charged, what's more, a shamelessly high rent every summer. Otherwise they had nothing whatsoever in common with them, and Alexandra Prokofievna, as a rule, hardly ever spoke to them at all, except to give them an occasional scolding. Of course, she felt sorry for Kolka . . .

These events happened to coincide with a very difficult time for Olga's mother (caused by the serious illness of Georgii Maximovich) and with the looming shadow of Darya Mamedovna. Everyone in the family got on Olga's nerves. She was irritated by her mother's inability to cope, by her daughter's selfishness, by her husband's muddled and aimless life – what *was* he doing all day while she was at work? – and now by her stupid mother-in-law and her preoccupation with the affairs of people who were virtual strangers, instead of trying to help by doing some housework or going to the parents' meetings at school, as all grandmothers and grandfathers did when the child's parents were working. It was no use expecting Sergei to be any help, and Olga was run ragged. If only the old woman would go to the post office and pay the gas and electricity bills during the daytime, when it wasn't crowded – was that really so difficult? Everything was too difficult. Much more difficult than taking the train out of town in bad weather, sloshing along muddy country roads, sitting for hours in court on behalf of people she hardly knew. Much of it was an act, a show of martyrdom. As always with that woman.

One day, in a state of extreme irritation induced by all this – not so much irritation as a wave of such total exhaustion that one's brain ceases to function and one gives way to all the subliminal irritants at once – she told Sergei that Kolka's fate interested her far less than Georgii Maximovich's illness. And would Alexandra Prokofievna with her show-off philanthropy kindly leave her – Olga — alone. It was an unfair thing to say. Alexandra Prokofievna actually bothered her least of all, but Olga couldn't help hearing the ceaseless legal consultations over the phone, the detailed bulletins over the dinner table, on top of which Sergei would later repeat more news that he had heard from his mother. Besides, Olga had just come back from seeing her mother, who was fluttering around aimlessly, distracted with grief as she watched her beloved husband die. Georgii Maximovich had already been in hospital for two weeks, and he was getting steadily worse. Three days ago he had been operated on by Professor Rodin, a famous specialist; the hospital was excellent (they had difficulty in getting him admitted; it was eventually arranged with the help of string-pulling by Vlad, whom they had successfully tracked down), and everything humanly possible was being done for him. Yet even so, Olga's mother reproached herself: she was convinced that she should have given Professor Rodin two hundred roubles before the operation. Someone had given her this idiotic idea, but she hadn't done anything because she had heard about it too late. Now she was tortured by the thought that perhaps because of this the operation might not be effective. Professor Rodin had spoken to her in what she felt was a rather cold, off-hand, way, saying: 'Unfortunately I can't give you much hope, although I can't say that it's the end either.'

Olga's mother was utterly crushed by that remark.

'I think it's insulting to talk like that to the relatives!' she said indignantly through her tears. 'Who gave him the right? He spoke to me like a bureaucrat . . .'

Then she immediately started blaming herself and cursing herself for being so cowardly that she had failed to offer money to Professor Rodin. For although her friend had suggested this to her when it was already too late, she had, in fact, thought of it herself earlier but had been unable to make up her mind to do it. Now, after the operation, she had somehow to get hold of a rare Swiss drug, erythrin. The only way was to find someone who might be able to help. As she was now exhausted, and obliged to lie down with an attack of tachycardia, Olga spent two hours at the telephone. A few people promised to try to find out or to ask others who might know, but most said that they themselves were trying to find scarce drugs and couldn't get any. Olga returned home at about nine o'clock in the evening, drank some tea and then decided to ring her mother up, because she had left her in such low spirits, simply to find out how she was feeling and whether the tachycardia had subsided. But it was impossible to get to the phone.

Alexandra Prokofievna was talking to Lupovzorov, Kolka's lawyer; their conversation had already lasted exactly forty minutes. Finally Olga went right up to the old woman and whispered that she urgently needed to make a phone call. Her mother-in-law nodded irritably, spoke for another minute, then hung up the receiver.

'Lupovzorov was telling me about the trial. It's very important to me,' she said sternly.

Olga replied with equal firmness: 'And I have to call my mother. She's not well.'

No, Alexandra Prokofievna did not ask what was the matter with Galina Yevgenievna, whether she needed help or perhaps some medicine that she might be able to get at the polyclinic in Kirovskaya Street. She was hardly likely to be able to get erythrin, but she might at least have asked. She was not hostile to

Olga's mother, and had never quarrelled with her; if there had been restrained arguments between them, it had been long ago, when Olga's mother had been looking after Irinka and Alexandra Prokofievna had preached at her. In those days their common delight and love for the baby had occasionally given rise to tiny outbursts of disagreement, but it was all long forgotten. Now had come the time of placid indifference to each other. Any stranger needing Alexandra Prokofievna's 'professional' help was closer to her than her daughter-in-law's mother.

It was after that tiny little squabble by the phone, ending in a draw for both sides, that Olga made the remark about 'show-off philanthropy'. Sergei immediately flared up, like a watchful sentry reaching for his rifle: 'Kolka got three years instead of seven. You call that "showing off"? No, my dear, that's the real thing, something *you* are incapable of comprehending.'

She muttered something in reply, taken aback by the alacrity with which he leaped to his mother's defence. Well, maybe she had been wrong; in fact, she certainly had been wrong: there were times when her mother-in-law did help people partly out of pure altruism (although there was little meant in it for she did it mostly out of habit, instilled into her by her professional training) – but she should also be able to understand what a state Olga was in when she came back from seeing her mother. And now Sergei decided to take offence. She was suddenly aware that he was walking into the room dressed in cap and overcoat, with that expression of stony gloom, jaws clenched, which he put on at moments when he felt mortally offended. He circled the room, looking for something.

'Where are you going?'

'To Fyodorov.'

Having found what he was looking for – his briefcase – he threw a few papers into it.

Fyodorov, Sergei's friend from his museum days, was, to Olga, a complete nonentity, one of those idle gasbags to whom Sergei was strangely attracted and who dragged him down to their level. Nowadays they met less often, thank God, because Fyodorov had moved to some place on the distant outskirts of Moscow, beyond Kuzminki. She asked, 'What's the hurry?'

'No hurry, I simply promised to go and see him.' After a pause he added: 'Darya Mamedovna will be there.'

It turned out that Fyodorov knew her well. She would be coming later, after she had given a lecture. This news produced on Olga the same effect as if a bolt of lightning had struck the next room, flooding the room they were in with light and making an audible crackle.

In a weak voice – she thought it was all over and he was going away forever – she asked how he imagined he was coming back. It was half-past ten. He said he would stay over there for the night. He spoke calmly, even slightly querulously, as if she were pestering him with trivialities, and she lacked the strength to protest and shout: What the hell game are you playing? What makes you think you can just walk out of the house and spend the night God knows where?

He acted like a man who was doing something completely natural, but of course to go visiting somewhere beyond Kuzminki at half-past ten at night meant staying over there. What was so odd about staying overnight with a friend now and then? There was nothing odd about it, for God's sake! It was simply something that wasn't a part of *their life*. It had never happened before; yet here was Sergei exploiting a sense of grievance in order quite callously and calmly to introduce this novel form of behaviour. Olga said no more, dumbfounded by it all – and in particular by Darya Mamedovna. Sergei said 'Goodbye' and left.

In the past when they had quarrelled, they had sworn at each other furiously, and he had stamped out or she had fled to her mother, but this was different – quietly, without any door-slamming, just to pick up his briefcase and say 'Goodbye'. They were like strangers parting – for an hour or for a lifetime: it made no difference.

At the funeral of Georgii Maximovich Olga wept uncontrollably, until she almost fainted – it was a cold spring day, jackdaws were screaming in the air over the crematorium – and she had to be held to prevent her from falling. Indeed she wanted to fall, into oblivion if possible; to go on living seemed pointless, because on the previous day Sergei had said 'Perhaps' and then had gone out again until late at night. He had demanded that she *stop tormenting him*. It was impossible to make the most innocent remark: he would instantly flare up and walk out. She had simply asked him: 'I suppose you're having an affair with this Darya?'

Sometimes he would go to Fyodorov, sometimes elsewhere. He said that he was seriously interested in parapsychology, and in fact he was reading a lot of old books, rubbish like Madame Blavatskaya's *Voices of Silence*, journals such as *Rebus* and *The Afterlife Herald* – who gave them to him? – as well as new American and English magazines, from which he would transcribe passages, dictionary in hand. He even made jokes at himself, but to Olga it was no joking matter. As a biologist, she knew quite well the true worthlessness of all that junk. And he was being led astray by a woman who wanted to gain power over him.

'Why do you need all this?'

'I don't. I simply want to understand something that has occupied people for thousands of years. Besides, my Colonel Martinov was a spiritualist and a member of a secret society. Because of it, he actually got into trouble with his superiors in 1916 . . .'

When Sergei jokingly announced that he had been to a spiritualist seance at Fyodorov's place and they had summoned up the spirit of Pobedonostsev, the mentor of Tsar Alexandar III, who had uttered the obscure remark: 'Not thus have we conquered', Olga and Sergei argued furiously for two hours about what it might mean, until his mother could restrain herself no longer and created a scene. She shouted that Sergei's father would have died of shame if anything of this sort had happened while he was alive. The son of Afanasy Troitsky – a spiritualist! The son of a revolutionary, a comrade-in-arms of the great Lunacharsky! If his father were to rise from the grave . . . Sergei observed maliciously: 'Aha, so you do allow the possibility that someone can rise from the grave?'

In all this, of course, there was a large element of Sergei's incorrigible love of buffoonery and teasing, but it was also in part a form of escapism, an evasion of the failures that plagued him incessantly. And there was the worst part of all, of which Alexandra Prokofievna knew nothing: Darya Mamedovna. At first when he went miles out to the distant suburbs to Fyodorov's place for the seances he invited Olga to go with him, but she had no desire to go so far to listen to nonsense, and she refused, laughing and sneering at him. All to no purpose. Once Olga spent a whole evening reading *The Spiritualist* magazine of 1906 and several tattered brochures in paper covers that were lying around on Sergei's desk – they were simply appalling in their pathetic intellectual poverty. Sometimes they made her laugh, sometimes angry, but above all she was amazed that so much unbelievable drivel – all these mediums, planchettes, lower spirits, higher spirits, voices from beyond the grave – had actually persisted into the present day. Having read the magazine, she came to two conclusions, both of which frightened her. The first was that the most fervent enthusiasts for all this rubbish were women. Somewhere in all this was some hidden enticement for the female mind: the famous Blavatskaya, the authors of *The Spiritualist*, Bykova, Speranskaya, Shchegol-kova, a particularly active woman named Kapkanshchikova. 'Was it because they were rich, with nothing to do? They should have tried running from shop to shop, queuing for shoes . . .' The second conclusion was even worse: the empty futility of the whole business of conjuring up spirits and meddling with an imaginary 'other world' was so obvious that if he continued spending time on this nonsense it meant that there were *other reasons*. That was why, when he answered her question by saying 'Perhaps' and went out, her heart sank just because she had been expecting exactly that reply. And no one had wept more bitterly than Olga at Georgii Maximovich's funeral in the Donskoi Monastery.

Sergei supported her on one side, Vlad on the other. She could feel Sergei's granitelike calm. At one point he said, 'You must pull yourself together!'

Then Vlad solicitously led her aside – it was at the moment when the music started to play – to a seat by the wall, took a bottle of medicine and a small glass from his pocket and gave her a dose to drink.

As she looked into his ageing, pockmarked face she said, 'Georgii Maximovich loved you, Vladik.'

Vlad nodded mournfully but with a hint of restrained superiority in his demeanour. A black official car was waiting for him on the drive in front of the crematorium. Olga realised that everything would have been different if Vlad hadn't brought Sergei on that holiday, and she would not be suffering now. How quickly life passed. Without looking around, Sergei was standing very straight and now supporting Olga's mother. The music smothered everything. Afterwards they went to the studio in Sushchevskaya Street, where kind neighbours had arranged everything. In charge of it all was Henrietta Osipovna, an energetic and efficient lady from the Moscow Society of Artists, whom they did not know but who was exactly the right sort of person for the occasion – she called Olga's mother 'my dear'. The artists had very soon drunk too much and started arguing at the tops of their voices, talking about Georgii Maximovich in such absurdly exaggerated terms that they sounded hypocritical and insincere. All the objects in the studio – pictures, frames, plaster models, jars, brushes – seemed orphaned, unneeded and displaced. Uncle Petya, who had turned into a scrawny, white-haired old man, coughed noisily all evening and kept shouting 'Oh, stop it!' at someone.

Amid this crowded hubbub Olga's mother seemed lost, with the air of someone who happened to be there by chance. Olga was terrified when she thought about her mother: How was she going to live now? Olga stayed to spend the night with her mother, while Sergei, Irinka and Alexandra Prokofievna went home.

Georgii Maximovich's first wife was also at the crematorium and came on to Sushchevskaya afterwards but did not come to the gathering in the studio, although she was invited. Instead, in a tasteless and unnecessary gesture, she arranged her own funeral party – on the same floor, in rooms belonging to a woman artist. Some of the guests moved back and forth from one party to the other. Once Uncle Petya flung open the door and shouted menacingly into the empty corridor: 'I'll come over there in a moment – and I'll smash all the crockery. The idea – having two funeral parties at once!'

From the other party something was said in reply, but it was inaudible. Olga sat on a couch beside a bearded old artist called Likhnevich, who would not go home but repeatedly filled his glass first with tea, then with liqueur, and wept as he described their life together in Paris a hundred years ago, when he and Georgii Maximovich, young and brash, thought they would conquer Paris. Marc Chagall had been with them in those days, too – and how had it all ended? A funeral party in Sushchevskaya Street. He advised Olga to sell two drawings – a church in Montmartre and a self-portrait with a wry expression on the face – and to give all the rest away to anyone who would take them, because Georgii Maximovich had personally burned all his best work in the thirties; it was a foolish thing to do – a moment of weakness, and a whole life was smashed to fragments, like that piece of fallen plaster: it could never be picked up, never put together again. All his later work was just rubbish, despite his official rehabilitation, despite the committees he sat on, despite the commissions he received ('Don't think I envied him, Olga; I pitied him, poor Georges'). But Olga, having already cried for her stepfather and worrying about her mother, unable to imagine the future, was wondering why Sergei hadn't stayed with her – Irinka could have gone home with her grandmother. He should have stayed with her, but he had not wanted to. 'Well, we're off,' he had said. 'I'm taking Irinka home. It's time she went to bed.'

Sergei lived a separate life. His work had ceased to interest him; his dissertation was getting nowhere. Instead, he told endless stories about the funny answers and amazing prophecies that were produced at the seances he attended. She still refused to believe in 'that nonsense' – well, how could anyone seriously believe they had made contact with a Franciscan monk named Brother Arnulf, who had lived in Switzerland in the sixteenth century, and that now Sergei was holding regular conversations with him? She became more and more firmly convinced that Darya Mamedovna had bewitched him.

Olga saw her once, quite by chance, in the theatre. They had gone to a première at the Sovremennik and were walking in the upstairs foyer during the interval when suddenly Sergei squeezed her arm very hard – she had a huge bruise afterwards to prove how painful it had been – in a purely reflex gesture that felt like a nip from a pair of pincers, and he whispered, 'That's Darya Mamedovna over in the corner!'

Before looking towards the corner, she looked at him. He had gone red in the face. Darya Mamedovna was dark and thin, with streaks of silver in her black hair. When Sergei and Olga approached her, she looked at him with an unsmiling, even unwelcoming expression. Beside her sat an unshaven young man in a dirty white polo-necked sweater. Sergei said hello and introduced Olga. The young man was at least twenty years younger than Darya Mamedovna. She did not introduce him. No conversation took place, although Sergei shuffled from foot to foot for two or three awkward, unnecessary moments, in which Olga felt painfully embarrassed, before they moved away.

'I pity you,' said Olga.

'Why do you pity me? What nonsense. I don't know what you mean,' he blustered. Having decided to take offence, he didn't talk to Olga again for the rest of the interval.

The play was funny, but they did not laugh. It was then that she suddenly felt – like a wave of coldness – a premonition of disaster.

Another meeting took place in a house on one of the embankments, a house with caryatids and little rooms that recalled the partitioned room they had long ago occupied in Shabolovka Street. It was the home of one of Fyodorov's friends, a civil engineer, who was a spiritualist and a collector of books on magic and occultism. He showed them an old book called *Sorcery*.

Once again Sergei invited her to come to a seance and see what happened, but she desperately did not want to: she felt that his invitation was insincere, that he didn't mean it when he said, 'Come on, let's go together . . . We'll have a good laugh.'

In reality, though, she knew *he did not want her to go*.

Therefore she had to overcome her aversion, so this time she said yes. 'Their life' was falling apart, turning into something fragmented, a mosaic, as in a dream; a dream is always fragmentary, whereas waking reality is a unified whole.

Olga arrived at the seance with a headache. In the lobby of the flat there hung a poster that read: 'Silence – thou art best of all I have yet heard'. The air was full of a sweetish smell, as in a church, of candle smoke and hot wax. Everyone spoke in barely audible whispers and flung their coats in a heap on some chests in the hall. Olga noticed that the parquet floor had not been scraped for a long time and was grey with dirt.

She was filled with a blind determination, of the kind that one feels only in dreams: to talk with *that woman*. Darya Mamedovna, however, was not there when Olga and Sergei arrived; she came two hours later, when the seance was over. The people who had seated themselves round the table shared a look of tenseness and covert unease. No one joked or smiled; they tried not to look at each other, gazing instead at the middle of the table, where a small glass stood in the centre of a sheet of paper on which the letters of the alphabet were written out in a circle. There were five women and four men. Sergei had said they were mostly engineers or technicians, and one of the women, it later transpired, was a cashier in a theatre box office. Fyodorov was present, unnaturally silent and grim-looking. In charge of the proceedings was the civil engineer, a pale man with a red spade beard, who spoke in rapid, abrupt sentences. Every remark that he made sounded slightly like a command, which was unpleasant. The man himself, affectedly dressed in a thick-knit red woollen waistcoat, a bootlace instead of a tie, struck Olga as altogether disagreeable. He had long fingers tinged with white around the nails. Throughout the evening he never once looked at Olga, although she felt that he was keeping her under ceaseless scrutiny with all his senses. Someone said they should open a window, others objected, and this gave rise to an argument. The two women who wanted the window open argued with extraordinary heat and fury, and even threatened that if their demand was not met they would leave the meeting, which would then – so it was implied – lose all meaning. It was clear that the real matter in dispute was not fresh air but something of sublime, universal significance. The host, after hesitating for a while, found a solution by compromise; he opened the door into an adjoining room and flung open a window in there.

Sergei was sitting opposite her. His expression was impenetrable. What was he thinking about? Olga's heart ached with worry and with pity for him: he was as unhappy as she was. Back at home things were waiting to be done: housework, shopping, clothes to be taken to the laundry (it was open until nine o'clock in the evening, but every day tiredness or other chores prevented Olga from getting there on time) and she had to write a report, while his notebooks, folders and books awaited Sergei, all the material for his dissertation that was bogged down halfway along – and instead of tackling it . . . The man in the red waistcoat commanded them:

'Place your left hand on the right arm of your neighbour . . . Foot against foot . . . Form a chain . . .'

The little glass really did seem to come to life beneath the touch of nine hands; at first it jerked around indecisively, then darted briskly and convulsively across the paper from letter to letter, and after an initial spell of confused gibberish, sentences began to form. Father Paisios said, 'Be not chary of doing good, it shall repay thee an hundredfold, thou fool.' The word 'fool' caused some perplexity. Why should he speak contemptuously of someone who was doing good? One of the ladies explained that evidently the spirit of Father Paisios was being ironic at the expense of earthly morality, since by our cynical present-day standards the doers of good deeds were regarded as fools. The spirit of Torquemada held a long and muddled conversation, but to the general disappointment his remarks were for some reason couched in banal journalistic clichés.

Then followed an experiment in psychography: one of the women held a pencil poised over a sheet of paper while the others sat around the table as before and tried to summon up the spirit of Alexander Herzen. At first the great man obstinately refused to appear. Someone suggested they should leave him alone, others did not agree, until the host in an angry whisper demanded that they cease arguing and get on with the task in hand. The lights were put out, the tension rose until amid total silence they could all finally hear the squeak of pencil on paper. The woman, sitting at a separate table, was actually writing! No one doubted that her pencil was being guided by the hand of Herzen himself. When the light was switched on, the woman was leaning back in her chair exhausted, her face streaming with sweat and terribly pale; she was immediately given a dose of valerian. Then they rushed to look at the paper, which was entirely covered with huge, sprawling letters.

Seizing the sheet of paper, the host read out in a voice hoarse with excitement: ' "My . . . rifuge . . . the river . . ." '

Olga heard Sergei giggle. She could not have been mistaken, because she knew that malicious snigger of his only too well, but when she looked at him, his face was as inscrutable as before. Voices were heard saying:

'What else? Isn't there any more?'

'Nothing more, only those four words,' replied the host, still in the grip of excitement.

The paper was examined, the scrawled writing was carefully studied, and again an argument broke out. What did 'the river' mean? And why 'rifuge'? They agreed that 'the river' was probably a symbol for time – the river of time – and the spirit of Herzen was no doubt expressing a conviction that time would vindicate him. The word 'rifuge', however, put them in a dilemma. Could the spirit of Herzen make such a crass error in spelling? The writer was sternly asked whether she was sure she knew how to spell the word 'refuge'. The woman – it was the theatre cashier, who was distinguished by her mediumistic sensitivity – indignantly rejected the suggestion that she could make such an elementary mistake.

'What do you think I am – illiterate?' she said, on the verge of tears.

Sergei remarked that, in that case, they would have to admit that Herzen was the one who was illiterate. This started another argument, with everyone talking at once, until the host cleared up the problem: spelling mistakes were of no significance; the important part of the message was its content, not its form. He explained that when the writing on the wall had appeared at Belshazzar's feast – *mene, tekel, phares* – it had never occurred to anyone to discuss whether the words were correctly spelled: everyone who saw it was just seized with horror. Incidentally, in the Book of Daniel the words were given as: *mene, mene, tekel, upharsin* – a normal example of tautology and transposition of letters that occurs in psychography . . . Feeling that her headache was getting worse, Olga could no longer bear sitting there and went into the next room to lie down on the divan. It was cold. Someone came in behind her and shut the window.

It was one of her very worst attacks of migraine, accompanied by nausea. Sergei brought a glass of hot tea and a tablet and covered her with some kind of rug. She wanted him to stay and sit beside her – just to be alone together for a while. She held him by the hand and asked: 'You do realise that all this is nonsense, don't you?'

He said that he did. Through the terrible pain that was boring into her temples, another pain thrust itself in like a needle: 'If he realises it, then why does he come?' But she did not ask that question; she felt too weak.

'It's all auto-suggestion . . . It's third-year psychology stuff,' she whispered.

About twenty minutes or half an hour later someone came into the room and switched on the table lamp.

'How are you feeling?' a woman's voice asked, and Olga saw that it was Darya Mamedovna.

With a great effort she raised herself and sat up. Sergei was not in the room. As before, her head was splitting.

'Better,' she said.

She looked at the woman's dark, sharp-chinned face with amazement. Why had she come? More than once Olga had imagined this: she would talk to this woman alone, choosing words of venomous hatred; yet now all those words had suddenly vanished, her malice dissipated as though by a draught of air, and the only thing Olga felt was a faint asthmatic shortness of breath.

'I wish Sergei wouldn't spend his time on all this rubbish,' she said, gasping slightly.

The woman held out a glass. 'Drink this.'

Obediently, Olga drank it down.

Darya Mamedovna sat down beside her on the divan and said in a calm voice that she, too, thought Sergei was wasting his time on nonsense. Although, in fact, it wasn't so much nonsense as an amusement, a game. A Saturday entertainment for tired, overworked people. Some gambled at poker, some played mahjong, others were chess fanatics . . . And more such banalities. But the effrontery of the woman: *she* was against it too! No one in the world beside Olga had the right to be against anything that Sergei chose to do. 'Stupid woman!' Olga thought. 'And everyone says she's so intelligent.' This insight calmed her greatly and even made her head ache a little less.

Darya Mamedovna said, 'I've been wanting to talk to you for a long time . . .'

'Why can that be?' Olga wondered, quite without alarm. Aloud she said, 'Do you want to talk now?'

'If you feel well enough.' Darya Mamedovna produced cigarettes and a lighter from her purse, and without asking Olga's permission – a charming and characteristic trait – lit a cigarette. 'Sergei once told me that you were working on problems of cell compatibility . . .'

Ah, so that was it! Was that all she wanted to talk about? Darya Mamedovna went on to say that some of her research was concerned with questions of incompatibility. So she was interested in it from the opposite angle. Olga told her a little about her work. Darya Mamedovna enquired about Olga's colleague Andrei Ivanovich, whom she had known at university. Then she began talking about her own work on extrasensory perception, about all the different kinds of tests, trials, and research projects, about the thousands of experiments that had been done abroad and how Soviet research had fallen behind and needed to catch up. 'You, as a biologist,' she said, 'studying problems of communication and biological incompatability, must constantly come up against this. What about bats and their locator mechanisms? And what about fish? You must agree there are no *a priori* grounds to deny the existence of special, extrasensory means of communication in the structure.'

Olga didn't want to argue with her, but even so, gasping for breath a little and in a weak voice she said: 'There is too much fraud involved in parapsychology. In no other science – if you can call it a science – are there so many swindlers. Why do you think that is so?'

'Because, Olga Vasilievna, people remain in a permanent state of self-deception: they think everything is known already.'

Olga said, 'Talking of incompatibility . . . One of the great riddles is still the problem of allergy. Do you know that there are people who exhibit a morbid reaction to a particular person: they start coughing, suffer from shortness of breath . . .'

'Oh, yes. Of course. The question is, What is the mechanism that produces this effect?'

As Olga replied, looking at the other woman's dark Caucasian forehead, she thought: 'They want to dig down into everything, to reveal the structure, find the means of communication that transmit hatred, jealousy, fear. And love. Then if they find the means of communication – will they then want to control them?' Someone opened the door, wanting to come in. Darya Mamedovna said sternly, 'Shut the door!' – and it was shut.

'Darya Mamedovna, I want to talk to you . . . about a certain thing –' Olga suddenly said in a miserable, quavering voice. 'If only Sergei wouldn't get wrapped up in all this, interesting though it is . . .. You see, he's no longer exactly a young man, his health isn't too good, he has his own work, he has responsibilities.'

Darya Mamedovna widened her dark, blue-rimmed eyes in a strange fashion, and bent her head over towards her right shoulder. 'What do you mean? I don't understand.'

'I mean, Darya Mamedovna, that he is destroying himself. Everything has stopped, his dissertation is not getting written . . .'

'But my dear, what can anyone do about it? His dissertation's not getting written?' She suddenly laughed. 'And a good thing, too! Please don't be offended, Olga Vasilievna. The fact is, I don't like – no, that's not true, it isn't that I don't like – I pity people working in the humanities, all these literary scholars and historians, all the scribbling brotherhood who are forced to do nothing but talk, talk, talk, nothing but talk – and it's all so much hot air. I pity them, poor creatures. Really, to think of devoting one's entire life to such rubbish – and it really is rubbish – as finding out about all the informers who used to work for the czarist secret police in Moscow. Who needs it? I laughed when he talked so enthusiastically about those, you know, discoveries he had made in that tiny little microcosm . . .'

A burst of laughter was heard in the next room, someone thumped on the wall with his fist and shouted, 'Nigmatova, come here!'

'. . . and this at a time when the fate of the world is in the balance – when people are literally faced with Shakespeare's question: "To be or not to be . . ." '

Then quite suddenly she started to tell Olga how she became interested in parapsychology. Several years ago her husband Nigmatov, an artist, had died in an air crash. That night in a dream she saw his face, distorted with terror.

She described it quite dispassionately, simply as one of the facts of extrasensory telepathic communication. Olga felt no pity for Darya Mamedovna. She thought: 'If Sergei is in love with this woman, then he is profoundly unhappy.'

It was late. Irinka, for whom she had promised she would do something that day, was waiting for them at home; so as soon as Sergei came into the room she said they must go home, and she got up. He gave them both a rapid, penetrating look; he was evidently satisfied, because he said calmly:

'Good, let's go.'

Usually he had to be dragged home with a tractor.

Out in the street, he said that everyone had been intrigued to know what she and Darya Mamedovna had been talking about for so long. 'It's not like her. She's not a great talker. That means she must like you.'

'Yes. She liked me,' said Olga. 'We were talking about you. She pities you.'

'Me? She pities me? Let her pity me; there's plenty to pity me for.'

'She thinks your work is so much rubbish.'

'Oh, come on!' He laughed and gave a sly wink, like someone who can't be fooled.

Even so, she felt relieved.

Yet after a few days it all started again – he would go out, he disappeared, lived a separate, unknown life, and Olga suffered torments.

In Irinka's early childhood, when she was about seven or eight, strange things had happened to her. She used to get up at night and go sleepwalking, bumping into things, and once at the flat in Shabolovka Street she had frightened her parents' guests by appearing in the doorway like a little ghost, in a white nightdress. She had walked up to the table – looking asleep, eyes closed – and said as she stretched out an empty hand: 'Would you like my gypsy?' She meant her favourite doll, a gypsy girl. After that it occurred less and less frequently and by the time Irinka was ten it stopped altogether.

Sergei remembered about these strange incidents in Irinka's childhood, and he decided that they might mean she was one of those 'psychic' persons that he was seeking in order to pursue his hobby. He was becoming seriously interested in parapsychological experiments. He exasperated everyone at home with his attempts to guess what they were thinking about or what they intended to do, and by his efforts to project his will on to them. To begin with, of course, his will only involved something trivial, like picking up a box of matches or switching off the light in the hall. Once he joyfully exclaimed, 'Bravo! At last! For half an hour I've been willing you to shut the window.'

Sometimes, equally unexpectedly, he would show irritation and annoyance, even sounding resentful: 'No, really, you are so thick-skinned, it's impossible to get through to you. I've been sending out waves of suggestion and you don't even . . .'

All this was simple boyish fun, reminiscent of the games played by inquisitive schoolboys in the 'Psychology for Fun' club, and Olga might have treated it as such, half jokingly, and half approvingly, because it actually seemed to enliven Sergei; it made him more cheerful, the tone of his life visibly improved and his cheeks looked pink, which showed that his new enthusiasm was doing him some good. Like everything else it was good if taken in moderation, but this game was turning into something bigger. Olga was alarmed to catch hints that all this was simply a series of preliminaries, a search for a method, and that when he had freed himself of some of his commitments he was going to take up the full-time study of psychology and parapsychology. She said this sounded somewhat naïve, it was like saying one intended studying physics and metaphysics.

'Aren't you afraid of turning into a Jack-of-all-trades and master of none?'

He looked at her vacantly. 'Be more careful in choosing your jokes. Right now it is the only thing in life that interests me.'

After a remark like that, what was there left to do? She stopped joking and waited to see what would happen. At any rate, it seemed to her that his infatuation was over.

God, what a mistake that was! She shouldn't have waited. She shouldn't have stopped fighting, shouldn't have surrendered him to the absolute power of Darya and her crowd of table tappers. What a naïve fool she was: it was, after all, obvious that he was moving away, casting off, like a ship slipping its moorings from the quayside, having hoisted all sail and flags – and she kept waiting for something, hoping for something. She didn't realise that he was going through the midlife crisis. Her chief torment was her failure to understand him. One day she decided to act positively, as though nothing had happened, as though his damned hobby had not come between them like a wall; without telling him she bought tickets to a film that the whole of Moscow was fighting to see, so that the tickets were like gold dust. He said he was sorry, but at ten o'clock that evening he was busy. Busy? What with? Was he going out? No, he would be at home. But from ten o'clock onwards he was busy.

She felt extremely hurt, but she did not try to make him change his mind; swallowing her pride, she went alone. In the cinema she could not hold out for longer than a quarter of an hour, and she ran home. Surely on top of it all he hadn't started lying to her? She felt powerless: if he were unfaithful, it was only because he had finally got himself so hopelessly entangled and disorientated – he had never been unfaithful to her before – that he was beyond her help. There is no greater agony than incomprehension and a total inability to help. But when she came rushing home she saw that he had been telling the truth – he really was busy.

He was shut in their room, a look of grim concentration on his face as he laid out his pack of Sehner cards, special cards with squares and stars for parapsychology tests. It appeared that he and Darya Mamedovna had arranged to have a seance at ten o'clock that evening: acting as the 'percipient', the person who has to guess the cards, she was sitting in Bolshevo, at the Film-Makers Club.

He had driven Irinka nearly crazy with these cards. At first he had told her that she was very gifted, that her percentage of correct answers was significantly higher than the median of probability.

'You could become world famous. I'm not joking. You'll be invited to go abroad, and Mama and I will go with you.'

Fairy tales of this nature were meant to keep up her interest and encourage her, because soon, of course, the business began to bore her. Gradually her success rate got worse and worse. Sergei became nervous and bad-tempered. She never again achieved such high scores after the first few days.

'Think! Concentrate!' he would say irritably. 'What's the matter with you?'

In the past, too, he had lacked patience when he tried to help Irinka with her homework, and his efforts always ended in a quarrel. Now it was just the same. One day Irinka burst into tears. Sergei's mother thumped the table. 'That's enough! I can't bear to watch you crippling this child's mind. You may send yourself crazy with all this obscurantist nonsense if you like; you're a grown man and can answer for yourself – but leave Irinka alone.'

They began to argue. As always, their arguments were conducted without shouting and without rudeness but with extreme venom and, probably, with a mutual infliction of pain. Alexandra Prokofievna was also inspired, no doubt, by memories of the celebrated disputes over metaphysics that took place in the 1920s between Lunacharsky and Archbishop Vvedensky.

'If you admit even for one second the existence of life after death and a higher power, namely God . . .'

'I didn't say that. You're not in court now, so don't try your old lawyer's trick of misrepresenting me.'

'What is it, then, if not agnosticism?'

'In your view, I suppose, the train has reached the last station and stopped, has it? And the track leads no further forward?'

'Your track, Sergei, is not leading forward but backwards to the Dark Ages. But I can't understand why you lead a double life. Take your beliefs to their logical conclusion: put on the black habit, shave the top of your head, take your vows and go and live in a cave or in an abandoned stone-quarry on the road to Paveletsk, sit there and contemplate your navel, like a Tibetan lama. Live on locusts and wild honey. Your wife can bring you locusts from the pet shop –' There were times when the old woman could turn out a brilliant line in sarcastic wit. At the same time she could never admit that the disgraceful state of affairs was Sergei's fault alone, so she had to drag Olga into it. 'But that wouldn't suit you, would it? You'd have to leave the institute, which pays you a salary.'

'I might leave it. By the way, that's not a bad idea of yours. If they do set up a laboratory for the study of extrasensory perception in one of the research institutes, as has been promised, I would gladly go there.'

At this stage, all this was said in the heat of argument and with the aim of annoying his mother. Again he assured her that he was interested in science and science alone. But in this universe of ours there were still too many mysteries – anti-matter, quasars, mysterious particles that had neither fixed mass nor electrical charge – so why could one not predicate the existence of suprasensory means of communication as yet unknown to science?

'Sergei, I am horrified to see that after forty years your head has filled itself with the most incredible jumble . . .'

'Whereas over the same period you, Mother dear, have remained totally undisturbed by a single new idea. I suppose that in itself is an achievement of a sort.'

'And I'm proud of it. I don't think about death, as other old women do. I know that when I breathe my last, I shall vanish from this world without a trace – and so will everyone else. There's nothing to discuss.'

'Yes, yes, there's nothing to discuss,' Sergei mumbled, nodding. 'How wonderful to see it with such clarity. And what about the death of those you love, your family? Will they too disappear without a trace?'

'I hope those of my family that fate has so far spared will not go before I do. But if – God forbid – such an injustice were to happen, then as far as I'm concerned the people who are dear to me – I repeat, as far as I'm concerned – would not depart absolutely without trace. For me, they would still be here.' And she slapped the spot in the middle of her chest where, at times when she felt a touch of heart trouble, a mustard plaster was applied.

Olga could not bear listening to conversations of this kind. She only knew one thing: she could not help. And this reduced her to despair. When she came back into the room a little later, she saw that Sergei was alone.

He was standing in an attitude of indecision, half turned

145

towards the window – it was not clear whether he was about to walk away from the window or step towards it! – and looking down into the yard. It was as if he were reflecting on something with enormous concentration. Olga saw his bent back, his stooping shoulders and the grey among his thinning hair. It suddenly seemed as if an old man were standing there.

'My old man,' she said quietly, walking up to him and putting her arms around him.

He did not turn, did not respond, but remained standing and looking down into the yard. The summer was over. It had been an unhappy one for Olga: her mother was slowly expiring with loneliness in the flat in Sushchevskaya Street; it was the first summer in which they hadn't rented a *dacha* – a foretaste of homelessness to come. Faïna's eyes had opened wide and shone with voluptuous curiosity; she pitied Olga, pitied her with all her heart, she even groaned with pity: 'I'll go to the Scientific Workers' Union. I'll teach that Darya to keep her hands off married men.' Her voice shook with anger. Nothing is sweeter than compassion for one's best friend. She didn't go to the Union, thank God. But she told Mara. And it all started to move and to grow, like a magic tree that a fakir conjures up out of nothing before one's eyes. She did not learn the details until the day when they went out to the woods on a mushroom-picking excursion. She knew only one thing; that he had handed in his resignation.

It had suddenly seemed the best thing for him to do.

That autumn, on a day in October when it was still warm and the leaves were still on the trees – everything was over, except the warm weather, except the mushrooms and the forest – they left the institute by bus at four in the morning. Almost everyone from Olga's laboratory came on the trip. Sergei was sitting beside her, his head on her shoulder, asleep. It was such a pleasure to feel the weight of his head. She wanted everyone to be quiet so that he could sleep, wanted it with all the force of her will power. Grey, misty, the countryside around Moscow flowed past the window; first there were mounds of dirt churned up on building sites, chalky-grey slabs of new blocks of flats, fields of watery green, birch trees, aspens, then fir trees. The road dipped downhill, more new houses rose up among the fir trees, a shower of rain flattened itself in a watery layer on the window and then suddenly disappeared. By the time they got out of the bus fifty-two kilometres outside Moscow, beyond Pakhra, the rain had stopped. The forest was wet, smelling of tired, sodden grass. Under the trees, where no grass grew, the layer of brown pine-needles covering the ground looked dark and swollen with moisture. There were not many mushrooms to be found. All the others on the outing had scattered in different directions.

Sergei said that if he had publicly admitted himself to have been at fault in having attended those idiotic seances, if he had stung himself with his own tail like a scorpion, the institute officials would still not have left him alone. Klimuk was now deputy director of the institute, having successfully levered Kislovsky out of the job, and a young man called Sharipov occupied Klimuk's old post as academic secretary. This Sharipov, twenty-eight years old, was a real go-getter, with a master's degree and several books to his credit. He had conducted the 'case' against Sergei with an unwavering hand. There was no reason, indeed, why he should have found it difficult. He had never shared meat or drink with Sergei; they had met for the first time on the staircase, when he had stopped for a moment and enquired briefly and amicably; 'Excuse me, Sergei Afanasievich, is it true that you go to spiritualistic seances?' Sergei had replied equally casually: 'Yes, I used to go last winter out of sheer curiosity. I've also been looking for people who are receptive to extrasensory stimuli, because I'm fascinated by parapsychological experiments. It's very interesting. Parapsychology is undoubtedly the science of the future.' Sharipov listened, smiling sympathetically. Careerists like him have a gift for asking sudden pointed questions, smiling sympathetically, and running rapidly upstairs. Klimuk kept himself clear of the affair. He signed no statements on behalf of the institute, although he could have – the director was away in Bulgaria – and he invited Sergei into his office, where he made a show of trying to persuade him to withdraw his resignation and even mumbled a few absurd, patently insincere remarks, such as: 'How is Olga? . . . You must call us up sometime . . .' at which Sergei simply laughed and said, 'Are you joking?' Nothing terrible actually happened, no positive action was taken against him, but he was nevertheless glad that the episode had taken place, because the moment had come to start another life. Hell, there was so little time left for another life; but he must, finally, take the plunge and start. Start what? Start doing what truly excited him. Everybody had something that truly excited him, but you have to struggle and claw your way up to get there.

It amazes us that we don't understand one another. Why don't other people understand us? This lack in our lives seems to be the source of all evil. Oh, if only we were understood. There would be no more quarrels, no more wars . . . Parapsychology is

147

a visionary attempt to get inside another person's mind, to surrender oneself to another person, to heal oneself through understanding; it is an age-old desire that shows no sign of abating . . . But then why do we, wretched creatures that we are, strive to understand others when we cannot understand ourselves? We should try understanding *ourselves*, my God, for a start. But no; we lack the strength, we lack the time, or perhaps we lack sufficient intelligence or courage. There is Olga, for instance, a biochemist, in charge of a laboratory; she is in good standing, she wins prizes and earns bonuses, but is this her real vocation? She herself has said, 'How I wish I had gone into applied art. I so love making things with my hands, modelling, carving.' And used not Sergei to say that history was a magic mirror in which one might foretell the future, that he was prepared to spend his whole life studying it, staring into it? Yes, he did say that, he did! He felt it, he thought it. Yet perhaps in thinking it, there was a quite different, concealed, unadmitted motivation at work: to study in order to foretell. Because he now felt that all those minuscule details of details, those crumbs from the tables of banquets long past were of no use to anyone except perhaps five or six people in the whole world. If one thought only of oneself, to whom these few details were of most value, then perhaps there was some point in continuing one's work, but it was so boring to think always of oneself. And one day the boredom became quite intolerable. Suddenly, like a faint gleam, like the feeble light of dawn through the tree trunks, came the idea: another life . . .

Olga felt her heart contract with fear. Where, for God's sake, was a new life to be found? What could possibly bring it about? Moving from one house to another? Buying a new briefcase? Going to this office every morning instead of to that one? Basically, things were the same everywhere. Sergei objected:

'Oh no! To talk like that is like saying that all women are the same. But how awful to spend one's life with a woman one doesn't love. Which, of course, is the way most people live.'

He said this calmly, as though discussing something extraneous that had nothing to do with Olga and himself, but even so it was terrifying. As they were talking, they had wandered deep into the forest, completely forgetting that they had come to pick mushrooms. In any case, there were few mushrooms. They met a woman with a bucket half full of white milk-cap mushrooms. They asked her whether that kind was edible. The woman explained how you had to boil them down, pour away the liquid, and then marinate them in diluted vinegar.

Having told them this, the woman disappeared, and they forgot to ask her the way back to the road. The aspens and birch thinned out, giving way to a dense fir plantation, heavily sodden with the damp. Here there was absolutely nothing to be found; they pushed their way through the thicket of conifers, because somewhere ahead there was a glimmer of brighter light, a glimpse or two of a glade or a clearing. That was where another life would begin.

They sat down on a tree stump; Sergei was tired, his face was grey and he was breathing heavily. Then they moved on again. The humidity in the pine forest was oppressive, the smell of rotting wood drifted up from the dead branches underfoot, from the depths of gullies and ravines. Here and there they found themselves on black, swampy ground as they walked on and on, talking, enticed by the brightness ahead. The cloudy, overcast weather cleared up a little, but still no pathway, no clearing opened out beyond the trees. She already realised that they were lost. Suddenly Irinka appeared beside them, and Olga tightly clasped her cold little hand. Irinka was now only twelve. Olga had to ask Sergei something painful that concerned only the two of them, and Irinka's presence was embarrassing. But later Irinka went away, and Olga asked about Darya Mamedovna. Was it true? One thing alone worried her? Was it true? Sergei laughed and said that it wasn't. Then she asked him: 'And what about the money that you borrowed from the credit union? After your death they came and demanded the money back. What did you spend it on? Please tell me truthfully – no one can hear us, we're in the forest.' He said, 'I didn't spend it on anything: I just lent it to various people and they never gave it back.'

How absurd – and how like him. He mentioned some names, all of them unknown to her. Even so, she believed him, instantly and totally. She wondered how she was going to live in this forest alone. They really should run, or they would be late; the bus was waiting on the road, but they had no idea where the road was or which way to run. So they just ran – straight ahead, jumping over gullies, plunging through the dead, mildewed fir-branches that covered the ground or scratched their faces and hands. Finally they came to a fence. It was high and solid, painted dark green and they only saw it when it suddenly loomed up close in front of them. What was behind the fence? Nothing could be heard or seen, except that the same fir trees appeared to be growing on the other side.

They walked beside the fence along a not very clear path –

obviously few people ever came here – and the farther they went, the less hope there seemed of finding the right way. Four men and a woman were sitting on a bench alongside a gateway in the fence. One of the men was huge and pudgy; he had a large prominent forehead, little piglike eyes, and a face with that expression, obtuse but good-natured, typical of people suffering from Down's syndrome. The others were an old man who continually nodded his head, and two of middle age, one bearded, who stared grimly from two eyes like glowing coals, the other short, with a flat, unhappy face, whose little legs dangled from the bench without touching the ground. All four men sat silent and inactive, while the woman, in a grey hospital gown, was reading a newspaper. Olga asked the way to the road. The men did not know. The large man with Down's syndrome said there was no road in these parts. Sergei started to get angry and insisted that there was a road: they had come here by bus, and the bus was waiting on the road. No, they said, no bus comes out this way and there is no road. Sergei grew even more heated. 'Don't argue with them,' said the woman, laying aside her newspaper. 'They don't know. Come on, I'll show you the way.' When they had gone some distance away from the men, who remained sitting on the bench, the woman said, 'They're patients. They don't know where the road is.'

The woman led them through the thick of the forest, where there was no path. No doubt it was a short cut. Olga squeezed Irinka's hand. 'Please forgive us for putting you to this trouble,' she said to the woman. 'We're late, and the bus is waiting for us on the road.'

'I understand,' the woman replied. 'That's why I'm taking you by the short cut.'

Twilight set in and it began to grow dark. Almost imperceptibly, the daylight was fading away. They had to clamber down between fir trees growing on a steep slope, then plunged once more into the dense undergrowth. 'We'll soon be there,' said the woman. They were very tired and barely had the strength to go on. Suddenly the woman said, 'Here we are.'

They were standing in front of a small woodland swamp. 'What's this?' Olga asked.

'This is the road,' said the woman. 'There's your bus – over there.' She stretched out her arm, pointing to a clump of sedge growing on the far side of the swamp. Olga felt herself turning numb and very cold, gripped by a sudden icy lassitude that struck like a flash of lightning. Just then a noise cut through her consciousness. A moment later the news arrived from the other world: Time to get up . . .

The alarm clock rang at seven, wrenching her out of clinging, enervating oblivion. So it continued for many days, each one like the other, although at times it was sunny, at times it rained or snowed. One day, though, she woke up before the alarm. She walked barefoot over to the window, pulled back the curtains and looked out towards the park: there, above the treetops, above the jagged dark horizon of roofs and chimneys, the red globe of the sun was sliding up into the faintly glowing sky. She opened the little casement at the top of the window. The wind blowing from across the park caressed her tired skin, and her breasts tautened with the cold. Through her bare feet she felt the floor quiver from some vague, subterranean rumble.

Whenever they had two or three hours of free time, they would ride out to Spasskoye-Lykovo and take a walk there: by trolley-bus to the last stop, then a short walk and a half-hour trip on the riverboat. The village was perched on the top of some high hills, thickly grown with pinewoods. Moscow had long since sent out its tentacles on all sides of this ancient semi-rural, semi-residential township, had flowed around it, surging westward, but had somehow not quite swallowed it up: the pine trees still stood unfelled, the water-meadow shimmered in its lush green, and high on a hilltop over the river and above the pines floated the bell tower of the old Spasskoye-Lykovo church, visible from far away on every side. After stepping down from the wooden jetty onto the path that wound along the bank, they would walk on and on, talking, breathing the river air, walking around the anglers and looking disapprovingly at the little cars that somehow or other managed to drive here, blocking the path at the very water's edge, even though there was no proper road leading to the riverside. This was their refuge, their riverbank, their grass. Anyone else who found the way here was an interloper, an alien.

Moscow was no place for them. Too many people knew them both, and none of these people, friends and acquaintances, would understand. Olga, too, could not understand it; she could only marvel and feel ashamed that another life had begun so suddenly and so quickly. Once they had dreamed of another life, searched and striven to attain it. But it is not something to be attained; it comes, if at all, by itself. He had weak lungs, easily caught cold and always suffered badly; a little chill would last a long time because he had an unusual constitution and could not tolerate antibiotics. He lived as though in the nineteenth century, treating himself with raspberry juice and herbal tea. Olga worried about him, because she could not be near him when he was ill. She felt that the people around him could not give him the kind of care he needed. As they climbed a slippery path up the hillside, she told him news of her job, about experiments; she told him about Irinka, who was planning to marry soon, telling him without embarrassment her innermost thoughts about Irinka. He, too, told her about all his concerns, about difficulties at work, about the people who worked under him, and asked her advice; but he did not care to talk about his home. And she understood him.

One day they climbed up the bell tower of Spasskoye-Lykovo church. It was an exhausting climb, he stopped to rest twice on the stone staircase, and when they came out at the top, under the bell, his heart was thumping very hard and they each took a sedative. But their reward was to see Moscow stretching away in the twilight. The towers shone for a moment, then faded, the light faded, everything turned blue and blurred, like a memory; but if they strained their eyes Olga could just make out the slablike skyscraper of the Hydro-project building near her house, and he could discern the faint spire of the skyscraper on Vosstanie Square, next to the building where he lived. It was windy up there, and suddenly it hit them with a violent gust. She stretched out towards him to screen him and save him from the cold, and he took her in his arms. There was nothing wrong in what she was doing, she thought. There was nothing wrong, because another life was already around her, as inexhaustible as that cold, windy expanse, vast as that boundless city fading from sight with the coming of evening.

Stephen Wright

Meditations in Green

'Just pumping in the penicillin,' is how the captain at Griffin's training unit describes America's role in Vietnam. Until he arrives there, young James Griffin has no reason to disagree. His job – interpreting aerial photographs of carpet bombing and defoliation – his youth, his vanity, his education: all flatter his ability to survive. But in a war so unreal and stalemated that leisurely atrocities on both sides are standard practice, it is not possible to stay untouched . . .

FICTION   0 349 13756 0   £2.95

Also available in ABACUS paperback:

FICTION

ENDERBY'S DARK LADY	Anthony Burgess	£1.95 ☐
QUEEN OF SWORDS	William Kotzwinkle	£2.50 ☐
ROSE UNDER GLASS	Elizabeth Berridge	£2.95 ☐
ACROSS THE COMMON	Elizabeth Berridge	£2.75 ☐
SING ME WHO YOU ARE	Elizabeth Berridge	£2.95 ☐
THE HOUSE ON THE EMBANKMENT	Yuri Trifonov	£2.50 ☐
FOREIGN EXCHANGE	Ed. Julian Evans	£3.50 ☐
BABIES IN RHINESTONES	Sheila Mackay	£2.75 ☐

NON-FICTION

STRANGER ON THE SQUARE	Arthur and Cynthia Koestler	£2.95 ☐
NAM	Mark Baker	£2.95 ☐
PETER THE GREAT	Robert K. Massie	£5.95 ☐
IRISH JOURNAL	Heinrich Böll	£1.95 ☐
KAFKA – A BIOGRAPHY	Ronald Hayman	£3.25 ☐
TERRORISM	Walter Laqueur	£2.75 ☐
THE GREAT EVOLUTION MYSTERY	Gordon Rattray Taylor	£3.95 ☐

All Abacus books are available at your local bookshop or newsagent, or can be ordered direct from the publisher. Just tick the titles you want and fill in the form below.

Name _____

Address _____

Write to Abacus Books, Cash Sales Department, P.O. Box 11, Falmouth, Cornwall TR10 9EN

Please enclose cheque or postal order to the value of the cover price plus:

UK: 55p for the first book plus 22p for the second book and 14p for each additional book ordered to a maximum charge of £1.75.

OVERSEAS: £1.00 for the first book plus 25p per copy for each additional book.

BFPO & EIRE: 55p for the first book, 22p for the second book plus 14p per copy for the next 7 books, thereafter 8p per book.

Abacus Books reserve the right to show new retail prices on covers which may differ from those previously advertised in the text or elsewhere, and to increase postal rates in accordance with the PO.